C000165037

THE HONEY TREE

JO SPARKES

OSCAR PRESS

First Edition 2023

Epub ISBN 978-1-7355631-1-4

Print ISBN 978-1-7355631-2-1

CONTENTS

A Note from the Author

Twenty years ago, Maggie came to me. She stood there in my dreams, first at night, then during afternoon daydreaming. I saw flashes of events, feelings, people she loved. And others she did not.

Though fascinated, I still refused to write it. The thing that stopped me was simple:

What could a White woman *really* know about being a Black slave?

But Maggie is nothing if not persistent. She drew me into her world, her story. She gave me no peace, and it became impossible to ignore. So I recorded her tale. At the end of the day, I'm merely a storyteller.

She would tell you this isn't just her story. So many people lived and died quietly, and nobody knew them. Their stories deserve to be told.

I didn't choose Maggie—she chose me. If her story touches just one heart, it's worth it.

BUTTERFLY

"AIN'T NO COTTON IN the sky," Maggie whispered, sparing but a glance at the new girl while her own fingers stayed busy. The girl—name of Elvira, Maggie remembered—went back to picking. Back might hurt, but you had to keep going. Had to keep your head down, back bent. Had to fill the sack.

Working in a whole world of fluffy and prickly white, Maggie set a rhythm plucking cotton. Snag the bloom, twist the puff clear. Mind the sharp bits. Most important, keep your head down in case Booker looked your way. Never draw attention. She kept herself non-descript, as her mammy would have said. Average height, average face, blend-into-the-background demeanor. The only thing that stood out was the purple scarf covering her hair. She couldn't bring herself to give that up.

Another movement caught Maggie's eye. This time it was a butterfly snagged in a dewy web, blue wings beating frantically against the white fluff.

"You caught, little thing." She shook her head. "Ain't no point fighting it." The garden spider appeared, sizing up its prey. "I'm sorry," Maggie whispered. *Bad way to die*, she thought.

A bristle bit her finger. Keeping low, she sucked the puncture.

The web shook as the spider approached. The butterfly's blue wings gave a last burst of energy, and it broke loose. Popping clear of the web, it hovered for an instant beyond the spider's reach. Beyond anyone's reach. Then it soared off over the Mississippi.

Free.

"Ain't no cotton in the sky," Elvira giggled.

Maggie realized she'd straightened right up, staring after the insect. Dropping back into that awful stooping position, finger still stinging, she hurriedly picked cotton. But despite all the white before her, she couldn't unsee that blue.

Still Missouri

Mark Hueron was a tall man, thin and blond and aged thirty-three years, though with Sweetgum's problems he felt past forty. As he stood on the veranda, he watched the clouds, trying to decipher their water content. It was March—still early in the month, but March all the same. April approached, and with it the Missouri rain.

Sweetgum had been a thriving plantation, its crops sought after and even garnering a premium. On the Mississippi and farther north in the state than most of its brethren, it had been a source of pride for its owners and the town of Blanten. Some townsfolk had even called it Blanten Tobacco.

That had all been before the place was sold to Mark's father. Reading that King Cotton now stood greatest among crops, yielding fortunes across the South, Kurt Hueron had ordered the land scoured of tobacco and planted with the white stuff. No doubt, no fear of the work, no hesitation at the cost ever assailed him. Certainly no thought was given as to whether the climate of northern

Missouri suited a plant that had been successful in the southern states of Mississippi and Arkansas. Mark hoped to squeeze out enough money from this endeavor in the next few years to convert back to tobacco.

A flicker caught his eye, and Booker sauntered out of the trees. The man saw him and hesitated before his feet got to moving again. Booker was Sweetgum's overseer, his father's man that he'd kept on—another decision Hueron was starting to regret. He'd been advised that a strong, trusted slave could be a good overseer without the cost of a salary, but his father had insisted he use a White man. "You get what you pay for," the old man had told him.

Which, come to think on it, Kurt never did. The man overpaid for everything.

"Yes, sir?" Booker was taller than Hueron, yet somehow managed to appear small. The man hunched in his presence, snatching his hat from his bald head. The shabby bowler had belonged to his dad, so he said. He stopped at the steps, knowing better than to climb them before being asked.

Hueron didn't invite him to. "Another day's gone, Booker. Where are those men?"

"Should be here tomorrow...or day after."

"Better be strong men this time. You spend far too much of my money bringing me female slaves." Somehow every task was always in the works with Booker, never actually done. And if something did finish, it never failed to disappoint.

The overseer nodded, staring at the ground.

Bad sign, that. He'd kept Booker on due to his familiarity with the plantation and was now regretting it. The man was lazy and spent too much time watching the women instead of watching the work. Hueron asked, "How many hands you buy, Booker?"

"Five, sir."

"And no change from all that money I gave you? Better be strong men."

Booker's feet shuffled in the grass. "Prices always higher this time of year—"

Hueron cut him off with a gesture. "Real strong, Booker. Else my next hire is a new overseer."

⟫⟫⟩ ⟨⟪⟪

Maggie heard Buster and Tweed before the two boys burst through the cotton, bare feet padding against the dirt and then leaping over her basket. Buster was all of six, muscles already swelling beneath his ebony skin. He'd be real strong someday, like his daddy. He grabbed a handful of white before she could stop him.

"Yaw git now. I don't need ya here."

Tweed, littler legs taking longer to reach her, kept running till he slammed into her thigh. Hugging both her legs, he grinned up at her with that sweet little face. His skin was the color of honey, like his sister's, and he had her delicate features right down to the long lashes above his gold eyes. He was a year younger than Buster, though it seemed like more. Buster would grow strong enough to survive the world, but Maggie worried Tweed would need his brother's help to do that.

"But, Mammy, we can help!" Tweed said. His upturned face grinned.

"You hear me? Go fetch water for supper 'fore it gets too dark."

Tweed spun around and raced away, only too happy to escape any work.

Buster gave his mother a long, puzzled frown. "But we gots to help."

Despite herself, Maggie smiled. "Not today, honey child. I'll be there quick as I can."

"Quick as a bullfrog catching a bug!" Buster sped after his little brother.

Their hair was getting long again, making them look like little wild men running through the plants. She'd ask Cook to cut it.

The truth was, she could've used their help. They were getting stronger, and Maggie was getting older—all of thirty-five, near as she could figure. But tonight she needed to talk to Squint alone. He was the oldest slave on the plantation, with a squat body and patch of gray hair atop his head. They all figured his years past sixty, and so—feeling the accumulated wisdom—he tried to keep them all out of trouble.

The sun had sunk below the trees when Maggie emptied her bag atop her gatherings in the basket. Rule was, you picked until the sun set and quickly dragged it to Squint before it got too dark to check it. Squint hefted each slave's gathering, making sure it was weighty and not just fluffed up, while Oliver emptied the cotton.

A good man, Oliver. Young and helpful, but not so strong with his bad arm.

"Your kerchief's come askew," Oliver told Maggie, beaming as he used the word, proud of his vocabulary.

It was her mammy's kerchief and reminded her of watching the large, loving figure in the fields, wearing the bright purple cloth with a big bow to secure it. The purple had faded some, but the memory stayed strong.

Oliver was a bit of a tattler, so Maggie pondered how to get him clear so she could speak to Squint alone even as she straightened the cloth on her head.

Squint's skill, on the other hand, had always been being observant of people. "Oliver, go see how much longer Hoby and that Elvira gonna be," the older man said.

Oliver strode away.

Squint carefully hefted her basket, feeling the weight as he eyed her over the rim. "You got something to say there, Maggie?"

Now that the moment had arrived, she hesitated. To speak it out loud was dangerous. What if it was Squint who'd told on Hank?

Eyeing her, the old man stretched himself real tall and rubbed his back in a familiar field-hand gesture. Maggie remembered a day long ago when the plantation grew tobacco and she was Honey's age. Squint had been trying to help her harvest the tall plants. The large blades too awkward for her, she'd cut her foot instead. Her tears fell into the dirt, the overseer but a row away. He'd'a flayed her back for that. Useless at reaching the flowers atop the plants, she remembered Mammy Miri was always whispering she *had* to make herself valuable to Sweetgum while Maggie could only sob and bleed.

It had taken her years to get good at cotton, secure her place, get noticed in a good way. To upset the apple cart now, maybe wind up like Hank... But she kept seeing that butterfly.

"Hank spoke to you pretty near those last days," Maggie said.

The old hand snatched up her bucket, emptied her gatherings.

"What'd you tell him?" she prodded.

Squint set the empty basket in the stack. "He won't help a female. If you get caught...he get caught."

"Who gets caught?"

Squint just stood there, quiet.

"I gotta ask..."

"Maggie, you done asked. Answer's no."

She asked again the next evening, and the next. On the fourth day, she found another possibility.

⤜⤜⤜ ⤚⤚⤚

Honey grasped the round knob and turned it. The door swung open, and she stepped out onto the second floor—a huge hallway lined by doors with handles made of genuine crystal. Stepping on wood floors was amazing. So smooth and even, and you never tripped over nothing, except maybe the rugs. She loved polishing them, making the planks gleam as the sun poured through the windows. The big house was plumb full of wonders. So much nicer than working the cotton fields.

Honey was all of sixteen, considered fully grown. Maggie had talked Bibby to death—so Bibby said—to get her this position. Now, only a week after being promoted to the house, here she stood above stairs. The bedroom floors needed polishing too. She hauled her pail to the farthest door and caught her breath. Behind it was the master's bedroom. Always clean that first, Bibby had instructed, so it'd be good and dry before anyone wanted to enter. She reached for the handle reverently.

"Weena!"

Honey almost dropped the pail.

"Weena!" It was the mistress's voice coming from inside.

Uncertain what to do, she opened the door. Miss Marianne sat before a dainty table ladened with bright-colored bottles. She was as pretty as one of them fairy stories Cook used to tell about the princess with the silky black curls dangling down her back. The flesh of her shoulders contrasted against it, so pale was her skin. The whitest white, so pure it didn't seem real.

"Weena went to town to fetch lavender oil, ma'am."

The lady never turned her head, but suddenly Honey saw her face. Miss Marianne was looking right at her through a fancy glass—a mirror—just like they had in Everett's Emporium in town.

"She'd better fetch it quick. I look like a hag."

"Oh no!" Honey burst out, stepping onto the thick rug. "You're beautiful, Miss Marianne! Why, we all brag about you all the time."

Miss Marianne blinked, and Honey worried she'd get a whipping for that. She had never been whipped, but she'd seen a few.

"You've no business talking about White folk," the mistress murmured, but she didn't sound angry. "What's your name, girl?"

"Honey, ma'am."

"Come brush my hair, Honey." And a silver brush, gleaming in the sunlight, was offered.

Honey hurried to grasp it.

Cook used to tell them all stories back when they were little mites racing around the place, making too much noise outside. The old mistress had liked quiet in the afternoon, and there used to be a lot of slave kids back then, so Cook would get the roast in the oven and come sit outside. While she shelled peas and peeled potatoes, she told stories of princesses and kings and people in the old days. Honey knew they was White stories, as all the pretty girls had pale skin, and Maggie would get mad. White stuff always made Maggie mad. She yelled and yelled at Cook for telling that nonsense. But Cook said she'd get in trouble for telling the other kind. Anyway, Honey loved the tales of beautiful princesses sleeping in the woods. She'd asked once if that was near the honeysuckle, and Cook had said it surely was. A handsome prince would find her and kiss her awake and then they'd live happily ever after.

⇝≫ ≪⇜

"Miss Marianne's hair is so soft!" Honey sighed, plopping down on the straw that was their bed. "Softer than cornsilk. Her skin so pale and clear. Not a mark on her anywhere!"

That's because she's never done a lick of work, Maggie thought. But no good would come from saying it aloud. Honey had a shiny new pebble.

When her daughter was Tweed's age, she'd collected pebbles from the river. She'd stuff her pockets full, bring them back to the cabin, even give each one a name. Hank grumbled that she was wasting time, but then it was hers to waste. Sweetgum Plantation put children to work at the age of six. Maggie felt they should do as they liked until the choice was taken from them.

At Sweetgum, young slave children were left with Cook and Bibby at the house till they were old enough to take off on their own. Buster had done that pretty early, dragging Tweed with him almost before his brother could walk. To stay near the house meant fetching this and hauling that, and the boy preferred to play in the woods.

Now Buster was past his sixth birthday and nearing his seventh, but Booker never kept records. Maggie prayed it would take the overseer a while yet to notice the boy's growing body and developing muscles. Tweed, so slight in comparison, was already five and a half. Sitting next to his sister as he always did, the boy gave Honey a big hug. Maggie realized the overseer was likely so busy watching Honey that he never noticed the boys. Booker did like the girls.

The door burst open, hitting the wall so hard Maggie feared it would break. Once again it held together, but there really couldn't be too many more of those smacks left in the wood.

"Buster!" Maggie forced herself to swallow an angry outburst. "Don't do that. You'll bust that door for sure." The old joke slipped out. "Now did you scrub your hands clean?"

"Yes, ma'am!"

They all looked to her, Honey and Tweed and Buster, and Maggie realized she was working herself up to a really foul mood. No good would come from that. "All right, child," she sighed. "Cornmeal's ready."

Buster carefully lifted the pitcher and poured water into the bowl. He stopped, poured a little more, and then grinned. His hand dove in, mixing the meal with the water to create the batter for their dinner.

Tweed leaned in to watch the process carefully. "No bacon fat, Mammy?"

"Tomorrow, baby. We get that tomorrow."

Buster dropped four globs on the hot stove, and the cabin filled with a comforting sizzle. Honey hopped up from the floor and snatched one of the wood slabs, ready to flip the cakes.

Hank used to whittle the wedges, making a nice thin edge with which to pry up the cooked cakes, but they were starting to splinter. One day they'd fail and new ones would have to be contrived. Hopefully when Buster was old enough, Maggie could trust him with the knife.

When Honey handed out the supper, they blew on the cornmeal to cool it off. Sitting round their table, Maggie watched the boys gulp down the food, having spent all their energy playing that day. Honey, too, ate well, happy in her new role inside the house.

Maggie was the only one in a bad mood, the only one to see they should all be in bad moods. For the first time in a year, it made her miss Hank something fierce. He was Honey's father. Buster and Tweed's father, Skeeter, had been sold a few months back, and she'd gotten used to that. But even after more than twelve years, she ached for Hank at the oddest moments.

Later she went to the stream herself, gently washing her kerchief in the water. It was comforting, somehow, cleaning her purple kerchief. Not headwrap. *Kerchief*. Slave women wore headwraps to show they were slaves. They often used old bits from discarded White clothing or burlap from empty feed bags, but Hank had cut her a kerchief from her mammy's skirts the very day she'd died. Mammy Miri had worn a purple dress with flowers on it, and Maggie had worn it proudly, even expecting to be punished for wearing it. But Sweetgum's old mistress had never noticed. Now some of the threads were starting to separate. But she'd wear it until there were no threads to tie round her head or use the piece Hank had cut for Honey. Maggie had tried to tie the cloth round Honey's head the day she set to working in the field, but Honey preferred the burlap the others used. The notion of defiance didn't interest her.

And how could it? How could Hank's child—or Skeeter's boys, for that matter—yearn for freedom? How could they know what the word meant? Having lived all their life in chains, how could they possibly understand that chains didn't have to be? Maggie herself had yelled at Hank for even thinking about freedom.

She'd be wiser now to forget the whole idea.

But try as she might, Maggie couldn't unsee that butterfly.

≫⟩⟩ ⟨⟨⟨

Preacher had run out of Poplar Bluff and never slowed through
Perryville. A dog caught him just outside Hannibal. Beating
the hound off with a heavy branch, he'd limped free, though
days later he could barely crawl. The pain had swelled, and his
strength had ebbed.

He'd avoided plantations till now. Old Merlin had told him
plantations were perfect—slaves helped slaves, and the masters
couldn't tell one from the other. But most slaves weren't tall
enough to look their master's prize stallion in the eye, and
Preacher could. And some slaves would turn you in for an
extra portion of bacon fat. He'd found that out the hard way
the night he ran. He'd stuffed food scraps into a feedbag as he
had taken to doing several times a week. The next step was to
snatch the last few scraps from the master's ancient hound.
The hound never minded—it ate too well and liked its sleep.
But that particular night, Old Ned had seen him. The man had
nodded friendly-like and started walking away—before Old
Ned's mother appeared and struck her son with a stick.

"He'll tell the master for bacon," she'd told Preacher. "Hell,
he'd tell just out of spite. You go on now. Get!"

Seeing the look in Old Ned's eyes, Preacher left the scraps
and ran. He ran for six days.

He'd been able to eat here and there, doing some hunting but more stealing from gardens. Hadn't ate much since that dog bit him. Last night he had crept into the plantation, dug up a potato, and devoured it dirt and all. The scent of honeysuckle had promised a sweet treat, but he found it too much effort to eat. So, he'd hidden in this bush, hoping the bit of food and rest would be enough to keep him going.

He woke to a sound.

"Snatch it off careful," said a boy's voice, innocent and unaware of life's burden. "Now bite round the end, but not all the way. See? Like this."

"And that drop's the honey?" said another boy, seemingly younger still and full of wonder.

A movement caught Preacher's eye, long and black and sliding through the grass toward his bad leg.

"That's the honey."

Preacher crept his hand into position. Saying a quick prayer, he grabbed the serpent farther down the body than he'd wanted, but close enough it couldn't bite him. That dog had outsmarted him, but no damned snake would do the same.

"I thought honey came from bees."

The reptile thrashed about, rattling the bush until two little heads popped through. "What you doing, mister?" asked the older boy, his eyes wide.

Preacher showed him the black snake. "Looks like I'm saving your ass."

"Shoot. That's just a king snake...he can't hurt nothing."

Preacher held it out to the boy, who pulled back. He then twisted around and threw it as far as he could.

"What's wrong with your leg?"

"Hound dog got it."

The little one finally spoke. "Booker had a hound dog."

"Buster! Tweed!" called a far-off voice. "You youngins hear me?"

Both boys looked over their shoulders.

"Don't tell on me," Preacher whispered. "We men take care of each other."

The older boy seemed affronted at the accusation. "We won't tell!"

"Where you boys at? Buster!" The woman's voice sounded annoyed but with an anxious tone creeping in.

"Our secret from the womenfolk." Preacher tried to smile.

Then the younger boy burst out, "Mammy!"

There was nothing Preacher could do but lie there and wait. When that third head poked through the flowering branches, the woman's eyes grew bigger than the boys' had been.

"His leg is hurt," the older one told her.

She didn't reply.

She looked old enough and then some to be the boy's mammy. Still had muscle, and she was a reasonable size as far as women went, with a faded purple scarf covering her hair. Her eyes were full of some emotion, but Preacher couldn't guess exactly what. He didn't know if he was safe or dead where he lay.

⇢⇢⇢ ⇠⇠⇠

Maggie could only stare. She'd prayed for a miracle, and here he lay.

"Buster, go check the path is clear. Shouldn't be no one about right now." Buster ran off while Tweed leaned into her leg. She patted him soothingly as she eyed the man. "Who you be, mister?"

"You don't wanna know. Just go way. I'll be gone by supper."

Maggie took note of his thigh, his trousers torn and showing dark stains.

"Well, by tomorrow," he amended.

She pushed past the honeysuckle, kneeling to examine his wound. Something had ripped through the material, ripped through the skin. It needed tending, but she'd seen worse.

"Please, woman."

"You can't go far on that leg." Maggie peered over her shoulder, checking no one was about. The house slaves should be fixing the noon meal, and the field hands never came in till sunset. The Whites would be heading toward their fancy dining room so they could sit while they ate. Booker had sent her to fetch some chicken from the kitchen. She could tell some tale about being late, but the longer she took, the less he'd believe her.

"Ma'am, you don't want to get mixed up in this."

Maggie turned, grabbing his arm to pull the man up. He was a giant, powerful and reassuring. He'd get his freedom, she just knew it. And they might get theirs by sticking close by.

Once on his feet, the big fellow moved quick. Maggie guessed that leg must be paining him something fierce, but he paid it no mind.

Buster popped through the vines, eyes widening at the size of the man. "Ain't no one nowhere...clean to the cabin."

Maggie kept telling herself they were safe, that no one would see. But when the door appeared at the end of the trail, relief swamped her whole body. Two other cabins sat near hers, both silent as the grave. The slaves were all where they should be.

When the wood door slammed behind them, shutting out the world, the giant man crumbled to the floor. He managed to land on the pile of straw covering half the space. The entire cabin consisted of straw, a tiny stove, and the old table—Hank's pride and joy. There were only three tables between all fifteen slave cabins. The man's skin glistened with sweat, and Maggie knelt to study the injury proper. His trousers stuck to the wound when she pulled, but she had to see it all.

"Buster, go get me some yarrow," she told her son. The boy nodded, leaping toward the door. Tweed started to follow, but she held him back. "The little white flowers, mind."

"And feather leaves." Tweed grinned. "I know." He darted out after his brother.

Maggie thought the man had done passed out, but his eyes were open and practically stabbing her with accusations.

"Why you doing this?" he asked.

"I'm helping you."

"Huh."

The boys took their time but returned with two good handfuls of the plant. Maggie chewed it in three lumps, using the spittle wads to pack the wound. She knew it had to give the man some relief, but he just watched.

"Where am I?" he asked.

"In our cabin," Buster said.

"What state?"

"Missouri," Tweed piped up.

The man leaned his head back against the wall. "Missouri," he whispered. "Still Missouri."

"Chicago?" Maggie prodded.

He didn't even look at her.

"You heading to Chicago?"

"Canada."

"They say Chicago's a big city. A *free* city. You can get lost in it and never be found."

"They catch slaves in Chicago. They catch freemen and say they ain't."

"Take us with you." There. She'd said it.

The man reached for his sack, which Tweed had brought, and made to push himself up. His leg didn't cooperate. "Can't drag a woman and her boys all the way to Canada. Can hardly drag myself."

"And my daughter. She's older...be a help to you."

"She'd be useless." He thrashed around, wincing. "Weather's cloudy, woman. I can't see the Drinking Gourd at night—can't see which way is north. Can't seem to find my way out of Missouri."

"Stay here for the night," Maggie urged. "We got a privilege cabin. My man's gone, so they let us stay here together. No one comes in, just us. I'll bring you food."

He pushed all the harder to try standing, but seemingly his leg at least had decided to stay.

"I'm Maggie," she told him. "I'll take care of you."

The big man just shut his eyes.

Reluctantly, she left. She'd been twitching to leave for a bit now. Booker was likely flirting with Maisey, busying himself for a bit. But only for a bit.

Then he'd be wanting that chicken.

⤜⤛⤛⤛

Preacher drifted in and out all that afternoon, dreaming. He walked the cotton rows in Mississippi, saw his mother's back whipped raw because the mistress lost an earring. His feet pounded through the swamp after she died, hearing Old Man Ember shouting his name. That hound appeared out of nowhere, tearing flesh from his leg. He climbed that old willow tree faster than a possum and sat there all night, afraid to come down. Afraid of the dog, of the pursuit. Of getting caught.

He woke to find himself buried. Thrashing for freedom, he cried out, "Not yet! I ain't dead yet!"

"Hush!" a woman's voice admonished. "Best let me tell my daughter. Got to be done careful-like."

Preacher stilled. His heartbeat kept its rapid pace, his lungs fighting for more air, but at least his arms and legs obeyed him. The covering over him was not earth, he realized, but a blanket. At the creak of the flimsy door, he held his breath.

"Maggie!" It was an angel's voice, pure and sweet and musical. Had he died and not known it? "I got to work upstairs all day," that lovely sound continued. "Miss Marianne says I'm the best ever at fixing her hair."

"Just what do you know about fixing hair, Honey?" Preacher recognized that other voice.

"I saw those ladies in town last month, remember? When I went to fetch Cook's flour. They had pretty combs holding strands atop their heads. Miss Marianne said she couldn't see proper for all her hair, so I showed her."

Preacher slid his fingers up to his nose, carefully lifting the corner of the blanket. Then he saw her—a genuine angel. She was so small, yet standing so erect. No bow in her shoulders, no hang-dog droop of her head. Pretty hair tumbling free down her back. And when she turned her profile, he glimpsed smooth skin, fresh and unblemished, the color of that milky tea the White folks drank. Most surely an angel, and with an angelic name. Honey.

"Help your brothers fix supper. Or are you too grand for that?"

"Can't, Maggie." Honey laughed. "I'm eating with Weena tonight! I'm a house hand now!" And with the softest smile yet, the angel up and disappeared.

"Guess what! We found—"

⇢⇢⟩⟩   ⟨⟨⟨⟵

Maggie clapped a hand over Tweed's mouth. Best to let Honey go without informing her of anything. Her daughter paused, smiled. With a flitting glance at each of them, she slipped out of the cabin. Maggie stepped to the entrance to watch her go. Honey disappeared up the path, and no one else was about.

Stepping back, Maggie shut and latched the door closed. Then she knelt by the lump in the straw and lifted the blanket. The man's eyes questioned her, though his lips never moved. She told him, "Best to keep this quiet. Tell nary a soul outside us."

"Not tell Honey?" Tweed asked.

Maggie thought it a mark of maturity that Buster said nothing. "Honey got a lot on her mind." She smiled. "It's best to keep this quiet."

Buster nodded. She hoped that meant he'd keep his little brother quiet.

"Go get me water." Maggie nodded at the pitcher.

Buster jumped to get it and ran out the door.

With Honey eating at the house, Maggie was able to fix the big man a big johnnycake. He ate it in silence, eyes closing as he finished.

Gently prodding the big man to slide over to the wall, Maggie put the boys between them. The nights were chilly, and she dug into the straw for warmth, as the trailing bit of blanket barely reached to cover Tweed.

It wouldn't be easy to keep Tweed quiet, but it was important. Telling house slaves anything was always chancy, and Honey was most definitely a house slave now. House slaves had a privileged position at Sweetgum. They didn't have the hard toil of the field, were better clothed, as suited the mistress's notions, and even got food scraps from the kitchen. Sometimes—not often—they would tell tales to the White masters. A slave would get yelled at or removed from handling the horses. Whippings were less common, but they did happen.

The next morning, Squint roused them without so much as opening the door. He roused all the slaves every morning and usually ate his breakfast in one of the cabins—hers more than most but fortunately not today.

Maggie bundled the boys out with their lunch johnnycake in their pockets, hoping that in the routine they'd forget the man who never moved. She did sneak a last look to be sure that he was still breathing. Buster glanced at the man and then at her, but never said nothing. That boy really was growing up fast. Soon even Booker would notice.

→→⟩⟩⟩ ⟨⟨⟨←←

Preacher dreamed of sunshine sparkling on snow. His daddy used to talk about snow in Chicago, the sun sparkling it up something fierce. Mississippi got the white stuff in parts of the state, but not the part Preacher had lived in all his life. "Hot as Hell," Daddy called it.

Daddy had been a freeman in the free state of Illinois. One day, a White man offered him work and bought him a drink in a bar. Next thing he knew, he was in a slave pen in Mississippi. Nobody cared if you were a freeman in the south, because nobody in the south thought Black men *should* be free.

Daddy had a bum leg these days, and anyway, loved his woman, but he'd always urged Preacher to run. "Follow the Gourd," he told him. The Gourd was a constellation—stars in the heaven pointing the way to freedom. "You ain't never been free, boy, but it's worth it. Whatever you have to do, risk your skin to the bayou or the hound or the whip, it's worth it."

Lying on stale straw, the chill seeping into his bones, Preacher wondered if God was punishing him. "Blacks better accept their lot," Master Baker used to say. "You're slaves, every one of you, so do your work. Don't get ideas above yourself. You wouldn't know what to do if you was free."

It was always that last sentence that made Preacher doubt the master. Of course he knew what to do! Get work like his daddy had done. Get his own food, find his own bed. Save his coin for better things.

And anything was surely better when you were a free man.

Footsteps snatched him out of his thoughts, and he resolved to tell that woman no. His own chances for freedom were slimmer than a spider web. Trying to free others as well would make it pretty near impossible.

"Honey, you sweet thing, you in there?"

Preacher looked up to find a white face peering round the door.

✦✧

Booker had never liked being an overseer. Oh, he liked being in charge, telling those slaves what to do, hearing that "Yassir!" from one and all. It made him feel respected, important. Like how folks treated Master Hueron in town.

Master Hueron, on the other hand, didn't seem to respect Booker. He'd kept him on when Sweetgum passed from the old master to him, agreeing that Booker knew the plantation and how best to run it smoothly. But the old master had taken Booker's advice without question. The young master had ideas of his own. If Booker told him a good strong buck cost five hundred dollars, Master Hueron told him it shouldn't cost more than four, or that that particular buck looked neither good nor strong.

This auction, Booker had really pushed his luck. Three of the five slaves he'd bought in Hannibal were females, and the two males weren't that young. Truth was, Booker'd used some of the money for drinking that night. And lost more playing poker.

With the new slaves due to arrive today, he found himself praying as his old mother used to pray, whispering, "Please, Lord. Please, Lord," without any real idea what he wanted the Lord to do. Maybe make the males turn up stronger than he remembered, or the females prove very skilled at picking cotton.

Thinking of the females made him think of Honey. She was a pretty thing, but working in the house put her out of his reach. She did still sleep in Maggie's cabin, but there was something about

Maggie he'd never quite trusted. If he chose to have his fun, Maggie should make herself scarce, but for some reason she saw it differently. The fact that she was Sweetgum's best cotton picker—and the master knew it—made Booker reluctant to push the point.

So when he'd seen Honey tramping away from the mansion earlier, he'd finished talking to the master, then headed toward her cabin. If he was gonna get fired anyway, he might as well have a go. His grin widened when he approached the place, for he heard a shuffling inside. With Maggie in the field, it had to be Honey.

But it wasn't Honey. It was the biggest buck he'd ever seen. Booker groped for his pistol, a big scary thing he knew frightened slaves and Whites alike. It fell apart if handled wrong, and he couldn't afford bullets, but no one knew that. He just hoped the slave wouldn't decide to charge anyway.

The buck was sprawled on the floor, making no move to get up. Probably afraid to move. Booker eased a step closer and saw the wet shine on the man's bare leg. His first thought was that this one wasn't going anywhere. His second was that even the master would admit *this* field hand was worth five hundred dollars.

As it turned out, moving the man wasn't as easy as he'd expected, and Booker hadn't expected it to be easy. The buck was big, real big, and lame. As Booker was used to waving a hand and having slaves scurrying to do his bidding, this presented a problem. Slaves rarely talked, and of course they did fear him, but it would be bad if word of this ever got to Hueron's ears.

The slave stood as soon as he was bid but would have fallen if not for the cabin wall. In the end, Booker got his own horse and draped the big buck over the saddle, legs dangling on one side and head on the other. Once in the wagon, Booker had to take a detour, driving the wooded trail to bypass the plantation gate, pick up the buck and put him the wagon with the other slaves, and then return by the same route. He almost skipped that part, but it wouldn't be good if Hueron happened to see the wagon coming from the wrong direction.

He rode in with the wagon, flashing his gun twice to be sure the new hands were properly intimidated. Most auctioned slaves were terrified to begin with, uncertain what the future would bring. But in that fear, you never knew what they might blurt out.

Normally he'd just take them to the field, but Hueron had ordered the new hands brought before him first. Not a good sign, that.

Looking over the wagon, Booker liked what he saw. Three girls, true, but two of them were young and strong. The two males were a bit scrawny and one had graying hair, but the addition of the big one overshadowed the rest. Even with a bum leg, he would have gotten a full five hundred dollars at auction. Well, more than four, at the least.

The wagon drove round the bend, and the house appeared. It was a few hours after breakfast, but the master had heard them coming and rose from the porch swing.

"Master Hueron," Booker said, waving his arm to introduce the new property to their owner. "I'll start 'em right away."

Hueron strode down the steps, eyeing each slave carefully. "Thought you said five slaves, Booker." The man's eyes lingered on the big buck, and though he looked calm, the question was barbed.

"Buck hurt his leg since I bought him," Booker heard himself say. "So I got 'em to toss in an extra."

Hueron leaned over the wagon side, studying the leg. "Can you work, boy?"

Booker swallowed.

"Yessir," the buck said.

"What's your name?"

"Preacher."

Hueron nodded. "See that leg is tended, Booker."

"Yes, sir."

The master mounted the steps, then turned around. "Don't push him in the fields today at the expense of tomorrow. And, Booker..."

"Sir?"

"Three days from now, that leg better be on the mend."

Fear swelling his throat, Booker could only nod.

Hueron gave him a steady look. "Looks like a good haul this time."

That, Booker knew, was high praise.

~~⟫⟫⟫ ⟪⟪⟪~~

Dust marked the approach of the wagon. Maggie saw it out of the corner of her eye as she plucked cotton. Corner of her mind too, as she thought about how to push the big man. Maybe if she got Honey to ask... Her daughter was skilled at asking for stuff. Everybody always seemed to help that child. But then Honey wasn't anxious to leave. Might be years before the child realized just what slavery was, what it did to the soul.

Slavery was a path, just like any path in the world. If you stepped exactly where you were supposed to, always pleasing the masters, it could go okay. Trouble was, you couldn't set a foot anywhere else. Your belly churning or your leg torn up by a dog, you still had to pick as much cotton as always. Master came to the slave quarters, you had to let him have his way no matter what that way was. And if they wanted to strip the hide from your mate before your eyes, you'd better not look away.

All Honey had ever been asked to do was brush the mistress's hair. So far at least. She was thrilled at being a house slave now, eagerly fitting in to house slave ways. And house slaves went that extra mile to stay on the master's good side. It was a privilege they didn't fancy losing.

As the dust trail drew closer, Maggie wondered if Buster and Tweed might not be the key. The big man seemingly liked them, after all, and Buster was both smart and nimble. If he could be brought to see the advantage in taking them...

"That's one big buck." The girl—Elvira her name was—straightened, a hand covering her eyes.

Maggie glanced up, an admonishment on her lips as the wagon slowed to a halt. First thing she saw was Booker's shit-eating grin. The second was her own big runaway man. His back was to her, but she recognized the set of his shoulders, the muscled bulge of his arms.

How can Booker possibly have him?

For a moment she wondered if he'd given himself up, figuring it was easier. Then she saw his face, and two things were blindingly clear. The big man wasn't there by choice, and he was furious. From his glare trying to fry her brain in her head, she guessed his fury was all for her.

⟫⟫⟫ ⟪⟪⟪

Marianne tired of waiting for Weena. She snatched the deep blue Norwich silk shawl—a better choice for this dress than Weena usually made—and headed down what Hueron called the grand staircase. Like all things in the South, it was a bit overblown.

She had sent an invitation to Miss Leonard and Mrs. Jevington to come enjoy a proper British tea. She'd sent it yesterday afternoon—late, perhaps, but surely they should have answered by now.

Baltimore had been so different. People were smarter on the East Coast, and more engaged. Debates occurred over abolition and women's rights. Indeed, Harriet Sitcomb had attended the Women's Rights Convention in Seneca Falls, and there'd been an uproar over the Missouri Compromise, whatever that was.

Slavery was so different, talked about so differently, in Baltimore. It was like a shiny new tea service, hand-painted in odd colors.

Everyone had an opinion and shared it. Here in Missouri, slavery was but a weed in the flower garden, distastefully ignored.

Her father used to say labor in Maryland was precious. The Maryland Chemical Works Company, where he worked, used slaves. They too had been concerned with slaves running away, but no one ever proposed using violence to change that. Instead, they treated them kindly but firmly, at least according to her father.

Not so in Missouri. Her first day in the state, traveling through Hannibal, she'd seen a Black man tied to a tree and whipped until his blood splattered the maple. Missouri wasn't a bad place, Mark had explained. It just wasn't full of abolitionists. The plantation owners understood the fiscal need. But Marianne had never forgotten the sight of blood raining down on the dead leaves.

Outside, a buggy drew up, a nice one drawn by two matched horses. That meant money and importance, which meant it must be Miss Leonard or Mrs. Jevington. Peeping out the window, Marianne saw it was both. She sped to the parlor and snatched up her embroidery as she sat down on the sofa. Taking a deep breath, calming her expression, she prepared a gracious smile.

Then something crashed in the hallway, sounding awfully like her prized Delft jar. She ran to the door to find Lucy standing in a sea of shattered blue porcelain. The girl's little face scrunched up, her skin tinged red, her eyes a plain brown. How could a child of hers be so plain?

"I'm sorry, Mother," Lucy said.

Marianne stepped over the broken shards and slapped her. Lucy had just turned eight years old and was getting out of hand. Perhaps the slave owners were right to be strict.

By the time the ladies entered and handed their shawls to Bibby, Weena had whisked both daughter and debris from the hall. If either lady noticed anything amiss, she held her tongue.

〰️〰️〰️ 〰️〰️〰️

It was early. Most likely, Mark was in the fields already, working. Marianne had meant to ask about arranging a proper dinner party with six couples. Her husband usually encouraged her to do as she liked, but he wasn't one for socializing. Probably he'd allow it, but probably he'd want a chance to say yes before she sent out the invitations.

He might still be eating breakfast, so Marianne threw on her wrapper and hurried down the stairs. The floor was cold, but she really wanted to start organizing today. Truth was, she was bored. Missouri was boring after Baltimore.

Slipping the door open, she peeped into the dining room. It was empty, the table clear. He must have eaten a while ago. Or... She hurried across the room to check the kitchen. For all she knew, he might eat there. Marianne remembered something about eating in the kitchen.

She'd been right, in a way, but it was a little blonde head she saw at the cook's table, not her husband. The child never looked around, and Marianne kept quiet. She found conversation with her daughter burdensome. Lucy never talked about the things a girl should talk about—pretty dresses or hair tongs—and Marianne had long since stopped trying to make her do so.

She sighed. She'd have to hope Mark came in at noon. As she weighed the idea of seeking out her husband in the cotton fields, the little blonde head inspected a biscuit before licking the jam off it.

A memory rose of Marianne at the breakfast table, using her tongue to taste the fresh strawberry jam. The sweet fruit in her mouth. Her mother slapping her face so hard her teeth sliced her tongue. The metallic taste of blood. The pain.

The cook later told her that good mothers taught their children well. A good smacking was the way to keep them on God's path. Marianne remembered looking at her mother through the tears welling in her eyes, and the harder strike that followed—the one with a fist.

Truth was, Lucy was difficult to manage. She did as she was told, of course, but only when told. And Marianne fancied the child didn't relish it much. She'd need to keep a good eye on her. It was duty, after all, and Marianne was one to do her duty.

⟫⟫⟫ ⟪⟪⟪

That evening, Maggie poured cornmeal into the bowl.

"Mammy, he's staying forever!" Tweed grinned. He'd been talking and talking about the man, and Maggie let him, hoping he'd get it all out of his system.

"I don't think he wants to stay," Buster told his brother. "I'll fetch the water."

Maggie handed her son the pitcher, then watched him dart out the door. She forgot to warn against tripping.

The big man didn't seem to be in trouble, which had her plumb flabbergasted. Masters always gave rewards for runaway slaves, and other masters always collected them. Oftentimes, they'd both beat the slave for the sheer joy of beating. Yet the story the field hands whispered was that Preacher had been bought at the auction, that the master was pleased with him, despite the leg injury, which Booker swore would heal just fine. Maggie couldn't quite figure it out.

Honey burst into the cabin. "Maggie, I'm going with Miss Marianne to town. Oh!"

Right behind her, Booker pushed his way inside. "Honey," he said, his hands clasping her in places Maggie didn't like. The man looked at Maggie and smiled. She knew that sort of smile.

"You got a full crew now, Maggie," Booker said, his hand stroking Honey's back as the big man stepped into the doorway. "This here's Preacher. You tend his leg real good."

"But..." Honey stared. "You can't put a man in our cabin."

Booker wet his lips, studying Honey, and Maggie itched to slap his face. "Well now, li'l darling, it's time. You're good stock."

Preacher stepped between them, his bulk filling the cabin and forcing Booker away from her daughter. "I won't be no trouble, miss," he said to Honey.

Maggie held her breath. Clearly Booker didn't relish the interruption, but he seemed nervous rather than angry. Being the overseer, he had a hold on the big man, but maybe Preacher had a hold on him as well.

Preacher. Of all names...

Buster popped through the door, staring up at the men.

Maggie prayed he'd hold his tongue.

At that moment, Booker noticed the meal preparation. "You get bacon fat tonight."

"Bacon fat?" Honey asked.

"For the buck! Proper men need to eat proper."

Buster offered the pitcher to Maggie, and Booker remained on the threshold, eyes devouring Honey. He'd had plans for her for some time now, Maggie knew, but between Bibby and herself, he'd never succeeded. In fact, Honey owed her promotion to house slave to their effort.

After a moment, Maggie poured the water in with the cornmeal and mixed it with her fingers. She heard rather than saw the overseer leave. Honey, she knew, hadn't a clue why Preacher had been bunked in with them any more than she truly grasped the danger Booker posed. Maggie'd explained it to her again last week, but while the girl nodded like she understood, she really didn't, because she really didn't understand men.

But Maggie knew that particular smile. When she was Honey's age, Master Jacob had snuck up on her one night as she fetched water. His eyes had glistened like the stream, his breath smelling so foul. His fingers had ripped the sleeve of her faded pink dress.

Just then, Hank had appeared, grinning, calling her name as if he did that all the time. He'd never seemed to notice her before, but he called her name that night. Smiled at Master Jacob and guided her away. For a minute, her fate—and Hank's too—had balanced on a teenager's whim. Then the young master had vanished in the dark.

Now Booker vanished out the door. Preacher had Hank's strength and protective instinct. He wasn't afraid of Booker and seemingly liked Honey, even if he blamed her mother for all his troubles. Maybe he'd take her with him to Canada once his leg was all healed up. Maybe he'd even take her family.

Shoot...they'd at least gotten bacon fat out of it.

⟫⟫⟫ ⟪⟪⟪

Puppies were playing in the barn, which Lucy knew because Cook had told Bibby. Weena had told her to stay away, but after she left with Marianne's tea tray, Cook just grinned and warned Lucy not to get her dress dirty.

The girl loved Cook. Cook and Bibby were nice, making sure she ate a good supper or was cleaned up before going to her mother. But Bibby loved her mother. Cook liked *her*.

Keeping clean wasn't so important these days. Mother rarely wanted to see her since they'd left the East Coast. Missouri, she'd declared, was nothing like Baltimore. And she was right.

But it wasn't all bad. Perhaps it was lonely here, like Mother said. In Baltimore, a lot of adults came for morning visits or afternoon tea, keeping the house full and always busy. But there hadn't been many children, and those that were there hadn't liked Lucy. Here, there was a river and a beach and woods and grass. And now a barn full of puppies.

She waited till Cook was washing up before slipping out the back door. Best not to attract too much attention. The barn was just a hop, skip, and a jump away, half in the woods and half out. Most of the farm stuff was kept in the other barn, the one closer to the cotton fields, so this barn had hay and horses and now puppies.

It wasn't *full* of puppies, but the five that were there whined and cried for their mother. Lucy found them in a back corner, resting in a nest of straw and old rope. Their mom was licking them, and after sniffing Lucy's hand, let them lick her as well, but the puppies were more interested in sucking milk than getting petted.

Scratching the skinny one's ear, Lucy heard a noise.

"They's in here," a boy whispered.

Lucy whirled around. Two Black boys stood halfway between her and the door, their eyes big as saucers. "Are you slaves?" she asked.

The little one spun around and ran as if a mean dog was chasing him. The older one nodded.

"Did you come to see the puppies?"

The boy nodded again, then raced out of the barn as well.

Lucy sighed. In Baltimore, one girl—who Mother promised would be her friend—had run away when they were alone. She hadn't wanted to play with Lucy either. So Missouri wasn't all that different after all.

~»»》 《«««

"I got a good rhythm going." Maggie straightened, rubbing her back. "I needs to finish this cotton."

She had to stifle a giggle when Booker slapped his hand with his riding crop and winced from the pain. "Go get me that chicken, woman. And be quick about it."

Dropping her bag, Maggie headed off, moving as slow as she dared. It was always better when the overseer went to the kitchen himself. That gave the hands a little freedom for a while. Lately, however, Booker had been sending one of them and sticking round. Probably figured he'd have better luck with Maisey here than Honey at the mansion.

As she made her way through the woods, a low branch caught Maggie's skirt and tore another hole in it. She always protected her head fiercely, fearing damage to her purple kerchief, which left her skirts more vulnerable. She used to darn them at night, but it just wasn't worth it. The holes came too often, and the thread not often enough.

It had been awhile since they last got new clothes. The old master supplied hand-me-downs every summer, but he'd missed the last two years, and this new master didn't seem to think much about slave clothes or supplies. Or food for that matter.

Things had changed since the old master. When Maggie was born, there had been three new mammies in the slave cabins that year alone. Mammy Miri had been hers. Big woman in purple, whose eyes had shone whenever she saw her baby. She worried about her too.

Maggie never took to tobacco. She never liked touching it, hated being in a field surrounded by it. When she was young, it had towered over her, shutting out the sun. She'd panicked more than once. The master soon sent her to work in the house. In fact, he'd sent her several times. The mistress would send her back, sometimes after a few weeks, sometimes that same day. She remembered this scrawny White woman standing over her in the kitchen, shouting, "Come get this thing, Bibby! She's too dirty!"

Mammy Miri had fretted that they'd up and sell Maggie to buy a more useful slave. Somehow the master hadn't, but the fretting had worn her mammy down. She died about the time Sweetgum was sold to a new master. When Maggie stood in the line of slaves to be presented, the tears had slid down her cheeks.

The new master had touched one of her cheeks and looked to the overseer, who told him the girl was no good at tobacco and was ashamed to face him. The master had simply said, "Maybe she'll be better at cotton."

Maggie decided then and there he was right. When cotton needed picking, it was white instead of green and never grew so tall she couldn't see the sun. Course, part of that was she was a grown woman herself by then. She became the best field hand on Sweetgum. If only Mammy Miri had lived to see it.

Now Maggie emerged from the trees and walked past the barn. Dust kicked up on the path, especially near the kitchen door, and she wondered how long they had till the spring rain settled the soil and ruined the cotton.

Maybe she'd make another run at Preacher tonight. He'd mellowed a bit, living in their cabin with Honey, but not to the point of talking to Honey's mammy. Squint was the only other man she could talk to about freedom, and she might as well ask a stone wall as him.

Rapping on the back door, Maggie waited on the doorstep. Bibby didn't like field slaves entering her scrubbed kitchen.

Cook opened the door and shook her head. "Booker sent you for chicken, didn't he. Master ain't all that happy with him, Maggie. Tell him he better watch hisself."

Maggie shrugged. She didn't care if Booker got himself in a little trouble.

"We don't wanna lose him." Cook moved off to snatch up a fair hunk of chicken—the leg and thigh. "Master Hueron's next overseer would be harsher, I promise you." That was Cook's way of looking at things. The woman was near as old as Squint, and near as smart. Maybe she knew the same stuff Squint knew.

Maggie wet her lips, glancing around to make sure they were alone. "You know anything about a man in town, supposed to help slaves..."

"Stop right there." Cook gave her a long, hard stare. "You gotta take care who you ask things like that." Cook turned, peering over her shoulder at the empty room. "Real careful, Maggie."

Maggie sighed.

Wiping her hands on the old apron, Cook stepped close. "Back of Sampson's Store. After dark. You knock once."

Maggie's heart stopped pumping altogether.

"No matter who opens the door, tell 'em that old mule threw his shoe. If'n he tell you to come back tomorrow, say 'yassir' and get your ass gone. But if'n he says, 'what mule,' you say Inky."

The world stilled. A faint puff of air tickled Maggie's hair.

"Likely won't help you," Cook continued. "Heard tell old Murphy done up and disappeared, which makes things tough. And being a female don't make them easier. Still, I ain't one to stand in your way." She set the chicken in Maggie's hand. "You go on now. Take that to Booker."

Maggie ran fast through the trees, her whole body feeling lighter than air.

Miss Helen wasn't under the bed. Miss Helen wasn't *anywhere*. Lucy scrabbled up from the floor, carefully replacing the lamp on the dresser. *Think*, she could hear the real Miss Helen say. *Where did you last see her?* Not in the kitchen, when she ate dinner. Not when she washed her hands after coming inside.

The wood. After Mother yelled over her torn dress and Weena bundled her away, Lucy had run out the kitchen door to the barn. Miss Helen was in her apron pocket.

They'd played with the puppies, and then they'd played explorers. Her daddy had once told her about Lewis and Clark and the courage it took to explore. That was why they had all traveled west, leaving Baltimore behind. That was when the real Miss Helen, her governess and friend, had given her a doll she'd stitched by hand. Lucy had named her Miss Helen too.

Today Lucy and Miss Helen had gone farther than ever, all the way to the slave cabins. They weren't supposed to go there, but the cabins were empty during the day. All the slaves were toiling away, as Weena liked to say. Lucy and Miss Helen had climbed on that log, sat right down, and stared at the tiny houses. They were made of logs stacked one on the other, and one of them had a window, just a single window among the three cabins so she could see.

As Lucy pointed that out to Miss Helen, the two slave boys burst from the bushes. She'd been so scared she'd fallen off the log. The boys stared at her, and she'd stared at the boys. The littlest had raced on.

"We'se going to the river!" the bigger boy announced.

Sprawled in the leaves, Lucy just gawked as he turned and disappeared too. Then she had scrambled to her feet and fled, leaving Miss Helen behind.

Now she was all alone in the dark. The doll was her first friend in Missouri, supposed to be followed by many more. But there hadn't been any more. And friends were important, the real Miss Helen used to say.

Lucy stuck her head out the window. The moon was shining, coloring the leaves a tingly brown. An owl hooted, but she couldn't see it. Would an owl eat Miss Helen? Maybe pick at her button eyes?

She should climb into bed and crawl under the covers. She wasn't allowed to do anything else once Weena had settled her down for the night. But Miss Helen was out there all alone, with owls and foxes and slave boys. And explorers had courage, her daddy said.

So Lucy tugged her coat down from its place in the wardrobe and pulled it on. She tiptoed down the servant stairs, peeking around the corners. At the bottom, she spied Weena carrying a silver platter to the dining room. Her parents always ate after she'd been tucked away for the night. It was easy to reach the back door without Cook seeing her. Grasping the handle, she let herself out. She'd expected to be scared, but she wasn't. Instead, she felt that surge of relief in being free of the house, free of adults. In the bright moonlight, she raced up the path, past the barn and into the woods.

Wind rustled the leaves, making their shadows dance at her feet. Lucy peered through the trees carefully but saw no owls or foxes or slaves. She did hear rustling and shied away. Being an explorer was scary. But Miss Helen needed her, so she hurried on.

Things looked different in the dark, and the path seemed longer than she remembered. She kept looking for the lights of the slave cabins, but she didn't see anything until a door squeaked open and a dim light teased the dark. The Hueron house was so bright at night, with lanterns glowing everywhere. There were no outside lanterns here at all.

"I'll get it, Mammy!" a boy cried.

Lucy froze as another door opened, and the slave boy from earlier raced out, carrying something. This was his house—the one with the window. That made him special, she decided.

She stepped to the side, looking for the spot where she'd sat earlier. The window should be more to her front...

There was the log. And there, as if she'd kept watch all day, was Miss Helen. Suddenly happy, Lucy snatched her up, brushing her dress clean of any owl feathers. Miss Helen was safe.

Lifting her eyes to the cabin window, Lucy noticed a light inside. It was easier to see it with the door standing open, as most of the light poured through that. She could see Honey in there, and the smaller slave boy.

"Mammy, I ate honeysuckle today!" he said.

Another woman hugged him. Lucy wondered if she was his governess.

The older boy came charging back, feet pounding on the path. He leaped for the door, tripped, and fell inside the cabin. Whatever he'd been carrying shattered into a million pieces. It sounded just like the blue jar when it fell. Lucy shivered for the boy.

He burst into tears. "I'se sorry! Oh, Mammy, I'se sorry!"

Framed in the low light, the woman wrapped her arms around him and hugged him tight. "Never you mind, baby. Never you mind."

If she didn't hit him for that, she doesn't hit him for nothing! Lucy thought in wonder.

"We ain't got a pitcher," Honey told her.

"Take the bowl to the stream, child," the mammy said. "More'n one way to skin a cat."

And that was that. No one got slapped. No one got yelled at. They just cooked and ate their supper together. Lucy watched them through the window, even though she mostly saw shadows. It was a long while till Lucy took Miss Helen home.

⇝≫ ≪⇜

The buggy jumbled down the road in a direction Lucy had never been.

"Jenny," Mother said.

"Jenny," Lucy repeated.

Mother nodded. "Now don't forget. It's impolite not to remember someone's name."

They never remember my name, Lucy thought. But saying that aloud would tempt another slap, and she wasn't to tempt a slap today of all days. Mother had warned her while Bibby pulled the pinafore out of the closet and Honey braided her hair in pigtails.

It was Jenny Leonard's birthday today, and her mother was holding a tea party for the girls. Martha would be there, and Elizabeth as well. Martha hated Lucy, and Elizabeth said she smelled like cow. Their only cows were in a far pasture, and Lucy took care never to go there again after that. She'd never met Jenny. Mother said she was a nice girl, nearly Lucy's age. The other girls were older. Jenny's house wasn't as big as Sweetgum, and Mother smiled as she said that. Mother liked to fit everyone in their place. Bigger houses, better dresses put them above the Huerons, so Jenny was below. Maybe she'd be nicer.

Lucy heard a lowing, as her mother called it. There were cows—lots of them—not so very far away. Maybe Jenny also smelled like cow.

Standing on the porch of the Leonards' house, Lucy looked beyond a grownup's legs as the door swung open. She saw Martha and another girl in the background, looking out a window. Seeing Lucy, the girl smiled. Martha stuck her tongue out.

They drank milk and munched cake as their mothers sipped at China tea. Or the cups might have been China. Afterward, the girls went outside to play.

"What are *you* doing here, cowgirl?" Elizabeth sneered.

"Lucy was invited," Jenny told her.

"Big mistake," Elizabeth said.

"Come on." Martha grabbed Elizabeth, and the two marched ahead.

Jenny stayed with her. "Are you a cowgirl?" she asked.

Lucy shook her head.

"We raise cattle." Jenny nodded off toward the cows. "Do you want to see?"

Lucy could see them fine, of course, and she really didn't want to get their smell on her. But Jenny was nice, and she hoped to keep her feeling that way. "Sure!"

They raced to the fence, made of wire and stretching farther than the white-painted fences around town. Many of the cows had horns, Lucy noticed. Sweetgum had four cows, and not one of them had horns.

"You must drink a lot of milk," she told Jenny.

"These are meat cows. They're the future."

"The future of what?" *Will milk go away?*

Jenny shrugged. "They just are."

"Jenny!" Two big men were wrapping more wire around posts. Mending the fence, they told the girls. "Your daddy will whip you good you go over that fence again."

Lucy stared at her new friend, who grinned.

Jenny told her, "We can get hurt by them hooves if'n we fell or something," as they veered off toward a patch of trees.

"Are all your slaves White?" Lucy asked.

Jenny shook her head. "They're hired hands. We don't have no slaves."

"Oh," said Lucy.

There was a brook running among the trees. Lucy and Jenny found flat stones and tried to skip them across the water. They never succeeded, but they had a lot of fun.

"I want to learn to swim!" Jenny said.

"Water's not deep enough."

"Imagine swimming in the Mississippi. How much fun would that be!"

Lucy guessed it might be fun, splashing and floating and all. Jenny was kind and didn't care if they got their dresses wet, so Lucy didn't either.

It turned out Jenny's parents were ranchers who didn't mind if their daughter played in the dirt and said slavery was a bad thing. Jenny's mother smiled at Lucy when they were leaving and said she hoped to see her again soon. By that time, both Elizabeth and Martha had gone.

As the buggy trotted past the cows, Lucy waved at the cow hands. Jenny's house wasn't as far away as town, so perhaps she would see her again soon.

"I like Jenny," she told Mother.

"They're not the right sort of people," Mother said.

Turning her gaze to her lap, Lucy knew she didn't have a friend after all.

⇒⇒⇒ ⇐⇐⇐

After the cornmeal was eaten and Maggie had tasted a piece of bacon fat, she walked into town. She'd made the trip twice before, once to get the master's new reins for that Dancer horse of his and once when Miss Marianne wanted Cook to hurry home and fix her tea. But this was different. Cloud cover faded the moonlight to almost nothing, and it was a long hike. Maggie would have been wise to wait for a better night, but then she couldn't sleep neither. Might as well get her answer now.

The town was quiet, so quiet she could hear her own heart pounding inside her chest. Her feet took the back way, avoiding the main street and hugging the shadows. Her feet had more sense than her head, Maggie realized. If anyone saw her...

Finding the path to the back of Sampson's Store proved difficult in the dark shadows. Her legs got scratched by a nest of thorns, and by the end, her breath was loud and harsh in her own ears. Staring at the door, she had to force her hand up to knock.

Maggie waited in drowning silence, wondering if anyone was even there and if they would open to the likes of her.

Light blinded her when they did. A small Black man stood there, a scar on his chin and his eyes gazing straight into hers. She waited for him to say something until the truth dawned on her. He *wouldn't* speak first.

"The mule," she rasped out. "That old mule threw his shoe."

The man didn't even blink. Behind him, someone bigger stepped forward, a White man. Bald and scary, with a nasty sneer.

"What mule?" he growled.

"Inky, sir."

Maggie felt his anger swell and braced herself.

"Sending me women now?" He turned to the small man, waving a hand at her. "What am I supposed to do with a woman?"

Answers rose to Maggie's tongue, but she knew enough to keep silent. You didn't talk to a White man without him talking to you first.

"Ain't heard from Rufus in months. Months! How can I send anyone to Quincy?" He strode off, then whirled back to glare at her. "Quincy! Murphy in Quincy takes the slaves—or he did. I sent Rufus more'n a month back. Ain't seen him since. More'n a month. No Rufus and no Murphy. Can't send anyone now, let alone a woman. How you gonna get there by yourself?"

Maggie put her hand out but didn't touch the man. She had that much sense at least. "I'll go where you say, do what you say. Just...say. Please, sir."

"Can't tell ya what I don't rightly know." The man grabbed the door, swinging it closed.

Maggie impulsively stopped it, then dreaded his reaction.

Yellow eyes glaring, he snarled, "Whatever you thought you knew, woman, keep your tongue between your teeth."

The door shut gently in her face.

When Maggie got back to the cabin, the others were lying in the bed. Buster was snoring just as loud as a full-grown man. He lay between Honey and Preacher.

Hank used to snore. After that night when Master Jacob tore her dress, Hank took to sleeping in her cabin. Mammy Miri had eyed him up and down and started feeding him.

A gleam caught Maggie's eye—the moonlight sparkling off Preacher's face. The big man was awake. "Were you heading to Quincy?" she asked.

For a moment he was silent, then said, "Ain't never heard of no Quincy."

Maggie parked herself on the table bench. "That's where they were sending Hank."

"Hank?"

"My man. Honey's father. He was Hell bent on running away..."

Barely a week since she'd fixed his leg up proper, but Preacher moved without much of a limp. One instant he lay there on the straw, then suddenly he was looming above her.

Grabbing her arm, he hauled her outside and into the trees. "Have you no sense at all?" he said. "And you wonder why no one will help a woman!"

Her jaw dropped.

"It's against White man's law to help a slave. They've burned their houses down, thrown them in jail. They hurt 'em all they can as an example to the others. If you think masters get mad at us for running, you ain't seen what they'll do to one of their kind helping us run."

"But...Illinois a free state."

"Ain't no free states." The big man paced, his angry stomp belying his calm face. "Slave catchers hunt you down in Chicago just as fast as Alabama. Hell, they catch free men too, and as long as they skin is black, ain't no one gonna stop 'em."

Maggie felt a rush of excitement. "So you know 'bout running! You *were* heading for Quincy."

"No, ma'am. I was heading for Canada. Following the Gourd. It points north, or supposed to at least. Ain't much good if you can't see it through the clouds." Glaring, Preacher stepped close, and she wondered if he was going to hit her. "Just...*think*, woman. Use some sense. If the wrong man hears about Quincy, or anything about White men helping, they put a stop to it. Burn him out, kill his family. They stop it permanent." Preacher turned toward the cabin.

"They dare hurt White people?"

Preacher sent her a glare over his shoulder like she was stupid not knowing all this. But how could she know all this?

"I only asked slaves!" she said.

Preacher spun on his heel. "You think no slave will tell on them? On you? Tell for a bit more bacon fat, or a new dress? Tell just to please the master, curry favor? Or maybe save the skin off their back? Damn, woman. And you think Honey's naive."

That leg had healed up, all right. Preacher's heels dug good into the dirt as he marched off.

⤛⤜ ⤚⤛

"Fine morning! Fine day! Best eat quick or you'll miss it!" That was Squint's voice, carrying through the pre-dawn air as he roamed between the cabins.

Already mixing lard into the cornmeal, Maggie felt her lips form a sneer. Anger at the man outside and anger at the man inside was welling up inside her like that stream in the wood after a heavy rain. Squint swore he knew nothing more about the men in town. Apparently, Cook had let him know about their conversation. He knew nothing about Murphy or Quincy, and when she asked about Rufus, he denied knowing about that as well. Said it didn't bear knowing.

Preacher hadn't spoken to her since that night. He might have been planning an escape, he might not, but he'd never breathe a word to her.

Maggie watched Honey roll to her feet, shaking Tweed in the same motion. "Up, sleepy…" Her daughter's voice trailed off as she spotted the big lump on the other side of the blanket. It'd been three days, and Honey still hadn't gotten used to the man in their bed.

So far, Preacher hadn't touched her. Whether that was due to his sense of honor or lack of privacy, Maggie didn't know. But she was grateful, and oddly touched.

"Any vittles to spare, Maggie?" Squint called from the other side of the door. He wasn't gonna let her ignore him.

Maggie dropped another johnnycake on the stove as Honey opened the door. The old slave stepped in, grinning when Preacher sat up in the gloom. "Well now, I forgot you were in here." He slanted Maggie a look. "That's extra bacon fat for this cabin now."

She bit back her retort. The old slave ate breakfast in different cabins each morning, frequenting hers most. They had a table, he used to say when others asked, or even when they didn't ask.

Honey passed out the wooden slats, and everyone scooped a share.

"Hurry up," Squint grumbled around his portion. "Sun's waking."

Tweed, who'd downed his food fast, looked at Maggie hopefully. "What about lunch, Mammy?"

Maggie turned to slide her scoop under two of the cooked cornmeal blobs on the stove. "Mind, put it in your pocket till noon, honey child."

The boys each took one.

"That's all there is?" Preacher spoke mildly, but she caught his piercing gaze.

Honey answered, "We ain't got the garden to grow stuff. You can have mine. Cook gives me nice leftover bits."

Preacher cut Maggie another shriveling look, but he smiled gently at Honey and tucked away the two blobs for his lunch.

Filling the gourds with water, Maggie stoppered them with corks and passed them out. She gave Honey's to Preacher. "Boys come by around midday and refill your gourd if'n you ask."

The man looked right past her to Squint. "Where you want me this morning?"

Licking his fingers, Squint stood. "Follow me."

The two men led the way—the two who could help her and refused. Buster and Tweed followed.

Watching them, her gut twisted. Those boys deserved freedom. One way or another, Maggie vowed, they were going to get it.

THE MAMMY

HUERON RODE SOUTH FOR a full half day, reaching Daunton Place just after noon. It was a prosperous tobacco plantation owned by Richmond Daunton, his best friend this side of the Mississippi. Sitting astride Dancer, Hueron now watched the fifty slaves in the field, noting their smooth movement, quick pace, sheer skill. Very different from his twenty-two hands back at Sweetgum.

"I thought you disliked slavery," he prodded his friend.

Richmond gently nodded. "Distasteful business, not very Christian. But without them there's no profit."

Aye, profit. The one thing that had eluded Kurt. There'd been a large store in Baltimore, quite profitable until his grandfather died. His father had run it for less than five years before selling, claiming it was time to move west, to new opportunities. Hueron had only been thirteen, but even then he'd recognized the decline in custom, the inventory piling up as the salesmen left. At fourteen, he'd found himself in Missouri, on Sweetgum Plantation.

At sixteen, he'd run back to Baltimore and gotten a job working for his uncle's shipping company. A shrewd businessman,
Uncle Jay had taught Hueron the power of numbers. Adding
the income figures, subtracting the expenses. Keeping an eye on
that key value—profit. Kurt, Hueron knew, looked for 'signs'
of good things—people saying what he wanted to hear—instead of at cold factual numbers.

Sweetgum had been, or so he'd been told, a thriving tobacco
plantation. Now, twenty years later, its fields were cotton and
the profit his father had prophesied barely paid the upkeep.
Barely. When Kurt had died and Sweetgum became his, he'd
hesitated to claim it. He liked living in Maryland, liked the
Chesapeake and the city of Baltimore, but his uncle had three
sons of his own and Hueron would never be more than a family
employee at the shipping company. Perhaps not even that when
his cousins took control.

Uncle Jay said one business was much like another. Understand where your income came from, what your expenses were,
and then apply your brain to increase profit. Simple.

Five months later, the Sweetgum profits didn't seem to have
improved. Cotton plantations could grow five to seven crops a
year, though Kurt had only achieved four. Every phase of the
growing cycle took work, be it planting or picking. Booker, the
manager, blamed all the problems on a troublemaker slave named
Skeeter. Skeeter'd been punished and sold four months ago, but
the numbers hadn't improved. So Hueron had decided to consult

Richmond, his best friend from his teenage years. His plantation yielded rich results.

"Slaves are a resource," he said. "You have to manage them like a resource. Feed them, keep them healthy. You took care of those ships in Baltimore. A slave's no different. They're an expensive tool. Keep them in good order."

"They're lazy creatures," Hueron said. "You gotta make them work harder."

"Well now, there are bad slaves. There are bad overseers as well." Richmond looked out across his tobacco, smiling at the steady rhythm of the field hands. "Why did your family decide to plant cotton?"

"King Cotton. Surely you've seen the figures. Ever since the cotton gin, demand just soared."

"Cotton is the most profitable crop in Alabama. And Arkansas...Mississippi. States with milder weather."

"There are other cotton plantations in Missouri."

Richmond eyed him a moment, then nodded. "Southern edge. And not as profitable."

Should have guessed, Hueron thought. None of his neighbors grew cotton. None of his neighbors were stupid.

Richmond patted his shoulder. "You got pretty near 800 acres. How many hands out in the field?"

"Eighteen. Four more in the house."

"It's March, Mark. Rain's coming soon. Gotta get the cotton picked before the rain. Buy yourself more field hands. Experienced, if possible. Fit and strong, if not."

Slaves weren't cheap, but Hueron couldn't afford to lose this crop. "How many you reckon?"

"How much money you got?"

⤜⤜⤜ ⤛⤛⤛

Lucy knew better than to follow the slave boys. Mother had told her and told her to keep a proper distance. Father said no decent woman would approach a Negro. Even Miss Helen in Baltimore wouldn't allow "mixing with that sort," so she knew it was wrong.

But the children in town were far away, and they didn't like her. Jenny Leonard did, but Mother said she wasn't the right sort and that Elizabeth Jevington was much more suitable. Lucy didn't tell her that Elizabeth thought she smelled like a cow.

Buster and Tweed played a lot. They ran and jumped, skipped stones on the Mississippi, and snatched bird eggs right from the nest. Well, only one so far. Another time, they raced leaves in the river. They jumped out on three big rocks to stand above the water. Each dropped a sycamore leaf into the current and waited to see which one traveled faster. Lucy had been amazed how quickly those little green boats sailed away.

The boys laughed a lot and had adventures. She wanted adventures too. It was the day they built the Indian fort that it all happened. Lucy had followed them the day before, but—keeping her distance—lost them in the wood. So she smiled when, eating her breakfast, she spied them outside the kitchen door.

"What you boys want?" asked Cook, slicing bread.

Tweed stuck his head inside. "I'se wanting to tell Honey there's a hummingbird out here."

"Honey ain't got time for hummingbirds."

"But it's pink!"

"Shoo!"

Tweed frowned and disappeared.

Licking toast crumbs off her fingers, Lucy waited till Cook was storing away the jam pot to dart out the door. Ahead, Buster and Tweed ran past the puppy barn, into the woods, which made it easy to follow. She could stalk them just like an Indian, ducking behind trees. She guessed they were heading back to the river to skip stones, but they stopped in a hollow of sycamore. Buster dragged a big branch to the center, stacking it atop a small pile. Tweed puffed away, trying to pull a bigger one, and his brother went to help. They struggled mightily to get it set on the others.

Tweed ran to another branch, and Buster shook his head, saying, "Not straight enough. Gotta be flatter, like a wall."

They are building a house, Lucy guessed.

"This one is perfect." Buster tugged a thick piece of wood to their structure. Both boys squatted, lifting one end up, but it was too heavy.

"Why don't you help us 'stead of just watching," Tweed huffed.

Lucy realized he was talking to her. Picking up her skirts to run home, she hesitated. They didn't seem mad, nor were they calling her names.

"Come help us!" Buster puffed, tugging for all he was worth.

Seeing his struggle, she took a deep breath and hurried over to help.

"What you building?" she gasped as the three of them yanked the branch into place.

"An Indian fort," Buster said.

"Indians don't live in forts."

"You know 'bout Indians?" Tweed asked.

Lucy nodded. "Father knows 'bout everything."

"The soldiers live in forts, so they can chase the Indians away," Buster explained. "Skeeter used to tell us all bout 'em."

"Father promised Mother the whole state of Missouri was empty of Indians. He says the government removed them."

Buster shook his head. "They sneak. They can sneak back."

Keeping an eye out for sneaking Indians, they built their wall.

It took three days to finish the fort. Lucy didn't want it to end. When the walls were as high as they could reach, she dragged a big log around to stand on so they could reach higher. They made a sort of roof with two big branches and set more branches covered with leaves atop them. Next, they built a partial window with short pieces, although they couldn't build it square. When all of that was done, Lucy snuck the broom away from the mansion to sweep the floor into a flatter surface. She even brought out the rug from her bedroom, but Buster got so scared that she put it back.

That morning they sat in their fort, playing soldiers and planning how to relocate the Indians. They relocated Tweed twice, and then it was time for the noon meal.

"Let's eat," Lucy said.

Tweed said that was a great idea and pulled his cornmeal from his pocket.

"What's that?" she asked.

"Johnnycake." He handed her his half-chewed piece.

She sniffed it. "What's it made of?"

"Cornmeal."

Turning her nose up, she solemnly handed it back. "Let's go ask Cook for something."

"Can't," Buster piped up. "If'n Honey comes looking for us, we can eat anything she brings. But if we beg at the back door, we gets a whooping."

The roast chicken from last night's supper lingered in Lucy's head. She loved roast chicken, and Cook always tucked some extra away for her the next day. Returning home, however, meant she'd have to sit at the kitchen table and eat proper, like a lady.

"Let's eat here." She sighed.

Buster pulled out his piece and broke it in half. "Here ya go."

Munching it, Lucy decided it wasn't so bad. It'd be better with molasses, but then maybe they didn't have any. Besides, it'd be rude to ask.

They played a while longer, but the johnnycake hadn't really filled her stomach and that eventually drove her home. Lucy left Buster and Tweed trying to turn a tree knot into a water bowl by scraping it out with a rock.

Cook fed her when she got home. The johnnycake wasn't bad, but she liked roast chicken better.

⤜⤜⤜ ⤛⤛⤛

Making her way home, Honey caught the snap of the branch and the immediate quiet afterward. She pretended not to have heard, picking her way through the woods.

When he pounced, she was ready. Catching him in a hug, she whirled him round and laughed. "What you playing at, Tweed?"

Her little brother wiggled in her arms, then hugged her knees when she dropped him. "I love you, Honey!"

"I love you, sweet boy."

"Can we eat honey?"

The mistress wouldn't be needing her till later, she knew, so she grabbed his hand and they dashed up the Honey Trail. It was just another path through the woods, really, but it had an old arbor, parts falling down and parts holding up honeysuckle vines. The vines spread to the huge tree nearby and seemingly draped the whole area. It was Honey's favorite spot in the world. The sun always lit it up, even in the rain. The nectar in the flowers was thick and sweet, and when you hid there—which she'd done many times when she was Tweed's age—no one ever found you. She couldn't walk past without feeling the warmth from the sky and happy memories.

Tweed raced ahead. Most of the flowers were too high for him, but he snatched a pale-yellow honeysuckle within his reach. He waited, eyes agleam, while Honey surveyed the flowers, choosing hers with care. Mustn't be greedy, Maggie would say.

Tweed carefully bit round the end of the blossom, then held it out for her to see. He often bit too hard, severing the flower stem within as well as the petals without. The stem had to stay intact in order to scrape the honey dew when pulled. Today, he'd done a better job. Honey nodded, and then they both grabbed hold of the bit piece, eyeing each other and grinning.

"One...two..." Honey began.

"Three!" Tweed finished.

Gently, they tugged, and the stem slid through the flower, dragging a bead of nectar with it. Honey wrapped her tongue round it, and Tweed quickly did the same.

"Mmm mmm!" He laughed.

Honey scratched the top of his head.

She got along well with Buster, of course. He was older, more mature, and watched out for his young brother. But she and Tweed had always had this special connection. Tweed made her think that she would like a boy of her own someday.

"Want to pick berries?" he asked her now.

"You know I can't do that. Gotta go work for the White folk, honey."

"You're Honey," he scoffed. His favorite joke, and she always laughed as if she'd never heard it before.

"Silly!" Another head scratch, and Honey turned toward the house.

❯❯❯ ❮❮❮

The next day, Lucy was a soldier just like Buster and Tweed was the Indian. He didn't want to be, but Buster insisted. The boy then snuck around the fort looking for his chance to scalp them.

Lucy giggled as Tweed tried to sneak up on his older brother twice while Buster marched around the fort. Both times Buster heard him, whirling to aim his rifle before Tweed dashed into the woods.

Feeling bad for him, Lucy pretended not to hear Tweed's next rush behind her. She was scalped, or so the boy declared, dancing around her and waving his twig, a pretend bowie knife. Buster was disgusted with her.

"I didn't see him," she said.

"You gots ta listen," he told her. "Injun's sneak up behind you. You gots ta listen."

"I was quiet!" Tweed announced.

"I heard you inside the fort," Buster declared.

Patting her stomach, Lucy realized she was hungry.

Before she could say a word, Buster told her, "Don't go back yet. Eat with us."

"There's not enough for three."

"We can make more." Tweed grinned.

The boys led her to the cabin with the one window. Stepping over the threshold, Lucy touched the table she'd seen them all sit around. They all sat together, the mammy and the boys. She wondered what that would be like, sitting at the table and eating with her mother and father.

"What's a mammy?" she asked.

"Mammies love you and take care of you forever," Tweed told her.

"Our mama," Buster added. "Like the mama dog takes care of the puppies." He snatched a bag from over by the tiny stove and poured its contents into a bowl. "Get the water," he told Tweed, who took the bowl and raced out the door.

"Can't cook it," he explained to Lucy. "But it's filling either way."

Looking around, Lucy saw a single shelf by the stove with stacked plates—wood slats, really—plus a brownish dish cloth and a broken pitcher. Unlike the mansion's kitchen, this one didn't have much. "Where's your larder?" she asked.

"What's a larder?"

Tweed popped back in, bearing the bowl as if it were a valuable possession. Buster set it on the table, and then both boys stuck a hand in to stir the contents.

Peering inside, Lucy wasn't so enthusiastic. "What's that?"

"Cornmeal," Tweed said, before shoving a glop into his mouth. "It's good," he told her around the portion.

Buster stuck his own fingers between his teeth, then shoved the bowl toward Lucy. She hesitated before sticking a finger in. The mixture was rather like thick porridge.

"Gotta cook it to get a johnnycake," Buster explained. "We ain't allowed to cook."

Truth was, it didn't have much taste, but the boys thought it special and Lucy didn't want to be rude. "You can't cook?"

"Mammy cooks. She does everything for us."

Lucy sighed. "Mammies sound nice."

~>»>> ‹‹‹‹‹~

The sun had peaked. To Preacher's amazement, the field hands took a midday break. There was no official stop, no call to rest, but one by one those around him slowed, straightening to rub backs and massage fingers. Do that in Mississippi and the overseer would whip your back raw.

An old slave lugged around a bucket of water and a tin cup, and sure enough, every hand got warm water to pour down his throat. Things were different at Sweetgum Plantation. Maybe vittles would be next.

Scanning the field, Preacher spied Booker standing near Maggie, smiling at Honey. Preacher didn't trust that smile.

In the bright daylight, the girl was as beautiful as he'd thought. So young, gazing out at the world as if it were no enemy of hers. Her dress was the same one most slaves wore—faded beyond color, ragged, and stitched in a few places to keep it together. But her smooth skin and pretty face weren't slave-like, and her sparkling eyes sure didn't look like those of any slave he'd ever seen. She actually laughed and gave Maggie something—something Maggie put in her mouth.

Then, looking up, Honey smiled at him and approached. "Got some chicken, mister." She held out a drumstick. "Sweetgum chicken."

Preacher took it carefully, half afraid of startling her. "Where'd you get this?"

"Leftover from dinner last night. There's always leftovers at the house. Miss Marianne don't eat enough to keep a bird alive."

Slaves scrambling for any scrap of food while White folks threw away last night's supper. That was more like what he saw in Mississippi.

Honey turned to go.

"Thank you, Miss."

Turning back, she leveled liquid eyes oozing with happiness. They were soft as a doe's and just as large and gentle. "I'm not Miss. Call me Honey."

"They call me Preacher."

"Are you a preacher?" She stared at him.

"I've been known to pontificate from time to time."

She let her eyes linger a moment longer, probably trying to figure out what pontificate meant. He hoped she wouldn't ask, as Preacher didn't know himself. It was just what his old master used to say, back in the days when his daddy still lived and the world seemed sweeter. Later, Master would say his father had to be punished for even thinking about running. How could they kill you just for thinking?

Preacher blamed himself for his daddy's death. "Don't get comfortable," Daddy used to tell him. "When the time comes, run away. The worst day of freedom is better than the best day in chains."

"I don't got chains, Daddy," Preacher would answer him.

"Just 'cause you don't see 'em, don't mean they ain't there."
It wasn't till the day Master beat Daddy to death that Preacher
began to understand.

Now Honey smiled and turned away, faded skirt swishing
gently through the rows of cotton. Booker watched her like a
hunting dog sniffing some scent.

As his teeth ripped into the drumstick, Preacher made a
promise to the overseer. *You'll never touch her.*

⟫⟫ ⟪⟪

Hueron took a different path that evening, walking through the
trees to the house as the sun's last rays tickled the grass. It was a
good home, this. Just lacked good management to bring it up
to a respected place in the area.

Weena and old Phil worked in the kitchen yard, with her
gathering washed sheets and him hammering furniture, assembling an old bed.

"What are you doing?" Hueron asked, hoping it wouldn't
delay his supper.

"Getting Honey's room together lickity split," Weena told
him. When he just stared, she added, "Mistress wants her sleeping here tonight."

Hueron found his wife where she often was these days—her
dressing table. Honey was twirling her hair up into a pretty
confection, making him smile despite his annoyance.

"Darling." Marianne stretched out a soft hand that he raised to his lips.

"Honey, we won't need you tonight. You're dismissed," Hueron said, and kissed Marianne's palm when she would have protested.

The girl actually curtsied—he hadn't seen that before—and left.

"But I've got a surprise for her!" his wife told him. "A bed with the house slaves."

He knelt, caressing her fingers. She was so like a child he tended to forget she'd mothered one. "Darling, Honey needs to sleep with the field hands for now."

"Why?"

"We've got a new..." *How to say it?* "We've got a new man, a good man. He's to take care of her." He'd ordered Booker to place the big buck in Honey's cabin when he first arrived. Good stock, that. He didn't want to change it now.

"But she's a slave." Marianne stared at him. "*We* take care of her."

"He's gonna be...like her husband. Slaves have children. Families, you know. He's to be her family now." For a moment, he wasn't sure she grasped his meaning. Then he caught the flush on her face.

"But they're not married!"

"Slaves don't marry, Marianne. You know that."

"It's not proper!" she said.

She meant it too. He could see the shock in her eyes. Arguments assembled in his brain, but he thought better of it. *"You don't have to fight every battle,"* Uncle Jay had said. *"Just the ones that matter."*

"Then we'll have a wedding," he said with a smile.

⤜⤜⤜ ⤛⤛⤛

Maggie had chicken duty that day. Being in a good mood, Booker had sent her to the kitchen for some of last night's chicken. "Tell Cook to get me a drumstick. Two, if she's got 'em." He seemed to still be pretty puffed up with the master's satisfaction over Preacher. He occasionally scored himself leftover vittles, but sending a slave away from the fields seemed risky. Maggie worried over what to say if she was caught.

"Hurry there, Maggie!" the overseer shooed her off.

So hurry she did, supposing the master would be angry at seeing her not picking cotton. Hopefully he'd ask and then take up his anger with Booker. But White folks' anger didn't need no sensible target.

The barn door opened as she neared it, stopping her heart altogether. Hardly able to stand upright, she had to lean a hand against the old barn as a little blonde head peeked out—that White child, Lucy.

She weren't much bigger than Tweed, really, but she could have Maggie thrashed just for startling her. The eyes—blue eyes, like her father's—pinned Maggie where she stood.

"Hello."

Maggie managed a nod.

"Are you Mammy or Maggie? Honey calls you Maggie."

Maggie swallowed to work up proper spit to talk. "I'm Mammy to my boys."

The child frowned.

"You best call me Maggie."

Lucy nodded, staring up as if she was seeing the devil himself.

Maggie's worry started rising up again.

"There's puppies in there." The girl pointed at the barn. "Want to see?"

Maggie shook her head, already skirting round the little girl. "I gotta fetch something." She hurried past, before her annoyance appeared on her face.

Stupid child had put her in a bad situation. She could get in a heap of trouble doing what that youngin wanted, and even more trouble *not* doing it. Whites were good at grudges, and the little girl would grow to be a full mistress, sure as Hell.

Maggie practically raced the last bit from the barn to the door. Fortunately, it was open. Fortunately, Cook saw her coming.

"Well now." The woman could put a wealth of meaning in two words.

"Booker sent me," Maggie huffed, trying to catch her breath. "He wants a drumstick."

Shaking her head, Cook shuffled off to her table, plucked up her carving knife, and pulled a dishcloth off what turned out to be a half-eaten chicken.

"That girl Lucy asked me to look at puppies."

"Poor thing's lonely."

Maggie snorted. She'd love to be that lonely.

"That child ain't got it easy." Cook sent her a look over the fowl as she hacked away. "And Booker ain't got no sense."

"Is the master about?"

The old woman shook her head. "But Miss Marianne is. I don't think she'd like it if she saw this. You tell Booker that."

Maggie nodded. She wouldn't, of course. Booker wouldn't listen to her if she did.

Sensing her thoughts, Cook narrowed her eyes. "That Rufus, the one from the store. Rumor is they found him."

Maggie smiled.

Cook caught her smile. "No...not good. They *caught* him."

"They caught..."

"You remember Meachum? You were pretty young when he was here. Real bastard."

Maggie nodded. She had a few nightmare memories thanks to Meachum.

"You know what became of him? He took up slave catching. Pretty good at it, they say. Only thing is, if you want your slave back alive, you got to impress that upon him."

Cook laid the knife on the table and wrapped the chicken in a cloth. "He's the one what caught Rufus, so they say." She waddled over and handed the cloth to Maggie. "Tell Booker I need my napkin back."

⟫⟫⟫ ⟪⟪⟪

It was pitch black by the time Maggie got to the cabin. Booker'd been full of himself all day, strutting round and tossing out orders just to hear himself speak. Wound up making Squint count the cotton bags over and over, then felt each bag himself to be sure there wasn't any slacking in the contents.

A tiny suspicion rose when Maggie first saw the shelf, but it wasn't till she emptied the bag into the bowl that she knew. "Half this cornmeal's gone!"

Buster's face told her everything, but it was Tweed who spoke up. "We ate luncheon," he said.

"I gave you food this morning."

"Lucy wanted luncheon. We were playing Indian fort."

"You gave that White child our food?" Maggie worked to keep her voice calm, but she must have failed. Both boys were staring at her with scared eyes. "White folk eat anything they want, whenever they want. Cakes and chicken...white bread with butter and jam, all toasted and warm."

Honey stepped through the door, Preacher behind her. He'd taken to walking up to the mansion to fetch her.

"We'se sorry, Mammy!"

Honey looked from one of her brothers to the other. "What happened?"

Maggie took a deep breath. *What was done was done,* she heard Hank say. Of all the Whites to cause trouble, she'd never thought the youngest would turn out to be the worst. "We're a little low on cornmeal."

Honey frowned. "What..."

"We'll be fine," Preacher broke in, gazing at the two boys. He stroked Buster's head in a gesture so exactly like Hank's, Maggie blinked back a tear.

Tweed walked into her, throwing his arms about her legs and clinging fiercely. She bent to hug him close.

Hank always did the right thing in his own time. Maybe Preacher would as well. He was already watching over Honey. Maybe when the time came, he would get them all to freedom. Maggie hoped so, because the store in town wouldn't be helping anytime soon.

⤜⟫⟫ ⟪⟪⤛

Finding one tress firmly knotted, Honey tugged the brush too hard.

"Ouch!" The lady glared at her.

"I'se sorry, Miss Marianne!" Honey stilled, wondering if a slap would follow, but none came. She'd only been slapped twice in her whole life, both times by Cook. Even she knew how lucky she was.

"Start at the bottom and work your way up," the mistress told her. "Gently. Always careful, Honey." She traced one of her perfume bottles on the table. "I'm a little grumpy this early in the morning."

Nodding, Honey began again, running the brush through the lower piece, each stroke moving higher toward the scalp. It had been hours since Honey ate her breakfast, but Miss Marianne woke long after the rest of Sweetgum was up and working. She wondered just how much a lady could sleep.

"Have you seen a new field hand? A male field hand?"

Honey nodded. "They arrived a couple of days back. Five new slaves, Miss Marianne."

"This would be the biggest, I believe."

Setting the brush down, Honey slipped a thin strand up from either side of the mistress's head and twisted the two together. Plucking a comb from the dresser, she deftly fastened the hair in place. The style made Miss Marianne's face look more rounded and showed off her eyes.

Glancing in the mirror, the lady suddenly smiled. "My, that does look nice. Thank you, Honey."

Honey smiled back, turning toward the wardrobe. The pink shawl would set off the dress best.

"One of those was a big man?"

"Yes, ma'am."

"Do you like him?"

Lifting the shawl, Honey turned. "Yes, ma'am."

Miss Marianne was frowning something fierce. Honey wondered if maybe she wanted a different shawl. The mistress rose, gliding to the window. "I know you all don't marry, but— You know what that is, right?"

"You're already married." Honey frowned.

"Yes. No, not me." The lady strode quickly to her, clasping her arms. "You, Honey. He's gonna marry you."

Marry?

Miss Marianne positively glowed.

Honey knew marriage was a church thing for White folk. The men promised to stay with the women and own all the children they'd have. She'd never heard of slaves doing any such thing.

Slowly, the mistress released her. "There, now." She smiled and took the shawl. "This will do nicely."

She glided out the door, popping back to grin like a mischievous child. "Come now, Honey. I got a lot of work to do."

⤜⤜ ⤛⤛

The sun was shining strong, warming Honey's arms as she rolled up her sleeves. The air was March cool, chilly despite the bright day. Still, she'd be hot soon enough. The parlor rug hung on the clothesline, waiting to get beat. Beating the rug meant dust flying round in the air, filling the lungs, choking the throat, and tearing the eyes. Weena said to stand with your back to the breeze, but it seemed to Honey the wind always changed as soon as she struck the carpet.

Marriage.

Long ago, she'd asked Maggie about that. Not so much about the White folks' events but about having children. Maggie had said it would happen when the time came and there was nothing a girl could do to change that. "Best not to think about it."

There was Slave Wisdom, which everyone knew from an early age. Honey knew to avoid being alone with men, particularly White men. She knew Maisey did the opposite. She knew White men married White women and toyed with slaves, and slave men sometimes chose a slave woman to be with. That, so Weena had told her, was when babies came.

Honey had thought she might like a baby. She'd never thought about the men part of it. But...*marriage*. No slave had ever done so that she'd heard tell of. What would that mean?

Preacher was a big man, big enough to hurt her without even trying. But he was a kind man too, with warm eyes and a gentle way. *Still*...

"Gotta hit it harder," Bibby said.

Honey swung harder, putting her thoughts into that swing. The dust blast nearly choked them both. "Sorry, Bibby," she said as soon as she could speak.

Bibby was leaning over, hands on her knees, spluttering. She slanted Honey a look and started laughing. "You're whipping that rug but beating something else."

Honey dropped the broom, hurrying over to touch Bibby's arm. "Oh no! Did I hit you?"

The housekeeper straightened, still chuckling. "Not me, child. You're hitting Miss Marianne and that preacher."

Honey stared at her.

Bibby sighed. "You're hitting at this notion of you getting married."

Denial rose to Honey's lips, but she saw the truth in the words. "I'm not even sure what it means, Bibby."

Her friend grinned. "For White women, it's a promise. She'll bear the man's children if'n he promise to take care of her forever. Fair exchange, that. It's in the Bible, and they swear it before God."

Honey nodded. She sort of knew this but had never heard it put into words. "But Black folk don't get married," she said.

"Slaves don't get married, child. We can't make such promises."

Honey pondered that. "So Miss Marianne is saying Preacher and I will always be here? Together." *So it is a gift? A White-folk promise?* "Preacher and I will always be together?"

Bibby gave her a dry look, the look she used when Weena swore she'd finished the laundry and it was still waiting in the basket. "The only promises made will be by you and Preacher." The woman turned, heading back to the house.

"Bibby," Honey called out, then hesitated when her friend turned back with that questioning eyebrow lifted. "Is it bad? The...the making babies part?"

"You'll be fine. We women always are." Bibby walked away. She had smiled, but such a faint smile. Not enough there to reassure.

Honey snatched up the broom and beat that rug near to death.

The next day, Maisey appeared at the back door. Honey opened it for her, as Cook's arms were covered up to her elbows in flour.

Maisey grinned. "Booker wants his lunch."

Cook called from the table where she kneaded dough, "You tell that man he better watch himself. Master would not be happy to find out he's feeding him on top of paying him."

"I'll tell him," Maisey called.

Honey knew she wouldn't—and if she did, it certainly would have no effect. Now the girl looked Honey up and down, as if sizing up a catfish on where to gut.

"Heard tell you're being put with Preacher. I'm jealous!" Maisey giggled. "He's a man, proper-like."

Honey always found jawing with Maisey awkward, as they thought about stuff differently, but this girl had knowledge that she lacked. "Maisey." Her voice low, Honey leaned in close. "Does it hurt when...?"

The slave girl smirked. "Nah. Well, a little, 'specially at first. My mammy use to say, 'If they's real good, it feels good.' "

"Slice a bit of that roast from last night," Cook called, her eyes narrowing. The thing about Cook was that she didn't move much on account of that bulk, but her eyes never rested. The woman saw plenty that others wished she wouldn't.

When Maisey ran off with the meat, Cook slanted Honey a look. "Don't pay Maisey no mind," she told the bread dough. "Life has a lot of bits to it. Natural bits. If you don't already know, you'll find out soon enough."

Honey sighed.

"Child," Cook added as the white dough slammed against the wood table, "ain't a woman at Sweetgum don't wish she were you. Be grateful."

Honey sped off to fetch the pail and scrub brush.

⟫⟫ ⟪⟪

Marianne talked to Weena, and Bibby, and Cook. She'd loved to
have asked Honey a few choice questions, but it was more exciting
to make some things a surprise.

Reverend Jessop said the church couldn't house such a thing.
While God appreciated her holding to Christian values, he didn't
want Negros sitting where proper folk sat. But holding the wedding outside meant they needed to have sunlight, and Mark had
firmly refused that. The April rains were on their way, after all,
and Sweetgum couldn't afford to have crops in the field when they
arrived. So, it was decided that the wedding would be in the slave
clearing, the area between the slave cabins. Marianne thought that
was a bit silly, but Mark said that way all the slaves could attend.
Otherwise, they'd have to walk miles at night. He'd even agreed
to a little dancing, with Squint playing his fiddle. The reverend
didn't want to attend anything heathen, let alone preside over it,
but Mark had had a word with him. He would marry Honey to
her beau.

The wagon pulled up before Marianne, and she stepped down
from the veranda. She was going into town with Weena to find
some lace for a new ball gown and, perhaps, find a gift for Honey.
Mark didn't think it necessary, but she dearly wanted to give the
girl something. Maybe a hat, as Honey loved to set hats so allur-
ingly on Marianne's dark curls.

Baskets of flowers! Marianne smiled to herself. *To decorate the
ceremony. Surely no one could object to that.*

Weena helped her into the carriage, sparing Squint the climb
down from his seat. It was funny, really, how Squint always washed

his hands up to the elbows and Weena still never let him touch her. The truth was, Marianne was grateful. The old man always smelled of dirt and manure no matter how much he scrubbed.

"Do we take Miss Lucy?" Weena asked.

Startled, Marianne saw that the child was right there, biting her little lip and clutching that foolish rag doll. Truth was she often forgot she had a daughter. The doll's dress was no more ragged than Lucy's, she realized. Perhaps a new dress for her, one she could wear to the wedding. "Yes," she said aloud. "Lucy may come."

The child sat opposite her, staring with those large eyes right up into Marianne's face. It annoyed her, till Weena smiled. "That child can't help staring at you. You're too beautiful, Miss Marianne!"

Marianne smiled back, relaxing into the seat. If she didn't completely believe it, she pretended to accept that reason for Lucy's regard.

The town of Blanten wasn't large compared to Baltimore, or indeed Hannibal. It was seven streets total, including the main one where Everett's Emporium stood proud beside Sampson's Feed Store and the blacksmith. The saloon with its cafe was at the corner, with the town hall and the other warehouse. As far as Marianne could tell, the warehouse was a catch-all place, holding a market one day and storing beef and grain the next.

Everett's Emporium had been touted as the best dressmaker in town, which certainly grabbed her interest. As it turned out, it was the *only* dressmaker in town. Sadie Everette had skill with a needle, but the Emporium stocked many items beyond those necessary to a lady's apparel. This included everything the town had for non-farmers, be it food or pots and pans, just as Sampson's stocked everything for animals.

Marianne discovered the coveted lace beside the glassware and kitchen spoons, hiding beneath a heavy brocade that surely wouldn't suit anybody.

"Miss Marianne! Why, how beautiful you look today," Sadie Everette gushed. Annoying that she gushed so much, but more annoying that Marianne always liked it. "Just got a new blue silk—bright, brilliant blue. Everyone will want it, though no one could do it justice but you."

The white lace under Marianne's fingers would look good against that. Just a trim on the sleeves, décolletage. Black lace might be better. As she lifted it to the light, a large shadow suddenly startled her.

A man, shorter than her husband but much more muscular, had entered the store. Seeing her, he removed the hat. "Good morning, ladies."

"Why, Mister Meachum," Sadie crooned in the same voice she used with Marianne. "More of those cigars?"

The man nodded, but he was looking at Marianne. "Mrs. Hueron, isn't it? Sweetgum Plantation?"

She nodded.

"A lady like you shouldn't walk around town unescorted. It's not safe."

He sounded sincere, but Marianne wasn't fooled. Before her marriage, all the men had wanted to escort her, and while many streets in Baltimore could be called unsafe, Blanten's seven in broad daylight were not exactly terrifying.

Yet the man didn't offer his arm. Bowing slightly, he followed Sadie over to the counter. "Three cigars, I think," he said.

A big man, that. Almost as big as Honey's fiancé, yet polite. Marianne watched him stride out the door.

"Clinton Meachum," Sadie leaned in to tell her. "He used to be the overseer at Sweetgum, when it grew tobacco. Well, now, Miss Lucy. Are we to have a new dress as well?"

Marianne had forgotten the child. Straightening her shoulders, she turned to the shopkeeper. "Do you have something suitable?"

Sadie waved a hand to the shelf beneath the lace. "As soft a cotton weave as you'll find on the Mississippi."

Yellows and pinks stood out, along with a ridiculously ugly green. Unimpressed, Marianne caught sight of Lucy's little nose, which was wrinkled up as well. As she moved through the bolts of material, a soft rose came to light, a gorgeous shade that would look so good in a ball gown. Lucy's fingers reached out, and Marianne wondered if the child had inherited her taste after all. Maybe she could have a matching daughter dress made. They'd be striking, entering a room together.

"See any color you like?" she prodded.

Lucy's hand rested on the pink.

So she does take after me!

But what her daughter tugged from the pile wasn't the rose pink, nor the ugly green. Lucy's little fist grasped a wad of purple. Ugly, horrid purple. No one wore purple except horses and old ladies.

"Let's try the pink," Weena murmured, prying the cloth from the girl's stubby fingers.

⤜⤛⟩⟩⟩ ⟨⟨⟨⤜⤛

Preacher seethed as he walked. Booker didn't need his whip fetched, nor could he spare a hand from the fields with the rains coming. Preacher knew exactly why the man had sent him.

In the trees ahead flashed a faded pink skirt and the dusky wrap Honey treasured and used to keep herself warm. Preacher had overtaken her as Booker must have expected. Seemed the overseer licked his lips at picturing Honey being taken by some man. *Booker's a disgusting little weasel.*

She stood by the honey tree, sucking the honey from a flower. When she saw him, she froze and then averted her face. But her voice sounded calm. "You know how to suck the honey?"

"Yes, ma'am." Preacher's mouth just curled up at the corners all by itself. He never chose to smile, he realized. His body did all the choosing near Honey. It reacted before his brain could stop it.

Honey plucked another flower.

That was what bothered him here. In Mississippi, slaves never did nothing but work. Even if you weren't working, you had to look like you were. Overseers never left their whips behind, never spared your back. You learned not to give them a reason to strike. Most times they'd strike anyway, just keeping in practice.

"Dogwood." Honey fingered a blossom and smiled.

Preacher wondered if her muscles ever tired of that smile.

"I love the way the white flowers flow down from the top of the tree and the yellow honeysuckle bubbles up from the bottom. They reach each other and mingle so prettily in the center. It's a honey tree."

She doesn't talk like a slave...doesn't even think like a slave. Not knowing how to answer, Preacher snapped a blossom for himself.

"The honey tree on the Honey Trail. My favorite place." The girl turned her face to the sun, and the golden rays caressed her skin. "Whenever I need to find some happy, this is where I go."

"Well now, this is something special," Preacher acknowledged, plucking another flower to offset the fear dancing along his spine. His brain knew neither Booker nor Master would be along to whip him, but his body couldn't seem to believe that.

Honey's hair swung like a White man's window curtain over her eyes as she snatched a blossom to tuck behind her ear. He was astounded that her mistress wouldn't strike her for wearing it.

"My best memory is Maggie carrying me when I was littler than Tweed. I got scared of the shadows, and she snatched me right up, holding my face against her shoulder. Only thing I could see was her purple headwrap. She said, 'Nothing to hurt you, baby.' And she meant it so strong. Her arms held me snug, and I knew nothing could get me, not even a bear." Honey's face beamed with the memory. "She even sang to me. Whenever I step along this trail, I still feel that love."

Yet Maggie hated this place.

"Honey, you know they're gonna marry us? Tonight?"

She nodded, and for the first time, her smile faded.

"They be wanting us to make babies," Preacher told her gently, then could have bit his tongue for his stupidity. Now her head hung so low he couldn't see her face at all. Stepping closer, he stopped short of touching her. "I ain't gonna hurt you."

She froze solid, like a Missouri pond in January.

Impulsively, Preacher knelt down. "I ain't never gonna do nothing you don't want me to. I'll take as good o' care of you as your mammy."

Her startled eyes flew up to meet his. She might have been nervous, but she seemed to believe him.

To be sure, he made it an oath. "I swear to you, Honey. I'll take as good o' care of you as your mammy on the Honey Trail."

In the end, it was she who touched him. Just the softest caress on his arm, and then she was gone.

⟫⟫⟫ ⟪⟪⟪

Meachum planted himself leaning against a tree across the street. It was his casual look, the one he used when hunting a bear or a slave. Feigning disinterest.

He was a short man, likened to a hoary tree stump by his grandpa, with his bulging muscles and dark hair. The black curls grew thicker on his body than his head. He looked like his grandpa, and the man had always been in his corner. His grandma hadn't. She'd said he had mean eyes that got meaner as he got older.

Plucking out one of his precious cigars, he struck an only slightly less precious match and waited. Truth was, he didn't hurt for cash. When he'd left Sweetgum years back, Meachum immediately found work as a slave catcher. Slaves cost big money, and owners paid top dollar for their return. Finding one that wasn't being looked for netted even more profit. A Black might claim to be a free man in the north, but down Mississippi-Alabama way, there weren't no such thing.

Problem was, slave catching meant you were always on the run, and Meachum was tired of that. He'd just decided to settle down and raise a family when the plantation master had let him go, wanting a cotton crop and a cotton overseer from Mississippi.

Now Meachum had heard tell that Sweetgum wasn't doing quite so well these days. Seems Mississippi cotton didn't thrive in Missouri. Apparently, neither did Mississippi overseers. He'd meant to talk to Mrs. Hueron, lay some groundwork. He knew how to get the most out of slaves and the most out of the land. He intended to have a little conversation that would settle in, so she could pass it on to her husband. By now that man had to be getting anxious.

But Mrs. Hueron had turned out to be so damn young. The owners he'd worked for had wives who understood the business, knew what was what—oft times more than the men. He'd found them very useful in persuading their husbands.

This Miss Marianne was different. Meachum would wager all his cigars she didn't know the plantation was failing or that her husband couldn't manage the cotton and the slaves. She would have no idea that her dress allowance was in danger, and if Meachum told her, she'd just blurt it all out to her husband.

Hueron wouldn't hire him, furious the man had dared approach his wife. No. This was gonna take a little more strategy thinking.

Across the street, Miss Marianne emerged from the Emporium and daintily stepped over a puddle to her waiting buggy. Nicest buggy this side of the Mississippi, so Sadie Everette had claimed. When Meachum did look for a wife for himself, he'd aim for something like Marianne.

He watched her drive out of town. And as the hazy dust rose from the retreating wheels, another female came to mind.

Took a bit to find the place. It was a little farther out of town than Meachum liked, with not enough land and a house crying for an additional room. Still, pretty flowers bloomed around the front stoop and the fence was freshly painted.

Linda's house. He'd heard her father died a while back and her brother had gone to work in the Chicago stockyards. Such a property was a good dowry for a woman to have. She was a looker too, he remembered.

He was still smiling when he rapped on the door and Linda opened it.

She had the yellow hair and trim figure he remembered, but the hair was a bit straw-like, lacking that silky look Miss Marianne had. She had a scrawny body, really, like that chicken in the yard you never took for the pot 'cause it was worth more in eggs than meat. The one chicken in the yard that lived to a ripe old age.

"Well, Clinton Meachum, as I live and breathe." As soon as she opened her mouth, he remembered how smart she was. "What you doing back in Blanten?"

"You gonna invite me in there, Linda?"

He expected her to fling the door wide like she'd done in the old days. Instead, she pursed her lips, perusing him up and down. At last the door widened, but by then he knew she wasn't gonna be his girl again.

Minutes later he stood in her kitchen, one room of the house he hadn't spent much time in. "Junior Green? You can do better than him!" he said.

The old Linda would have laughed and tossed her head, encouraging him to sweet talk her. This Linda was having none of it. "He's a respectable blacksmith and good at his trade. Earns a steady living, Clint."

She poured two cups of tea and sat at the little table. To think of Linda pouring tea!

"Hell, darling, I make good money," Meachum told her.

"You used to, once upon a time. I don't know what you do now."

He started to convince her, but the ring on her finger changed his mind. No point in arguing when there was nothing to gain. Anyway, seeing her now made him think he could do better. "I hear tell Sweetgum ain't making the profit like it used to," he said, then cautiously took a sip. Tea, he decided, was an ungodly drink.

Linda eyed him over her cup. "Don't know about that. I do know they pay their bills."

"But they ain't selling much cotton."

"The father didn't sell much. The son's just starting in...and he ain't stupid. Folks round here think he'll figure it out."

Meachum nodded. "Who's advising the man? Steve Leonard or Bill Jevington? Or maybe Sampson? He's always got advice for any who'll listen."

"Or even my Junior?" Linda smirked. "Hueron listens to a lot of folk, from what they say. But he's the kind that sifts his advice 'fore he swallows it. If you're wanting to get in his head, you'll need to do some work."

He wanted to deny it but held his tongue. She'd always had a way of seeing right through him.

Watching his face, she suddenly grinned. "Your best bet, Clinton Meachum, is a direct approach. Not your strong suit."

That was something he'd need to chew on.

⤜≫ ≪⤛

Lucy hated Sundays. Church wasn't till ten o'clock, but she had to put on her Sunday best first thing and couldn't go outside in case she messed it up.

As Weena tied her sash, she glimpsed Buster through her window. He slipped into the barn, no doubt going to play with the puppies. Maggie and the other field hands would be working in the cotton, like always. Sundays didn't trouble slaves, but they sure troubled White folk.

She had to eat her breakfast in the dining room, a napkin tucked in her collar to shield her dress and Mother and Father on either side. They never seemed to look at her, but if she made a single mistake, Mother corrected her with a harsh whisper. They got to eat pancakes drenched in syrup, which dripped down the napkin if Lucy wasn't careful. Sooner or later, she wouldn't be careful.

Finally, they bundled her into the carriage and set off to church. Reverend Jessop always stood at the lectern, "righteous and full of vinegar," as her father would say. The organ ground out scary music before he would warn them of Hell and damnation.

Today, the reverend spoke in that scary voice of his. "And she answered, This woman said unto me, 'Give thy son that we may eat him today, and we will eat my son tomorrow.' So we boiled my son and did eat him."

Lucy shivered.

"And I said unto her on the next day, 'Give thy son that we may eat him.' " The reverend looked out across the congregation, Hell flames dancing in his eyes. "And she hath hid her son!"

Would Mother hide me? Lucy wondered. *Or would she make Weena cook me in the soup pot?*

"Do you begin to see how horrible the judgment of God is? Do nothing to be judged foul of God's law, lest famine so terrible be visited upon you! Lest you be forced to eat your own children!"

Lucy shuddered again and felt her father's hand on her head. Would he protect her, she wondered. Probably he would, from bad men. Probably not from her mother. Her mother would get Weena to roast her up with carrots.

>>>> <<<<

Meachum stood at the north corner of the field, watching the slaves. He recognized the woman on the far edge, seemingly better at cotton than she ever was at tobacco. That old buck's woman, Maggie. She'd been pretty meek, even if the buck had been a troublemaker.

There was a big buck working farther on, working good, but he could be made to work better. Meachum counted twenty-one—no, twenty-two—doing the work of fifteen, maybe sixteen tops. That Booker was gnawing on his lunch, watching one of the younger females. Lazy bastard, just as he'd heard.

When he'd seen enough, Meachum turned away and spotted two young boys running toward the river. Two who should have been working but instead, playing just like they was White boys.

One thing was certain. He could raise Sweetgum's cotton production forty percent.

An hour later, Meachum slipped into an empty back pew. The reverend hadn't changed. His sermons still rained down fire and brimstone, scattering indignation among a few of the women and boredom among most of the men.

The sunny day outside failed to reach the church interior. The closest it came was the red light flickering on Jessop's face from the stained-glass figure of some avenging saint. For a man of the cloth, he managed to appear more like the devil with which he loved to threaten his parishioners.

Meachum could just make out Hueron in the third pew from the front. How odd that that precedent still held—no one ever sat in the first two rows, not wanting to be that close to the good reverend.

"Think you know Hell? You have no notion what God's wrath will wield, step you one foot from the path!"

Eventually the sermon waned. Jessop ran out of words when the second family snuck out the back door and avoided the collection plate. Meachum made a show of dropping his penny, then strode out to position himself near the family carriage. It afforded him a view of Hueron's deft handling of the reverend, shaking the cleric's hand while slipping his wife and daughter past. The family spoke to a few others before making their way toward him.

By that time, Meachum was ready.

⟫⟫⟫ ⟪⟪⟪

Admittedly, Hueron had been preoccupied. The last two days had been ominously cloudy. There was yet a third of the crop remaining to be picked, perhaps more. It was a relief to emerge from the vestibule into the bright sun, but it was past noon. He needed to get back, so he ushered his family firmly along. Marianne could talk to her friends later.

A man stepped out as they neared the carriage. "Mister Hueron?" He was powerful, short but confident, offering his hand.

"Mister Meachum," Marianne exclaimed. "Mark, this is Mister Meachum. You were the overseer, were you not?"

How does Marianne know this man?

"Yes, ma'am," Meachum said, a touch of annoyance in his voice that could have been Hueron's imagination. "I was overseer at Sweetgum back when you raised tobacco."

Hueron shook his hand. "Mark Hueron, Mister Meachum."

"Clint," Meachum told him. "A pleasure, sir."

Hueron hesitated, then lifted his daughter into the carriage. "I need to get back. Harvest, you know."

"I know."

Hesitating again, Hueron studied the man's face. Something in his tone said he knew more than that.

"Tell Booker to push those slaves harder. They got more to give."

"Do they?"

Turning to leave, Meachum sent a narrow look over his shoulder. "Forty percent, by my reckoning."

Hueron pondered that the whole way home. He didn't quite trust Clint Meachum. The man certainly hadn't just happened to be standing by the wagon. But the man did know Sweetgum and didn't seem a fool. Lord knew, Hueron had had enough of fool overseers.

When they reached the plantation, Hueron veered round to the fields. Booker was there, leaning against a tree and watching one of the females, it appeared.

Looking over the others, he watched them work. Surely they could work a little faster? That new buck never rested, but shouldn't his hands be quicker than that? What if the cure to his bottom line wasn't more hands but a better overseer?

Marianne had set Weena to clean out an empty cabin while she was at church, and sure enough, it was clean. As clean as an old cabin could be, at least.

Inspecting it was a little jarring. For one thing, she'd planned to put her old bedroom rug in it, but the wool wouldn't last very long lying on raw dirt. Who'd have thought there weren't any floors? And the old curtains that matched the rug were just as useless since the cabin had no windows at all.

She had considered having Honey and her big husband sleep in the house, but as Mark pointed out, the man was a field hand. He'd be covered in field-hand dirt and smell very much like it.

In the end, she decided to give Honey the China bowl and pitcher Mark's mother had given them. The set was too good for slaves, but then Honey was special. And, anyway, the hand-painted flowers were such an ugly purple color. Purple always made Marianne's complexion look haggard.

Bibby suggested they forgo the fancy China, as there wasn't even a table in the small cabin. But there was some old furniture in the attic, and Marianne told her to find something appropriate. When it was all set up properly, the stove clean, and the floors leveled, Marianne was satisfied. *Who ever thought you'd have to level floors?* If her maid couldn't sleep in a decent house room, at least she'd have the best cabin a slave could have.

Buster spied a crawfish hole, reached below the water, and dug to find a wiggling thing. He plucked it free, shouting, "This is four!"

Ever since they found that bucket two days ago, he'd been thinking up new things to do with it. This one was important—getting food for his family. Crawfish was good eating. He was getting older, and soon he'd be old enough to work in the fields. Soon he'd be a man. A man took care of his family.

The air was chilly, but when you stepped out of the shadow, the sun warmed you real good. It felt good on the back of his neck. Beside him, Tweed started digging.

"Not there," Buster warned.

"But there's holes!"

"Not the right holes. See, gotta be this size, like someone stuck a finger in the sand. Those are too tiny."

Lucy leaned over. "Pin pricks." She wrinkled her nose.

They all dug a little more. Buster added three crawfish to the bucket, but Lucy only found one and got nervous at its wiggling. Tweed didn't find nothing. He was pulling Lucy's crawfish out when she stepped deeper into the river—all the way past her knees.

"Let's go swimming," she said.

"It's too cold," Tweed told her.

Lucy moved farther out in the Mississippi to a big branch floating by. It had lots of leaves, lots of little twigs, and spread out across the water. Catching it, she tried to lift it clear, but the river wouldn't let it go. The river did that, sucking things back sometimes when you tried to free them.

"We can float on this." Lucy struggled with the branch. "Hang on to it, and it will hold you up in the water."

Buster eyed it. "You'd sink it."

"Would not."

"Would too."

"Would too," Tweed echoed.

With a sudden splash, Lucy leaped upon it. The leafy raft bobbed up and down but held her up pretty good as it turned around slowly.

"Told ya!" She grinned in glee when she faced him again.

"Wow!" Tweed was already gliding farther out, seeking a branch of his own.

"Stop." It did look like fun, Buster thought, but scary too. *"Bad things could happen fast,"* Preacher said.

Lucy was already drifting downriver and farther from shore. And moving faster.

"Come back here," he burst out.

Nose wrinkling in annoyance, Lucy pushed back, sinking slightly and then slightly more. Her foot was reaching for the bottom, Buster realized, and not finding it. Suddenly clinging, she levered her body higher on the branch. When the river turned it so he could see her face again, he knew.

"I can't," she said.

"Go get Honey," Buster told Tweed. "Quick!"

Maggie had a good rhythm going, having found a particularly nice patch. As she picked, her mind churned ideas on what to say at Sampson's Store next full moon. If she told them she had a big man to help her...

The first faint shout didn't prod her brain. It was a girl-child's cry, not one of her boys. And anyways, children always yelled when they played.

The second scream held a genuine thread of fear. It was the boyish echo to that scream—this one sheer terror—that raised the hair on the back of Maggie's neck. Without thought, she moved.

The Mississippi often bore flotsam downstream, driftwood usually. Peering down at the river, Maggie saw a piece coming that was bigger than some, not as big as others. But the next scream came from it. The White child lay atop. *Lord God Almighty. The girl is twirling down the river.*

"Mister Booker!" Maggie's mouth acted all on its own, just like her finger was already pointing.

"Maggie!" he shouted in that terrible voice, the one that meant trouble. The next words, 'whip your hide,' didn't follow. Instead, Booker started walking, then trotting to her. "Jesus."

Funny how they all call on God, she thought, *when in doubt or trouble. Even Booker, who surely never spoke to Him at any other time.*

The other slaves looked up, though most kept working. Most wouldn't be able to see, of course, but you'd have to be deaf not to hear the shouting.

"Can you swim, Preacher?" Booker called.

Preacher straightened. "No, sir."

"You're gonna give it a try." The two men started down the hill, crashing through the brush.

Maggie went with them, all-out racing to the water. That White child was moving pretty fast. They'd have to be quick to catch her. *Serve them right to lose one of their own*, she thought, and felt a little ashamed for that.

Preacher didn't slow until the water swamped his knees. His legs kept pumping even then. At first it looked like he'd make it easy, but as the river dragged on him, Maggie wasn't so sure.

The Mississippi swallowed the big man up to his chest, with little waves washing over his shoulders. He struggled to stay upright. It was a mighty river, so folks said. You wouldn't have thought water could beat a big man, but it seemed it could.

It surely could.

Two arms wrapped around Maggie's legs. Tweed was holding on, his eyes wide and scared. Buster stood beside him, and her heart dropped all over again. They might blame her boys. Buster and Tweed had been there, seen it. Maybe caused it, maybe not, but White folk didn't need no proof. When they got mad, they'd hit out. And the madder they was, the harder they hit.

After this, they'd be furious.

⟫⟫ ⟪⟪

Preacher felt the sand beneath his feet tugging him out even farther. Too far, too fast. He lost his footing twice, both times yanked downstream. Damn river was strong. For an instant, he was tempted to quit. Pretend to flounder, pretend to near drown. He could even reach his arms out as if trying to get her.

And then he saw her face. He saw a little girl, eyes terrified, arms shaking something fierce. The white skin just added to that pale fright. The branch she clung to had caught on a half-buried tree, but that surely wouldn't hold.

"Swim to me," he called, his hands stretched as far as possible.

Looking at him, searching his face, she let go.

Trust. A child's trust.

He reached all the harder, even when his feet came off the sand. Her little hands grabbed his arm before he could seize her. He managed to pull her in even as the river pulled them on.

Clinging together, they watched the shore. Preacher's feet thrashed now, seeking purchase. Just when he was ready to give up, the bottom rose to meet his feet. The old Mississippi had dragged him across a shallower bit, shallow enough he could plant his numb toes.

Took him a bit, being burdened. The wound on his leg ached in a way it hadn't done in weeks, but he managed to drag them both halfway. By that time, Booker had caught up and he took the child. Rescuing the child, Preacher realized. If the master came now, he'd see Booker carrying his daughter from the river.

The master didn't show till much later.

Marianne had fun that afternoon setting up for the wedding. At first, she merely watched Weena and Bibby rake the grass clear and set the tables upon it. Somehow things had progressed from setting out a few lanterns to braiding daisy chains, gathering other flowers, and having the two dining room candelabras brought out to mark the reverend's place. Marianne would have even made big velvet bows if Bibby hadn't suggested Mark might not like it. She'd wanted to wait to see everyone's reaction.

Bibby reminded her it would be after sundown. "You'll need to eat before we go," she added.

"I can eat when they do."

"No, Miss Marianne. The master won't like it."

Recognizing the truth of this, Marianne sealed her lips.

⟶⟫⟫ ⟪⟪⟵

The sun dropped below the trees, and still they worked because, Maggie realized, Booker feared the master would arrive any moment. The parish buckboard had already walked past, the reverend not being one to try to trot his old nag, so this wedding was fixing to happen.

By the time the shout of "bring your baskets" rang out, it was so dark that Maggie was glad to rely on Buster's sharp eyes. She could hear the mule snorting, but she didn't see the wagon until she was practically on it.

"Very good, Maggie," Squint called out loud enough to be sure Booker heard it.

Didn't matter, though, as the overseer appeared preoccupied. Earlier she'd thought the overseer may be regretting Honey's wedding, but she didn't see how. It had pleased the master and wouldn't likely stop him doing whatever he wanted anyway. But something was preying on his mind.

Buster was dragging her basket and Tweed pulling on her hand, both eager to get to the clearing.

⇢⇢⇢ ⇠⇠⇠

Honey had dressed her mistress in silk and fastened her curls with two pearl combs. Then Miss Marianne had left her to tidy the room and turn down the bed, because tonight Honey wouldn't be there after supper. Bibby and Cook had waited downstairs and escorted her outside.

Lights beckoned through the trees, their warmth drawing her down the path. Slipping past the cabin, they rounded the maple to see the clearing glow in lantern light. Such a sight she'd never seen, might never see again. Fairy lights, right out of Cook's stories. It was beautiful.

All the slaves were there, standing as far from the light as they dared, faces astonished, disbelieving. Awed. Weena and Buster and Tweed—even Squint—looked startled. Mammy less so, though she too couldn't never have seen anything to equal this before.

Honey saw Reverend Jessop at the far end of the clearing, standing with Bible in hand. Beyond him were two old tables spread with baskets of apples and bread. Beyond those stood the master and mistress. He frowned, as stern as ever. Miss Marianne beamed her beautiful smile.

Bibby stepped back.

Preacher took her place, smiling down at Honey. "You want to be my wife?" he whispered softly.

She stared up at him, unable to speak.

People asked if you wanted to do something, to hang the laundry while the sun was out or go with Tweed to fetch water for supper, but they really meant "do it!" Slaves rarely had choices in anything, but that evening, with the gleam of the lanterns reflected in his eyes, Honey knew Preacher was offering her one. She could say no. Oh, they'd go through with this wedding thing of course, but nothing more. Even if he got in trouble, Preacher would honor her choice.

The "yes" she whispered to him came straight from her soul.

The big man gently set her hand on his. Together, they walked through the middle of the clearing and the others' faces flickering about them, to stand by the mistress's best candelabras. Reverend Jessop pointed to the grass before him, and Preacher took another step. The candle flames were so close, Honey hoped they wouldn't set fire to her dress.

"Dearly beloved," the reverend began, then looked around the clearing with a frown. "We are gathered here today..."

Honey lost track of the words as she gazed at Miss Marianne. To think she was actually getting married, just like her mistress had done. Maggie said she'd never heard of a slave getting married, as if it were a sinful thing. Surely it was the opposite of sin.

"Do you...er..." Reverend Jessop sputtered.

"Preacher," the master said. The reverend's mouth opened and shut twice without saying anything until the master added, "That's his name. Preacher."

The master had walked right up to Preacher earlier, thanking him for saving his daughter from drowning. Honey had been so proud she could have burst. Her man, her *husband*, had saved a White child, the mistress's daughter.

"Yes, sir," said Preacher beside her.

She peeked up to see him smiling down at her.

"And do you..."

"Honey," Miss Marianne whispered, but in the quiet everyone heard.

"And do you, Honey, take this...*Preacher*...to be your husband?"

In the silence, her voice seemed to echo through the slave clearing. "Yes, sir."

⤞⤝

That night, his Honey showed him their new cabin with the silly table and sillier China. Preacher laughed aloud to think how little understanding the White folks had of their lives. Honey thought it very kind, so he let it be.

He realized he was scared to touch her. She was so perfect, an innocent angel. So far above his touch. Still, when she walked right to him, his arms opened of their own accord. Gently, reverently, he made love to his sweet wife beside that silly table.

Later, holding her close, he asked softly, "Do you want to stay or go?" He felt her surprise. "If you want to go to Canada, or Chicago...or anywhere, Honey, I will take you."

"I...can't. This is *home*."

She shared none of Maggie's ambitions. Well, he'd suspected as much.

"Tweed needs me. And what about Buster? And Maggie? Miss Marianne..."

Her voice grew more anxious with each word, so his arms tightened protectively.

"Then we stay, sweetheart."

THE COTTON SCALE

HAVING WOKEN UP LATE, Lucy dashed to the kitchen. Buster had said they were dancing a rain dance today, and she didn't want to miss it.

"We let you sleep in, honey child." Bibby always said that whenever she woke up late. "You were plumb tuckered out."

Lucy knew her mother never missed her at all, so the slaves just left her alone. They were kind, of course, but "hands off," as her gram would say. She missed Gram, as she missed Miss Helen. But Gram was in Heaven and Miss Helen in Baltimore.

"Why are some mothers called mammy?"

Holding her knife above the cutting board, Cook eyed her. "What you want to know that for?"

"I just heard it the other day."

Cook sliced last night's leftover chicken, sprinkling it in a pie pan. Lucy grinned—she liked chicken pie.

"You be careful where you play," Cook told her.

"I won't play in the river anymore."

"You shouldn't play with those boys neither. Find some nice girls to play with."

"There aren't any nice girls."

The woman frowned, eyeing Lucy as she reached for a carrot.

"May I have some chicken to take with me?" the girl asked.

Cook slanted her the look—frowning lips beneath dancing eyes—before unearthing a napkin and spreading it on the tabletop. Bibby came in just as she dropped a few bits onto the cloth. White meat, Lucy saw, and an apple.

"Maybe more?" Lucy asked.

Cook slanted her another look, this one without the eyes dancing.

"You that hungry, missy?" Bibby asked. "Eat more porridge."

Lucy hung her head and held her tongue. Bibby watched her closer than the others and too often knew what she was planning to do, sometimes even before Lucy knew herself.

"It's best you come home for midday," Bibby told her.

The words hung in the air, a new rule for Lucy to follow. There'd been a lot of new rules since leaving Baltimore. Missouri Rules.

Bibby was polishing the parlor furniture when Cook snuck Lucy the napkin. It only held the three pieces of chicken and the apple, but it would be enough. After all, hadn't Mother warned her about getting fat?

The Indian rain dance took some setup. They had to have tom-toms, which were Indian drums. Lucy hadn't known this, but Buster explained it all. Warriors would paint their faces and beat on the drums while other warriors would dance to make rain.

"Do the dancing Indians paint their faces too?" Lucy asked.

"Of course!" Tweed scoffed at her. But as he loved to paint his face, she wasn't surprised at the answer.

It took a bit to find red mud, which made better paint than black mud. Lucy had been hesitant about painting her cheeks.

"Rain will wash it," Tweed scoffed again. He was in a scoffing mood this morning.

They found two wood bits that were round, or at least round-ish, and looked like drums should look.

"You slap it with your palm," Buster explained, as he'd seen a drum once, or so he said.

Whatever it looked like, it made no music, just a slap sound that hurt her hand. So Lucy sat cross-legged like an Indian and pretended to slap the drums, saying "bum, bum, bum, bum" as Buster and Tweed stomped their feet and shook their hands.

"It's not working," Tweed said after long minutes of dancing.

No clouds had appeared, storm clouds or otherwise. Only the ones already above them were there, and they did not swell with rain.

Lucy tried dancing with them, yelling "bum, bum, bum" to see if the extra dancing would make a difference. It did not.

Buster let out an Indian war whoop, and Tweed echoed him. Feet stomped, dust rose, and a breeze did rustle the leaves. Maybe it got a little cloudier, but no rain struck the land.

"It'll rain later," Buster declared after a while. They even ran down to the Mississippi to cup water in their hands and pour it on the land by the fort. Buster said it would help get things started.

The morning progressed from water pouring to skipping stones on the river, which Lucy had never done before. Buster showed her how, but it was Tweed who was best at it. Buster said his little brother had a real knack.

Lucy wondered if it was more to do with the stones he picked. Buster liked the big ones, but Tweed chose small, flat ones. When he flicked those with his wrist, they would skip three, even four times. Buster got two skips, tops. Lucy only got one thunk, even with the smallest, flattest stones.

They were sitting in the fort, the sun high overhead, when Lucy pulled out her chicken and handed a piece to each boy. They in turn produced their johnnycakes, each offering half to her. When they'd consumed their portions, she was still hungry.

"Can we make more?" she asked, licking her fingers.

Buster shook his head. "Nah. We're not allowed to."

Producing her apple, Lucy frowned. "Why not? Anyways, we need a knife to split this."

Buster studied the ground as Tweed explained, "White folks get to eat cakes and chicken and white bread toasted. Anyways, we ain't got no knives."

Biting her lip, Lucy then bit the apple, taking as big a chunk as she could. Then she passed the rest to Buster, and he and Tweed devoured it. After that, they ran to scout the woods for soldiers to scalp.

When she got home, Bibby made Lucy change her dress before her mother saw the mud. Once she washed her face and hands, she then ate her supper at the kitchen table. Cook was fixing a roast ham, which meant there wasn't any meat Lucy could sneak 'cause she wasn't allowed to handle a knife. Instead, she took her slice of apple pie and wrapped it in a napkin when Cook wasn't watching. Then she ran out to play with the puppies.

Running past the barn, she went to the Indian fort, where she found the boys. "Give me the napkin back tomorrow," she told them.

Tweed was already licking his fingers, sticky from holding the cloth. "What *is* it?"

"Pie."

"Real pie?"

Lucy grinned and raced off, needing to get back quick in case Bibby went looking for her.

⤜⤜⤜ ⤛⤛⤛

Maggie rubbed her back while waiting on Buster to fetch the water. Booker had been in a nasty mood, yelling and stomping about. He'd actually hit her with his whip before he backed off. He'd rarely whipped anyone that she could recall.

"Booker in a bad mood today." Preacher eyed her. "Why, do you suppose?"

"Don't think he liked you saving the master's daughter. He'd o' liked credit." Actually, Booker's mood seemed well beyond that, which had set Maggie's mind to working. She could even guess right enough but didn't want Tweed worrying none.

With a nod, Preacher headed out the door to fetch Honey. Buster burst into the cabin seconds later to set the precious bowl on the table. He eyed Maggie's hand.

She stopped rubbing her back. "We got bacon fat too," she said by way of distraction.

"And pie!" Tweed shouted.

Maggie stared at her son. "There's no pie, honey child."

Buster reached for something on the table bench, producing a napkin plumb full of something. A house napkin, neat and precious, instead of the rags they were used to seeing. Her belly went cold.

"Where'd you get that?"

Buster frowned. He must have heard the thread of fear in her voice.

"It's all right, Mammy. Lucy gave it to us," Tweed said.

"Lucy..." Maggie's voice failed.

The White girl giving her sons presents after she'd nearly died playing with them. Miss Marianne would smack her good for this, but the master, Booker...they'd punish the boys. Black boys near their precious daughter of the house. It didn't bear thinking of.

"You stay away from that girl."

"We play at the Indian fort," Buster told her.

"We share lunch," Tweed added.

They didn't understand. How could they possibly understand? Maggie sat down, putting an arm around each boy. "Listen to me. The master would be very angry at you boys being near his daughter. *Very* angry. He would punish us all."

Her urgency got through to Buster, though Tweed was frowning rebellious-like.

"You can't mess with her, you hear me? Ain't safe, honey child."

Honey came through the door, laughing at Preacher behind her. "I was done! Wasn't gonna wait for you to fetch me."

"You wait next time," Preacher told her, smiling and serious at the same time. "You're my wife, and you gotta wait."

Smiling still, Honey noticed the napkin. "What's that doing here?"

Maggie sighed. "Somehow the boys got given a treat. By that girl, Lucy."

"We didn't ask for nothing. She brought it to us," Buster told them. From his tone, he understood the seriousness of the thing.

Honey frowned, and Preacher went deathly still. He, Maggie knew, understood.

"I'll sneak the napkin back tomorrow. No one need know nothing," Honey said.

Both boys leaned in close, and Maggie hugged them tight.

Some dangerous things were easy to spot, like a rattler or a bear, but some dangers were more complicated. If the rattler didn't bite you, you were fine. But with Lucy running round, you could get proper bit and never know till it was too late to draw out the poison.

When supper was done, Honey clasped Maggie's hand and pulled her out the door. "I got a surprise for you."

Tired and heart-sore, Maggie shook her head. "Surprise me tomorrow."

"Won't take a lick of a puppy's ear!"

Honey dragged her mother through the slave clearing, pulling her to the farthest cabin, the one that now belonged to her. The inside was dark, of course, but it smelled of carbolic soap and beeswax. Then Honey lit the lantern.

Near the stove stood a fancy round table of polished wood, barely large enough to set two small stools beneath it. The surface was covered by a fancy white doily with a large painted bowl and pitcher atop it.

"What the Hell are you supposed to do with that?" Maggie asked.

Honey grinned. "I got *two* pitchers! Which one you want?"

She almost chose the old one. But why shouldn't she, just this once, get what she wanted? "Give me that purple one. It'll match my kerchief."

⇒⇒⇒ ⇐⇐⇐

The next morning, Lucy waited until Bibby was upstairs with Honey and Cook was in the larder. Tonight was ham, which the boys would like, she was sure, but it hadn't been in the oven yet and she didn't think they could cook it easily.

She spotted several bread rolls from Mother and Father's dinner the night before. Lucy snatched them up and stuffed them in her pockets. For a moment, she eyed the butter, but then she heard Bibby coming down the stairs. She dashed outside and headed for the barn.

The puppies were playing ferociously this morning. The black one, who was growing into the largest of the five, was growling and pouncing on his sister, the yellow one. She in turn nipped his ear, which made him leap backward and then bounce back. The little chocolate one with the white patch on his face stayed by his mother and whimpered. Buster had said he was the runt, and they don't always make it 'cause they're not strong enough.

So Lucy cuddled him and whispered, "You can make it if you want." But he squirmed in her hands, anxious to get back to his mother, so she let him go.

She'd thought it'd be too early at the Indian fort, but the boys were already there. Today they were fetching water to make a mud pie, so they had to hunt and hunt for a suitable pitcher. They found one too, after walking the river flat—a large, ugly bowl that had a sharp piece near the mouth where the lip had broken away. The water had smoothed the jagged edge a little, but you still needed to mind your palm when grabbing it. They made a wonderful mud pie with tiny stones for nuts on top. Then Buster and Tweed decided to have a pow wow.

"What is that?" Lucy asked.

"Indian talk," the older boy explained. "We're gonna plan to stalk Booker and watch him without him ever seeing us."

"And scalp him!" Tweed grinned.

"No." Buster shook his head. "Can't get that close." He plucked his johnnycake from a pocket, waving it in the air. "After noon, we'll stalk him real quiet."

Lucy dug in her pockets and pulled out one of the rolls. "Bread roll," she said, offering it to Buster.

He pulled back as if it were a bug. "Can't. We're not allowed anymore." But his eyes were large, and inside them, she could see he was hungry and wanted to eat it.

"Why not?" she asked.

"The master would be angry!" Tweed told her.

"But why?"

Tweed just shook his head. "Mammy says."

Buster looked at her odd, and for a moment, she feared she couldn't be an Indian anymore. Then Tweed bit into his johnnycake, and a moment later, Buster ate his.

So, she nibbled the bread roll. It was good but would have been better with butter. Better still with strawberry jam.

They stalked Booker pretty good that afternoon. Lucy found it turned out to be easy because Booker seemed to be stalking a field hand himself. She was Maisey, Buster said. And Booker weren't supposed to be stalking her no more.

The game turned out to be way too easy, so they tried stalking Mammy and then Preacher. That was also too easy, as field hands just worked the rows and you knew where they were going. The only exciting bit was when Preacher, seemingly working hard and looking at his hands, said, "You boys planning to scalp me?"

Buster jumped a mile, and Tweed burst out laughing. Lucy looked around in case they'd get caught, but no one else even blinked. Booker was off aways, still stalking that Maisey.

Preacher turned and chuckled at them, but when he spied her, his smile disappeared. "Good afternoon, Miss Lucy," he said. He sounded different than when he spoke to the boys—real formal like. It made her feel lonely again.

"Good afternoon, Mister Preacher," she tried, smiling her best smile.

He just bobbed his head and went back to work.

The boys had dashed two rows over to where the mammy worked. Tweed was hugging her leg, and after a quick glance at Booker, she hugged him back. "What you two up to?" she asked them.

"Stalking," Tweed told her. "We're Indians."

The mammy smiled, and her smile practically covered her whole face.

Mother's smiles, Lucy decided, always had other stuff mixed in. She looked angry or annoyed mostly, and sometimes just plumb tired. This mammy's smile was pure *smile*. But then she saw Lucy, and it faded.

Without really thinking, Lucy reached in her pocket to find the other bread roll. Slipping closer, she handed it to the mammy, who took it before seeing what it was.

She stared at it, then stared at Lucy. "Child, you shouldn't be giving me this."

Lucy looked around to see if anyone could hear. Only the boys could, and that was all right.

"Yes," she told the mammy. "I surely should." Suddenly uncertain, Lucy whirled around and ran home.

～≫⟫ ⟪≪～

It being Sunday, Preacher slipped out of the cabin after supper, up the path to the slave clearing. As their cabin was located where it was, he'd never seen the clearing till the ceremony. He wanted to see it again.

Rounding the second cabin, he moved off between two more, but didn't find anything, clearing-wise. He was having another look when Honey appeared.

"What you doing out here?" she asked.

"Wanted to see the clearing again."

"Why?"

With it being dark, he couldn't rightly see her face. "Impulse, I guess. Seemed like a peaceful place."

Honey wrapped her hands round his arm and tugged him down a little trail he hadn't noticed. They passed by two more cabins and stepped into the setting of their wedding.

Preacher had feared he wouldn't be able to see it well without Miss Marianne's lamps, but with the trees all hanging back, the moonlight sparkled down unobstructed and the light from two of the surrounding cabins helped a bit. One cabin even had a window, just like Maggie's.

"Used to play here when I was little," Honey said. "With Maisey. We played dolls."

"You had dolls, did you?"

She laughed. "Squint fashioned them from bits of rope. Arms, head, and the frayed bottom made a nice skirt."

Preacher chuckled, sitting on the stump in the center of the clearing. There wasn't room for Honey, and after a moment of looking at each other, he wrapped an arm around her shoulder and gently leaned her against him.

"This is better than any old church," he said, gazing at the moon.

"They sing songs in the church. Imagine that."

"You like songs?"

Honey nodded. "Ain't heard that many."

It was possibly because the moon was so bright, or the night so mild, or maybe 'cause he was so happy. Whatever prodded him, Preacher began to sing. "When Israel was in Egypt land, let my people go."

Honey's eyes widened.

"Oppressed so hard, they could not stand." Dimly, he realized his song choice might not be the best. But Preacher loved singing and couldn't bring himself to stop. "Go down, Moses, way down in Egypt land."

She leaned into him, resting her head on his shoulder as natural as the owl rests in the tree.

The door of the window house opened, and Squint came out. "Here, boy, you gotta be careful now."

"Preacher singing me a song, Squint." Now she was protecting him.

He had a proper wife, the sweetest little gal ever been born, leaning against him and defending him. Squint did make an excellent point, but Preacher couldn't simply stop singing after Honey did what she did. Best thing to do was change course. "Swing low, sweet chariot..."

Squint blinked.

"Coming for to carry me home."

Honey gasped. "I *love* this song!"

Shaking his head, Squint stepped closer, then suddenly joined in.

"I looked over Jordan, and what did I see? Coming for to carry me home." The men sang it loud, and by the last refrain, pretty near every slave had come to the clearing.

No sign of Booker, Preacher realized. Did that mean the man lived out of hearing? Or was he just preoccupied? Peering around, Preacher saw Maisey wasn't there either. So their overseer was most definitely occupied.

Afterward, Squint warned him that singing at night might not be approved of. Honey protested that, proclaiming it was beautiful. Surely Miss Marianne would approve of God Songs.

Preacher held Honey's hand on the way back to the cabin. With the door in sight, they kissed. And kissed again. He'd have kissed her a third time, but she put a hand to his chest.

"You can't do this outside!" she whispered.

He somehow withstood the temptation to prove her wrong.

It wasn't till the next morning that he spied the bunch of flowers set in her China bowl. No wonder he'd smelled honeysuckle in the night.

"When did you have time to pick flowers?"

Honey saw them and laughed. He loved her laugh.

"Tweed," she told him. "He must have picked them."

When Squint came round to get Preacher, the old slave also sent Honey to talk to Booker. "Can't sing like that without permission," he told them sternly.

So, choosing a day when she'd brought Booker an extra portion of roast chicken for lunch, Honey asked, and the man agreed. They didn't sing every day, of course. No point in pushing their luck, and anyway, slaves were too plumb tired to stay up most nights, but a Sunday tradition was born. Preacher would hold their own sort of church just as he'd done years back in Mississippi. Hopefully, this one wouldn't end so bad.

⟫⟫ ⟪⟪

For some reason, they needed the feed early. There should have been enough for the horses to last five, six days, but it seemed there was not.

Hueron studied Booker's face. "What happened to the feed?"

The overseer shrugged. "S'all gone. Somebody being too free with the shovel, I expect."

Words trembled on his tongue, but Hueron held his peace. Arguing would be a waste of time, and there really wasn't time to waste.

"Have Dancer saddled."

"Oh, but..." Plainly Booker had wanted to go himself, probably fool around in Blanten. Maybe he'd even sped up the feed use.

At least Hueron got the chance to exercise his spleen. Dancer, attuned to his mood, flew down the road, even jumping the fallen tree on the side near the crossroad without the slightest hesitation. They cleared it together.

Sampson agreed to have the feed delivered that afternoon and headed to the back to arrange things. Somehow Hueron had the impression that the shopkeeper wouldn't do that and Booker had always needed to fetch supplies himself. Perhaps the man hadn't actually lied, but he would never be one to push for the best outcome for Sweetgum. Booker only cared about the best for Booker.

Hueron was patting Dancer, promising to take it easy on the return trip, when Meachum appeared.

"Mister Hueron." The man nodded.

Hueron returned the nod.

Sampson came back and assured delivery of the feed before supper, without mentioning anything so crass as payment. They were polite in Missouri. In Baltimore, a seller would have confirmed money would exchange hands.

Sampson turned to Meachum, who apparently wanted a new bridle. Hueron needed to move on. He wanted to check the field, see how far they'd gotten this morning. He wanted to make sure

Booker was overseeing the field, not just the female slaves. He wanted to estimate how much money he was going to lose with this crop.

Sampson finished and moved off.

Meachum looked at him. "You all right, Mister Hueron?"

Hueron studied the man, trying to weigh his own mind. He knew Meachum would produce where Booker had not, knew he was smart and understood Sweetgum's fields. But there was something about the man he didn't quite trust. If he could just figure that out...

"Tell Booker to pull as many from the house as you can spare," Meachum said. "It's only for a few weeks, and it needs doing now."

The man did make sense.

"And tell him to put those two boys to work. They're old enough and then some." Meachum touched his hat in a respectful nod, turning away.

"You still looking for work?" Hueron heard himself ask.

⟫⟫⟫ ⟪⟪⟪

The kitchen door was half open, to Maggie's relief. She hated rapping on it when it was closed 'cause you never knew who might be on the other side.

Only person she could see was Cook. "Booker wants his chicken," she called.

Cook turned and shook her head. "That man gonna get hisself in trouble. You tell him that, Maggie."

Maggie shrugged. Weren't worth telling the overseer nothing, and they both knew that.

Watching Cook slice a drumstick off the roasted fowl on the table, Maggie was amazed that the White folks only ate the breast off their birds. Then Cook wrapped a checkered cloth round it as Miss Marianne marched up.

"What are you doing with my chicken?"

Maggie's instinct was to hide low behind the door, but she couldn't abandon Cook.

Cook replied, "Mister Booker sent for this, Miss Marianne. Sometimes he eats a little leftover when he's extra busy in the field."

Maggie had to admire Cook. The woman made it sound reasonable. She might have added that the family didn't eat much leftovers themselves, but that wouldn't have gone over so well.

Miss Marianne was turning away when she saw Maggie at the door. Her lips pursed out, and Maggie knew it hadn't been her imagination. The lady really did dislike her.

"Well, hurry up and send her on her way!" Miss Marianne snapped at Cook.

Cook hid her surprise and strode quickly across the room.

Miss Marianne turned to Maggie. "And you—tell Booker not to send you near this house again."

"Yessum, Miss Marianne." Maggie bowed her head and darted down the path.

Time was she'd have worried herself silly trying to figure out what she'd done. These days, she knew there was no figuring White folks. Best to just do what they said and move on.

There had to be a way to get to Quincy. Surely this Murphy couldn't be the only one ever gone there.

⋙⋙ ⋘⋘

"Maisey girl, don't miss that cotton lying on the dirt. Bend over and get it, darling," Booker sniggered. She was a sexy thing in that thin dress, and he wondered just how long old Hueron would be in town.

But glancing at the road, he saw the cloud of dust. Someone was coming, and there weren't many who'd be passing Sweetgum. Maisey would have to wait.

Maggie was still missing, which weren't good. Best to claim one of her boys hurt hisself at the river. Being a father himself, Hueron would surely see the need for her to help her boy.

Nodding to himself, adding details to his story, Booker saw the slave emerge from the trees, chicken in her hand. Frantically, he beckoned to her, but it was too late. Hueron's cloud drew close enough he could see the horse.

"Hide the chicken, Maggie!" he growled through his teeth.

The damn woman stared at him, still approaching.

"Git back to work!" he shouted loud enough for Hueron to hear.

And after precious seconds, she did.

The relief he felt was short-lived. As the master drew close, Booker noticed the second horse with Clint Meachum atop. Meachum, the man he'd replaced years ago by puffing off his cotton expertise and pointing out the man's cruelty hurt what should be strong men's ability to work.

With the skies clouding up for April, Booker suddenly realized how Meachum might turn the tables.

⟫⟫⟫ ⟪⟪⟪

Maggie stuffed the chicken in her pocket and went back to work. Not that she feared Hueron, but she sensed the coming confrontation and figured it best to watch it with her head down, picking cotton.

"There hasn't been much progress," the master was saying.

Maggie's fingers seemed to speed up all on their own.

"We pretty near got that whole row done," Booker burst out, a trace of fear in his voice.

Maggie pursed her lips to keep from smiling. She remembered a day, years back, when Honey was barely ten. Booker'd been watching her lately, and at the time, Maggie had been franticly worrying about him hurting her. She had actually confronted him, stepping in front of her daughter. Booker had looked up with a nasty gleam in his eyes.

Just then, Skeeter had stepped out of the cotton and into her life. He'd actually grinned. "Now don't get all bothered," he told the overseer. "She's just being a mama bear. You know what they're like, protecting their cubs and all. She don't know you're a real man...wouldn't go for no cub. Only a man can't get a woman go after a child." Skeeter directed the last part at Maggie. Booker left Honey alone for a while after that day.

That night, Skeeter had showed up with his bacon fat and claimed he was there to protect Honey, but it was always Maggie he sought. Buster and Tweed were his. He was a funny guy, never seemed to care much about nothing. But he disliked Booker and loved his boys, and he protected Honey. Last thing he told Maggie was she would have to be that mama bear. Whenever Booker got in trouble, Maggie felt a little smile tickling her lips.

"Booker, this is Clint Meachum."

The smile died. *Meachum.* He said, "We've met."

Maggie snuck a look up.

Booker had turned pale as the clouds rolling across the sun. She couldn't see Meachum's face, but she knew the smirk that would surely be there, beneath those Hell-spawn eyes. That's what Hank used to call them.

"Maisey, you lazy fool! You missed some!" Booker barked out hoarsely. Then, "Thought you'd moved on."

"Just moved back."

"Booker," the master spoke in that firm, quiet voice, the one that sent shudders down a slave's back. "Get your things and clear out. You're fired."

They were words Maggie had wanted to hear, had dreamed of every time the man licked his lips watching Honey. But now she heard the echo of Cook's warning. *"Master Hueron's next overseer would be much harsher, I promise you."*

Maggie's hands flew faster, even as the man's horse took several prancing steps into the field—closer than Booker ever came to the work. A shadow passed over her. It was either a cloud or Booker leaving, but she didn't dare look up to see.

"Rain's coming," the new man's voice announced.

Her stomach shriveled into an icy knot. That voice from the past, dredging up memories. Bad memories. "You will clear this field fast, or I'll know the reason why."

The man's boots approached, striding firmly down the row of white cotton. Maggie fancied she recognized the scratch on the toe, though that was unlikely. It was all she could do to keep her fingers busy.

Those boots stopped right near her nose. "You're the mammy of those two boys."

It weren't a question, but she nodded all the same.

"Go get 'em."

Her heart sank. "Yessir." Her feet started running all on their own.

Cook had been right all along. Booker was a lazy White, a woman chaser with his sight set on Honey. Meachum was the man who'd killed her husband.

It never actually rained, but that day would always be remembered as dark and dismal. No one got beat, but they felt that whip hovering over their backs just the same. Both Buster and Tweed picked cotton, bent low to the ground, bags hanging on their necks. Maggie felt tears on her face, ignoring the sight of her babies working as she ignored the muscle aches and insect bites.

At sundown, Meachum stood at the wagon, feeling every bag for weight, watching Squint and Oliver. He never said a word.

Squint had them already in the field when first light hit the crop the next morning. With Booker, they'd had a good hour before he appeared, usually dragging Maisey with him, but Meachum was already there, sitting atop his stallion and slapping his palm with a horsewhip. A whip, they guessed, that had never struck his horse.

Booker always had Squint and Oliver working, but sharing one row and resting as they needed. Now each had his own row and sack, and Maggie guessed they'd be measured just like everyone else. She winced when she saw Oliver, who'd always been just a bit simple, straighten and rub his bad arm.

Meachum swung a leg over the horse, sliding down the polished saddle. When he strode over to the boy, Oliver actually grinned warmly.

The snap of the whip split the day in two as it split the flesh on his arm. Blood splattered Squint, who never paused in his picking. The second blow brought the boy to his knees.

"Pick cotton, boy," Squint said clear as a crow cawing on the breeze.

Oliver stayed frozen for one more vicious strike, then reached for a bud.

The next blow fell across the back of his neck, and Maggie thought it'd killed him.

The boy's hands fumbled in the white, grabbing, twisting. The shadow of the whip marked his shredded shirt, poised above his head, and then slowly lowered. Sobbing, Oliver snatched buds, filling his sack faster than Maggie ever thought he could with that arm of his.

"I ain't Booker," Meachum said, seemingly to Oliver, but his voice clearly carried across the field.

"A man of few words," Preacher commented later.

Those three, however, were unnecessary. Every slave in the field already knew he wasn't like Booker at all.

That night Maggie waited till the boys were asleep before making her way to Sampson's. Dangerous, perhaps, but less dangerous than doing nothing. Slaves died quick under overseers like Meachum, and she had the boys to think about.

Maisey had said Booker was gone from his cabin, which likely meant Meachum was moving in. Maggie took the route through the woods to avoid his place just in case.

It should have been a three-quarter moon in the sky, but cloud cover kept the night dark. Low scrub tripped her, and her cheek got scratched by a sharp branch she never saw. Yet she kept going.

When she finally knocked on the back door, it took a fair time before it cracked open. That same small man stood there, gazing up at her. If he recognized her at all, he never showed it.

"That old mule threw his shoe."

The door widened, and the big White man grimaced. "Can't help you."

"Please," she whispered hoarsely. "My boys...we got a new overseer."

The man grimaced again, but he didn't shut the door.

"I know you can't guide us...can't show us nothing. But if *we* go...on our own?"

The man leaned his face against the door and sighed. "Meachum's a bastard," he said. "Ain't no denying that. But if you fear him now, think how scared you'd be if he caught you running."

Maggie waited, hopeful.

"That's what he did before, you know. Slave catcher, and a good one at that."

Her skin chilled in the cold night air.

"Trust me, woman, you don't want to be caught."

This time she didn't try to stop the door from closing.

~>>> <<<~

The firm knock on the back door startled Honey. Miss Marianne had sent her to fetch another candle so she could see the mirror proper. Cook was working away, preparing a goose for roasting. At the rap on the wood, they exchanged a frown.

"See who that is," Cook told her.

Honey hurried to open it, and then stared. Outside stood a rough-looking White man, slapping a whip against his palm and glaring at her. White men never came to the kitchen door—except Booker sometimes. This must be that new overseer. He looked vaguely familiar.

"Fetch me all the house slaves," he told her.

Bibby appeared at her side. "Mister Meachum. We heard you were back."

He frowned, his bushy eyebrows drawing low over his eyes as if expecting Bibby to do his bidding. But she weren't about to follow the man's orders.

"Now, I can't do that, sir. The house slaves working for the mistress right now. What is it you need?"

He struck her across the arm with the whip. "Get me all the house slaves."

Bibby flinched but stayed standing there. "Miss Marianne done give orders for all of them. If you'll wait—"

He struck her harder.

Honey caught her as she staggered.

"Bibby?" It was Miss Marianne's voice. They all waited silently as she tapped across the polished floor. "Why, Mister Meachum! How nice to see you."

"Miss Marianne."

Smiling at him as if he were a friend, the mistress said, "What are you doing at the back door?"

"Your husband gave permission for the house slaves to work the fields. Ahead of the rains, you understand."

"But...they're all busy. They're just women, not field hands."

"Women can pick cotton."

The way he said it sent a chill down Honey's spine. White folks had tones to tell you when they were getting angry, getting serious. She'd never heard them use those tones with each other until now.

Looking at Miss Marianne, she didn't think her mistress understood the danger it meant.

"All right," Miss Marianne said slowly. "Weena can go with you." With a quick nod, she sent Bibby off to fetch her.

Honey ached for Weena. She'd hate working in the field after being a house slave.

"I need more, madam." Meachum reached out and latched onto Honey's arm.

"Honey's my maid."

"She looks fit and healthy..."

Miss Marianne stepped in front of her, and Honey feared for her mistress. This White man wasn't one to mess about. "She's my personal maid. I don't want her getting dirty in the field."

For the longest moment, Honey's fate teetered in the balance.

And then this Meachum let go. "Very well, Miss Marianne. We'll let your husband decide."

Bibby returned with a wide-eyed Weena, staring hopelessly at her mistress. When Meachum spun on his heels and left, she hurried after him, tears rolling down her face.

Weena had been Honey's idol, queen of the slave quarters as long as she could remember. She'd been startled and thrilled to find herself stepping into Weena's place, the mistress's own maid. Now poor Weena was being sent back to the fields.

For the first time, Honey wondered if *she* would someday be sent back to the fields. If Meachum had his way, that day would come soon.

That night Preacher ate his dinner solemnly, though he smiled at her just the same. They ate with Maggie, as they often did, then walked back quietly to their cabin, holding hands. It was as if nothing had happened that day. Nothing had changed.

But when they were alone in the dark, afterward as he held her close, Preacher stroked her hair and whispered softly, "Do you want to stay or go?"

For the first time, Honey hesitated. Still, surely things would settle down and be all right. "Stay," she finally replied.

Honey felt his chin touch the top of her head. "Then we stay."

⤞⤞ ⤝⤝

Word came to Meachum on Monday. His scale had arrived. In the end, he'd told Sampson to deliver the damn thing since he couldn't leave the slaves to pick without him and he couldn't send one to collect it. April rains were on their way.

Sampson didn't like being told that, but then he didn't want to annoy Hueron either, so late afternoon, his wagon rolled down the road.

Meachum had seen the picture, of course, and read the dimensions, the weight. Still, the thing's size surprised him. It was a proper scale that had belonged to old Joe Brack in Mississippi. Sampson had acquired it when Brack sold up and passed it on for a fee.

Hueron—Karl, not Mark—had never fully committed to a proper cotton plantation. He'd missed key things, relying on others to handle the raw cotton. That had cost him money, more than he'd realized. Now young Hueron was planning to go back to tobacco as soon as he had enough money to do so. This posed a problem in that the master of Sweetgum didn't want to spend too much cash on cotton equipment.

At least he'd approved the scale.

→»»⟩ ⟨«««

"This here's to weigh your pickings," the overseer announced.

It was near dark, and Maggie stood with all the other slaves beside the cotton barn. Their baskets had been dragged here rather than loaded in the wagon. They were heavy, the cotton properly squeezed into the basket to hold a day's collection. Booker used to lift—often just half-lift—to see there was good weight to them. Now Meachum intended to properly measure each slave's daily work.

Oliver and Squint went first. Squint struggled getting his basket close to the scale, then Meachum tugged it onto the flat metal rectangle. The fancy pointer moved, sliding up to point at some figures.

"One hundred eighty," Meachum announced. "A slave should be able to pick two hundred pounds of cotton."

Squint hung his head—a protective gesture all slaves instinctively knew—and waited.

Meachum merely gestured for Oliver.

The boy had picked one hundred forty pounds. Maggie's own back twitched, worried for him, but Meachum waved Buster up. Her son's basket weighed two hundred ten pounds, and Maggie felt furious at herself for a surge of pride. Her basket weighed two hundred twenty. She actually got a nod from the overseer. Only one other basket exceeded the two-hundred mark—Preacher's.

When the last basket was pulled off the scale, their stomachs were rumbling with equal parts hunger and fear. No one dared move.

"Tomorrow, any slave with less than two hundred pounds will get a few chunks taken out of his hide."

As she headed back to the cabin through the dark woods with the others, Maggie shivered. The fear hung over them all like a swarm of hornets. Didn't matter that she and hers had picked a good amount. They were all slaves and, sooner or later, they'd all get stung.

The next day, the master himself watched the weighing. More than half had the two hundred pounds, and those who failed weren't actually whipped with Mister Hueron watching. The whippings came later.

⋙ ⋘

So the master of Sweetgum had bowed to his wife's wishes. Meachum shook his head, but he found himself smiling too. Most women knew how to twist men about their fingers, but she was so young and delicate he'd just figured a man like Hueron would know how to manage her. She surely didn't need three slaves keeping her company.

Yet Marianne got her way.

Sliding off Demon, Meachum plucked the whip from the saddle horn and stood gazing over the field.

Truthfully, the house girl wasn't near as good as the others, but having her was better than not having her. Much as that weakling boy was better than nothing, if only just. Even the old man had proved more productive. The bigger of the two boys was good, very good in fact. He picked faster than a lot of the older hands. The littler one, just a dab of skin and bones, was hardly worth putting in the field.

That Booker. Whatever qualities the man had sought in a slave, ability to work wasn't one of them. Meachum spied the house girl rubbing her back, using a fist to dig into skin. It dug into his mind, taking him back.

Katie O'Hallon.

His mother had been shouted at, threatened, beaten. She'd been lazy and needed persuasion to keep to her end of the bargain. At least that's what he'd been told. She hadn't been a slave but an indentured servant. As far as he could remember, there'd been no difference. She'd come over from Ireland having agreed to work four years to pay for their crossing. He didn't recall much beyond the pitching of the ship and the creak of the timber, but the captain had oft said they'd need to earn their passage.

Upon docking, Katie had found herself indentured to an innkeeper in Philadelphia. Meachum did remember him. The man

beat them both hard and often, and when Katie died, told him he'd
have to work eight years to pay their debt.

Meachum had worked every single day owed. When he made a
mistake, he learned from it. Soon he got the whip off his back, and
even occasional praise. Others got beat, and he shook his head at
them. Shut up, work hard, and do your time proper.

At fourteen, he'd been released and even offered a paying job
to stay. But he'd done his allotment and earned his freedom, and
the American West beckoned, so he'd hitched a ride on a wagon
train. Seeing the Mississippi river, he'd found his first real smile,
and upon fording it, decided to stick around. There was work to
spare for a man unafraid of it.

Meachum wound up helping on a tobacco plantation, liking the
chance to work outside instead of in. From there he rose to overseer, having observed exactly how to please the bosses. You didn't
complain, just worked through it. And as others didn't do that,
you stood above them. He had no time for sniveling. Weaklings
sniveled.

Now, as he advanced on the house girl, another movement
caught his eye. It was near the trees, moving toward the field,
toward that mammy of the two boys. Did she have another boy?

Meachum strode through the cotton, annoyed when his shirt
snagged on a plant. Whoever this was would pay for that.

But it was blonde hair that ducked from him. The little face staring up at him, eyes big and lips trembling, was White. Marianne's
daughter. What the Hell was she doing here?

"You're Lucy."

For a moment the child held still. Then she stood, staring up at him.

"What are you doing here?" He had to work to keep the snarl from his voice.

She just blinked, her mouth a slim line on her face. He had the impression she didn't smile much. She wasn't a well-favored child despite her mother's beauty. Lucy's little fist clutched a drumstick, left over from last night's dinner.

"What are you doing with that?" Meachum spoke very softly, a nasty suspicion clouding his mind.

For a moment, he didn't think she'd answer. He was just deciding how to force her to when she opened her mouth. "It's for the puppies."

"Puppies?"

She danced away, putting distance between them. "Barn's full of them."

"Why were you here?" he demanded.

"To see what you look like, of course." With that, Lucy spun on her heels and ran away.

Meachum had to smile. He'd always been attractive to women—even Marianne gave him the eye. Now he knew the effect spread even younger than he'd guessed.

Lucy raced for the trees and kept going.

Her mother liked the new overseer, had even commented on how smart he was. Lucy could see the smart but not the nice. He had a scowl on his face that never left, even when he smiled. As if his brows were still mad. Seeing that, she'd been afraid to tell him anything about Maggie. She'd told him about the puppies instead.

Hopefully he wouldn't hurt them, at least.

⁓⟫⟫⟩ ⟨⟨⟨⟵

Maggie's back was spared for the most part. Others weren't so lucky.

Meachum beat backs frequently, and hard. She'd never liked Booker, but he lacked the cruel streak that ran through the new overseer's core. Meachum's whip broke skin, leaving bleeding welts that took time at night to tend. He rode that stallion of his, picking his way down the rows, checking up on every cotton bag, every slave. Maggie didn't dare do so much as wipe the sweat off her brow.

She panicked anew over the White child. She'd told the boys not to accept the food, so the girl had taken to giving it to her. Sometimes there'd be a morsel left at the cabin, a piece of bread or a chicken wing. Sometimes she'd find Maggie in the field. If Maggie didn't take her offering, the girl placed it on the dirt before her. It was wiser to take it quick than to catch Meachum's attention.

Constantly she worried about the new overseer finding out, the master finding out. About what they might do. She'd explained this to the boys, to the girl herself. She'd asked Cook for advice, but

Cook had already warned the child. "I can't stop her altogether, Maggie. Ain't my place."

So Maggie had turned to Honey, who tried to talk to Lucy. But her daughter didn't get far, and she didn't see the danger. "The mistress is kind," Honey told her. "She would never punish you."

Maggie had seen kind masters beat a slave just as hard as mean masters.

Then yesterday, Meachum had caught Lucy. Maggie hadn't heard their conversation, but she'd utterly panicked over what he might do. The girl had run away, and he'd strode back to his horse without so much as looking at her. Her back itched that whole afternoon, fearing a blow that never came.

Well, it came the next day, and it was the child—not Maggie—who got in trouble.

Cook told her about it. "Don't think you'll have to worry no more," she said, wiping her hands on her apron. Maggie had come by to walk Honey home since Preacher had to handle the cotton bags after the sun set these days. Oliver was just another field hand now.

"'Bout what?" Maggie asked, her mind on the boys. They hadn't been beat yet, at least, and were working hard. But Tweed shouldn't have to work.

"'Bout Lucy," Cook told her.

That snagged her attention. "Why?"

Standing at the back door, Cook turned to check the kitchen was still empty. It was, but even so, she leaned in close and lowered her voice. "Miss Marianne caught her this morning, sneaking last night's leftovers into a napkin. I don't think she'll do it again."

So Maggie went back to worrying about Quincy, because now, more than ever, she wanted to run.

⫸⫷

The scale thing didn't work quite the way Meachum wanted. It should have forced the slaves to work harder, struck the fear of God into them. And in the beginning, it had. But then Hueron had taken to showing up, throwing the whole thing off. Meachum had struck Oliver and been told that was enough. It weren't enough.

Just like a dog, you needed to beat the slave when the mistake was made. Waiting till Hueron weren't there sort of took the edge off. Worse, it watered down Meachum's authority. Sooner or later a slave would take to tattling to the master, and Meachum suspected Hueron might actually listen.

The second time it happened, the littlest boy had dragged a puny offering up to the scale, beaming like he'd done good. Meachum slid off his horse, slowly unfurling his whip, when the words rang out in the silent barn.

"What do you think you're doing?" Hueron had appeared out of nowhere.

"Boy ain't done enough."

The master swung a leg over the horse, dropping down to the kid's level. He actually smiled at him. "You done all you could?"

"Yassir!" It was a toothy grin, and Meachum itched to slap it off his face.

Hueron, however, ruffled the boy's hair. "You ain't gotta work for another year," he'd told the boy. And that was that.

The man had no idea the damage he did.

Maggie, the boy's mammy, was Meachum's best worker. He couldn't threaten her easily, 'cause if he did, the others wouldn't work so hard. No point in working to avoid the whip if she got whipped. Using her children was the way to leverage her. Except the older boy worked harder than half the field hands, and now the younger was off the table completely. And her damned daughter was under Marianne's thumb.

Meachum had promised a forty percent increase in cotton yield, but he needed absolute control to wring out every ounce of that. He'd have to find another way.

→≫⟩ ⟨≪←

Lucy saw Maggie working in the field. She had a picnic basket, like Lucy's mother used to have in Baltimore, sitting on the ground beside her.

"Lucy."

Lucy lifted the lid and peeked inside. It was empty.

"Honey child, it's time to rise."

Maggie shook her shoulder, but when she opened her eyes, it was Bibby she saw. The sun streamed across her bed, and her heart dropped in her chest. Bibby only woke her on Sundays, to go to church.

"Do I have to go, Bibby?"

She turned to plead, and the housekeeper tsked and touched her cheek. "Go wash your face, child."

Lucy bit her lip. Mother had hit her good yesterday.

Bibby tossed the bedsheets back and moved to her wardrobe. "Blue dress today? You always look good in blue." That meant she had to go, of course.

Lucy poured the water from the pitcher into the basin. Dipping her hands in, she bathed her face. Her cheek stung, and her eye felt funny.

Bibby tsked again.

Breakfast was in the kitchen today. She didn't know where her parents were and hoped that they wouldn't take her to church, but after her porridge, Bibby took her outside. The carriage was there, her mother already up in it.

When Lucy's father lifted her, he stared at her face. "What's this?" he asked. He was looking at Mother, so Lucy didn't answer.

"Lucy's been stealing," Mother told him.

Father set Lucy on the seat and touched her cheek.

She kept her eyes down.

"Marianne..."

"We mustn't be late."

After a moment he climbed in, snapped the reins, and drove off.

"Marianne." Father broke the silence of the ride. "Can you spare any more of the house slaves? It's important that we get that cotton picked."

"We got to eat, Mark. Cook is old, too old to do much out in a field, but she does wonders in the kitchen. Bibby and Honey keep the house clean. With Weena gone, they have to work harder and there's no one to keep a proper eye on your daughter these days."

Her father wasn't happy, Lucy knew. But she also knew he wouldn't do anything about it.

Lucy could read, mostly. Miss Helen had taught her, and she'd practiced since the move—partly to honor Miss Helen, but partly because there was only so much to do at Sweetgum now that Buster was working in the field. Mother had promised Father that a new governess would be found, but so far, she'd found all the ones she'd interviewed lacking.

As her parents entered the church, Lucy read the sign. Slaves for Sale and Rent. She knew what a sale was, but the word "rent" confused her.

Her father, too, noticed the sign. He read the whole thing, top to bottom, or at least stood long enough to do so. Adults read fast, she knew, and understood everything instantly. Almost, almost, she asked what rent meant, but before she could, her mother grabbed her shoulders and marched her to the pew they always sat in.

Lucy pondered the word, imagining all sorts of possibilities. Sale meant you bought them and they were yours. Rent might be when you sold one, or a slave sold himself. Or maybe you rented animals, like horses or cows.

"Oh, daughter of Babylon, doomed to be destroyed!"

The sun poured through the stained-glass Jesus, and his blood made red dazzles on the pew. Lucy touched one in the silence. Maybe instead of working, a rented slave played games with you.

"Blessed shall he be who repays you with what you have done to us!" Reverend Jessop swept his glare across the congregation in righteous anger.

Lucy wondered why he was always so angry. Was righteous anger worse than regular anger?

"Blessed shall he be who takes your little ones and dashes them against the rock."

"The reverend is in fine form," her mother whispered to her father.

Eventually the service ended. They didn't linger, as Father had to get back to the fields. Mother wasn't pleased, but she didn't argue. Instead, she swept into the house, telling Bibby to dig out her copies of the *World of Fashion* she'd brought from Baltimore. She hadn't been able to get any more in Missouri.

Lucy slipped off to the barn. The chocolate puppy with the white patch on his face was nestled beside the mama dog. Buster called her Runt, but Lucy hated the name. It was so unfair.

She lifted the dog, holding the wiggling warmth to her cheek. Its soft fur felt soothing against her face. "I'm going to name you Ellen," she told her. "You'd like that better than Runt, wouldn't you?"

Instead of whimpering, the puppy licked her face.

Lucy smiled. "Ellen it is."

Buster and Tweed were working in the field, of course. She'd brought them chicken once, but Buster said they weren't allowed to take it. He meant it too, looking more scared than she'd ever seen anyone. All the slaves were looking scared these days.

Maggie was farther away, and that new overseer-man was on a horse, standing right over her. He wouldn't like Maggie getting chicken and not him, and Lucy wasn't going to give him chicken 'cause he must be a bad man. So she took the chicken to Ellen, and played with her all afternoon.

⟫⟫ ⟪⟪

Whoever said Sunday was a day of rest had certainly not been a farmer.

Hueron slid the curry comb through Dancer's coat. There was a time he'd have handed the horse to Squint, who would brush him down proper. Or perhaps he'd have someone else do it. Lord, he didn't even know who. But these days it was all hands in the field all the time.

Problem was, currying took no real thought, which meant the mind wandered. As it did, he recalled the bruise on Lucy's face. He wasn't the most loving of fathers. Girls were to be treasured, of course, but they didn't really do much. They were placeholders in a family. They learned needlepoint and dancing, one for use after marriage and one to get married in the first place. Their upbringing should be left to their mothers.

Sons were the responsibility of their fathers. They were the heirs, with men's jobs in the world. They had to learn, to grow into that responsibility. After all, they were the future of the name. Hueron lacked that missing piece. After Lucy, there had been a second child, stillborn. There had been no third.

Hueron wanted a son. Not just an heir but a boy, his boy, to grow beside him, to learn from him. He'd imagined him ever since the day he married. Watching his father, wishing the man would spend more time with him, Hueron had turned to his uncle for his mentoring and been rewarded. The thought had been to pass on all he'd been taught to a son of his own. To do for him what he'd had to seek himself.

His wife was still young, of course. He'd formed the intention to have a talk with her several times, but she would blush and quickly turn away if the conversation turned "ungodly," which it invariably did. He'd planned to overcome that, find a way to discuss it, but never truly made the effort. There was still time, but there was no denying that Lucy was getting older, and despite her youthful appearance, so was Marianne.

"Swing low, sweet Harr-ee-oooot."

It was a young boy's voice, and Hueron found himself biting his lip not to laugh aloud. Meachum swore both boys were useful, but the littlest appeared to him to be more in the way than anything. The overseer proved stubborn in his ways of thinking.

Dropping the curry brush, Hueron moved silently from the stall. The puppies lay in the haymow, still too young to wander far from their mother, and sure enough, the little slave boy was there, stroking two of them at once.

"How old are they now?" Hueron heard himself asking.

Lucy would have been startled, needing to work up to an answer. This young one, however, didn't fear him in the least. "Coupla weeks, Master. Four and a bit."

"And they're all getting along?" When the boy merely frowned, Hueron added, "All healthy?"

"Yassir. The runt is a female, but Lucy takes care of her. She makes sure Ellen gets her share of milk. That's what Lucy named her—Ellen. I sure didn't."

So his daughter was playing in the barn as well...and playing with the slave children.

"Lucy's good with 'em!" the boy added, sensing he'd said something wrong.

Barely five years old, and he knew he'd misspoken. Smart boy. "What's your name?" Hueron asked.

A big grin spread across the child's small face. "I'se Tweed, Master."

"Tweed." Hueron found himself smiling back. "You're a good boy, Tweed."

"I know!"

After a moment, Tweed ran off aways, then turned to look.

Hueron nodded his permission, and the boy raced out of the barn. Very smart, that kid.

⌁⌁⌁ ⌁⌁⌁

Lucy hid in the haymow. She'd ducked down when her father approached, knowing better than to get caught with a slave. Tweed had been surprised but hadn't said a word. The boy had talked to her father, speaking easily, without hesitation. And her father—her scary father who she had to be respectful of and not annoy in anyway—had actually *liked* him.

Why couldn't she get him to like her? Maybe he liked slaves better. No, that couldn't be true. Maybe...he liked boys better.

Of course he liked boys better.

⟫⟫ ⟪⟪

Maggie kept her head down even as Squint dragged the broken wagon wheel down her row. The master had taken to coming out to watch, and it was a good idea to be working when he showed up.

The wheel had broken an hour earlier, and Meachum had whipped Squint's back for it. The damage was his own fault, as Meachum insisted on treating the wagon as he treated the slaves, driving it hard and rough. He'd run over that big rock on the trail and then blamed Squint. Now the overseer was working fast, trying to get the wagon fixed before the master appeared. Meachum had had to pull Preacher off his row to lift the thing while they attached a new wheel and now kept looking over his shoulder as Squint approached. He'd have done better to have Preacher pull the wheel. The man was so nervous he wasn't thinking straight. Maggie chuckled at him even while keeping her back bent.

As Squint got close, he glanced over his own shoulder. "Quincy ain't so hard to find," he told her.

She froze to her core.

"It's the river that makes trouble. No matter how big you think it is, it's bigger." He kept his steady pace, dragging the wheel past as he talked. "Rufus was good with a boat. I know that he crossed pretty near here, but careful-like. Real careful."

"How?" Maggie asked, her hands busy with the cotton.

"I ain't rightly sure." Squint sighed as he passed. "That was all Rufus. That ole river's a son of a bitch, Maggie. Slaves die trying to cross it."

"It don't like slaves?"

"River don't like nobody." Squint moved on.

Maggie rolled his words over in her mind. The river was so wide that you couldn't see across it most places. The water rushed pretty fast, and she knew boats had sunk and people had entered never to be seen again. But the far side of that river was Illinois. Slave catchers or not, it was a free state.

The cotton rustled behind her.

She kept picking at a good pace. "Got more?" she asked Squint.

Then she heard a different rustling and a little white fist, tightly clenched, thrust out before her. Maggie spun round to see Lucy. The child's trembling lip was swollen, and not just from crying. It was split, with dried blood marking the spot.

Seeing Meachum was occupied, Lucy turned her whole little face to Maggie. The other side had a black eye forming, the lump there purpled up real good.

Dear God, someone hit a White child that hard.

The little fist opened. A piece of toast lay there, squished and soggy. Maggie was scared to death of Meachum seeing her, of getting her back torn to shreds over being caught taking food from this child. But then the little white fingers trembled, the girl even more frightened than she was.

Gently, Maggie took the bread. "Thank you, child."

"S'all I could get." Ducking down, her eyes on Meachum, Lucy darted away.

Maggie thrust the toast in her mouth. As she picked the cotton that day, she kept seeing that child's battered face.

WADE IN THE WATER

THE SUN HAD SET, and Lucy was supposed to be in bed. She leaned on the windowsill, staring out at the barn and the trees. Buster and Tweed would be running home now, to eat johnnycakes and hug Maggie. She wished she had someone to hug. Then she remembered Ellen.

Cook had said the puppies were too young to leave their momma, but she could get a goodnight hug. Ellen and her mammy wouldn't mind. Whirling, Lucy dragged her cloak from the wardrobe and snuck down the stairs.

Her parents were eating in the dining room, and Cook and Bibby were removing one course to serve the next. Used to be Weena helped Cook, but Weena worked in the fields with Maggie these days.

It was easy to sneak out the back door. The night was clear and crisp, with that honeysuckle tang in the air. Lucy stepped softly, making sure her father wouldn't hear nothing. Her quiet movement allowed her to hear the song in the breeze.

"Jim crack corn, I don't care. Jim crack corn..."

Her feet were padding toward the song before she even thought.

"...and I don't care. The master's gone away."

The song came from the slave clearing. Carefully, she kept to the brush, slipping through quietly as she neared. She rounded the first cabin, ducked behind the second, and then, staying low to the ground, peeked out from the hazelnut bush.

Between the leaves, Lucy could see a lantern set on the big stump, making a halo of light. It shone on all the faces, dark and gleaming, smiling as they sang.

"One day he rode around de farm, de flies so numerous dey did swarm."

That preacher, the one who'd fished her out of the river, led the group. His voice was strong and clear. "One chance to bite him on the thigh. The devil take that blue tail fly!"

There was Maggie, hugging Buster and Tweed. Honey stood to one side of Preacher, that old slave on the other side.

"Jim crack corn, and I don't care. Jim crack corn, and I don't care. Jim crack corn, and I don't care. The master's gone away."

Laughter followed. Not too loud, almost careful-like, but laughter all the same.

Lucy realized that, while all the slaves smiled, they never laughed—except for Buster and Tweed. And even Buster didn't laugh so much these days.

"Oliver's in a bad way," one woman said. "Honey, can you sneak some of that liniment outta the house? Meachum beat him pretty good."

"Mister Meachum, he expects him to work better tomorrow," the old one spoke up. "And he can't hardly move."

"Did you try asking Bibby?" Preacher's deep voice soothed.

All the other voices sounded small and scared, but his was strong, firm. Lucy loved the sound of his words rolling through the night air. He sounded more like a preacher than Reverend Jessop.

"She say she do what she can. But she ain't done nothing yet."

"What we gonna do, Preacher? That Meachum's a bad one."

The big man looked at the skinny man who'd just spoken. It was suddenly quiet, so quiet that even the insects stilled their noise, and then a trickling sounded, gentle and sorta blanketing them all. The leaves beside Lucy rustled very softly.

Preacher held his palm out. A slow grin spread across his face. "Well now, God done answered you. Looks like the rains have come."

Gasps erupted as the others held out hands or lifted their faces. Sure enough, everything was getting wet.

"Wade in the water. Wade in the water, children..." Preacher sang all by himself.

Maggie stared. "Ain't never heard that one," she said.

"I'll teach it to you."

Smiling anew, the slaves all joined hands and sang.

Lucy sang the words quietly so no one would hear. Nestling down into the grass, she stayed, pretending that she too was holding hands with Buster and Tweed. And Maggie. She'd dearly love to hold hands with Maggie.

⋙⋙⋙   ⋘⋘⋘

Preacher sung that night with one eye looking over his shoulder. Singing had always been special to him, and singing to God the best. When he was young, his old master had loved to hear him sing, and Preacher often got off work to sit on the porch and give him some of those songs. Better than church, the master used to say.

But Meachum didn't seem the kind to appreciate music. That man was vicious and didn't like slaves doing anything but picking cotton. Even with permission—and it was Booker who'd given permission, Preacher suddenly remembered—the overseer would delight in punishing the lot of them.

He had been punished for singing once before. The day the old master summoned him to the house and stood him on the porch, told him to sing the chariot song. The day his teenage voice kept breaking on the edge between boy chatter and man talk.

The master had guests inside, and they all laughed. The master sent him off. That night, Preacher felt the whip for the first time. The bite of it, that pain-streak digging a trench in his flesh, slicing through skin to sear his soul. A year later his voice steadied, and the master bade him sing again.

Fortunately, Meachum never showed. The next morning, working in the field as the sun warmed his back, Preacher kept an eye on the overseer. The man sat astride that horse he was so proud of, arms resting on the horn of the saddle, eyes gazing out across the field—gazing at him.

Preacher wondered if he knew. A slave mighta told him, or he could have seen something, maybe even last night. Though if he had, Meachum wasn't the type to just go away without doing something.

He heard the slide of cotton on leather before he saw the man's feet hit the ground. Striking that whip across his palm in a gesture every slave knew well, the overseer strode down a row. Best Preacher could tell, he was heading in Oliver's direction. Oliver, who was already beat pretty good just yesterday.

"Lazy...stupid..."

"Mister Meachum, sir, he already got whipped, remember?" It was Buster's voice.

Looking over his shoulder, Preacher saw Buster facing Meachum. Beyond him stood Maggie, frozen in place, her eyes terrified. Preacher didn't recall praying, but the answer to his prayers came trotting round the bend, still far off, yet just in the nick of time.

"Mister Meachum, sir," he called, keeping his back bent and his hands picking, "the master's coming."

The world seemed to hold its breath. In the stillness, the hoof beats approached.

"Buster, get your ass back to work," Preacher said, hoping that would tip the scale.

Buster gave him a confused look but obediently resumed picking.

Meachum didn't twitch, neither his whip nor his feet. The overseer still hadn't moved when the master pulled back on the reins, but at least he hadn't struck nobody.

"How are we progressing?" the master asked.

Meachum strode off to greet him. "We'll get that forty percent."

Preacher resolved to have a talk with Buster that evening.

>>>> <<<<

Days later, it seemed the master had calmed Meachum down a bit. At least Maggie thought he had. She'd been working as fast as she could, her fingers twisting the buds free 'fore she even had a proper hold. Her bag filled faster than anyone's, but that weren't enough for the overseer. He'd done marked every slave picking except her, and she figured it was a matter of pride with him. Now he sat on his horse in the middle of the field, close enough to kick her if the urge seized him.

The funny thing about Meachum was that he couldn't seem to strike without some sort of excuse. He'd whipped Oliver for tripping, and he'd whipped Elvira for back talk, though she'd only asked which row he wanted her on. He hadn't hit Buster yet, but Maggie suspected if she didn't get beat soon, he'd whip both her boys out of sheer spite. He was that type.

She was just thinking about pretending to fall so he'd get it over with when she heard the sound. Another horse approached, galloping up fast. She didn't dare fall now, as she might be run over.

Soon, the master was beside them, holding Dancer in check. Maggie had never seen the master this close. Dancer didn't like to sit still, and Master usually kept him out of the field so he wouldn't crush a slave accidentally. Or maybe it was just the cotton he didn't want to crush.

"Meachum."

"Master Hueron." Unlike Booker, the new overseer always added his name to the *master* part. Squint said he did it for respect, but it didn't sound like no respect to Maggie.

"I just came from the barn," the master said. "Seems like the amount of cotton has fallen a bit from last week."

"Surely not," Meachum said.

Maggie felt his eyes burning ribbons into her back.

"Surely so. I'm wondering if it's because you're down a slave."

So the master was aware of Oliver lying in his cabin 'cause he couldn't stand. Meachum had laid into him real good two days back.

"Slaves gotta know what'll happen if they don't work proper."

"Cotton count is down, Meachum. And the rains are due any day now. We've already had a sprinkle or two." Dancer trotted a narrow turn, and the master rode off toward the house.

Maggie decided not to fall. After a few minutes, Meachum's stallion walked away.

⟫⟫⟫ ⟪⟪⟪

Waking up early, Hueron decided to look in on the auction in Blanten.

Slave auctions were frequently held in Hannibal, over forty miles away. That meant a good three days by wagon. But Tuesday's auction being nearby meant that, while the selection would be slim, any slave purchased could be picking cotton that same afternoon.

He'd debated taking Meachum. The overseer was usually reluctant to leave the plantation, thinking his presence made the field hands work harder, and really, Hueron didn't relish Meachum's company. Truth was, he didn't like the man. Surely Hueron could do better at finding slaves than Booker ever did.

Saddling Dancer, he spied Tweed playing with the puppies. "You're up early." He smiled at the boy.

"Yassir." Two big eyes stared up at him, confused. "It's morning."

Hueron realized all the slaves were up, working in the field. All except this little guy.

"'At's a big hoss!" Tweed said, following him as he led Dancer out of the barn.

Gazing down at the beaming face, Hueron thought he could use the boy to fetch and carry if needed. And if not, he wouldn't mind the company.

The town of Blanten wasn't precisely bristling, but there were folk about. Jevington was there, talking to old Leonard and Richmond. With a wave, Richmond excused himself and strode over to Hueron, smiling.

They shook hands. "Mark! Here to add a few more slaves?"

Hueron plucked the little guy from Dancer's back. "Might rent a hand or two...if the price is right." The boy seemed very nervous of both the horse and him. Hueron almost dropped a reassuring palm atop his head but refrained.

"I'm only asking a hundred dollars for a year's use of each slave," Richmond told him. "That's a good price."

"What about a few weeks? Days, even—just until the rains come."

"Problem is, I got these slaves here now with people willing to rent them now. I rent to you short term, then I got them on my hands again."

Hueron nodded, though his heart sank.

"Who's the boy?" the man asked.

The shiny face turned upward and grinned. "I'se Tweed!" he announced.

Hueron found his hand on the boy's head again and had to smile.

Richmond smiled back. "Too little to work the fields?"

"Yes, unfortunately."

"Maybe..." Richmond eyed the boy. "Tweed, can you run as fast as lightning to that water trough and back?"

"Yassir!" Tweed took off, running like any five-year-old. He was beaming a huge smile all the way back.

"Show me your arm," Richmond told him on his return.

Uncertain, the boy held his arm out.

The man solemnly looked over the muscle, then winked at the boy.

Then they strolled to the town hall. Everette was the auctioneer, inspecting seven slaves and talking to Jevington. Richmond left to have a word. He returned as Everette faced the crowd.

"We got four slaves for purchase here, folks, and three for rent. First up is Nancy, believed to be about twenty-eight years old. She's been a house slave for as long as anyone can remember." A small woman stood, her eyes riveted on the dusty street. "Let them see your face, Nancy."

The bowed head jerked up. She had a scar running across her chin, and her cheeks glistened with tears.

A little hand grasped Hueron's. He looked down to see Tweed earnestly gazing up, his eyes big in his small face.

"Bidding starts at two hundred."

At the end of the afternoon, Hueron rode back feeling satisfied. His business instincts had not withered and died, despite the little voice in his head saying otherwise. He'd gone to town for help, and help he got without so much as wasting an hour to fetch the wagon.

Richmond drove his own wagon beside him, bearing the two newly acquired field hands. He'd offered to carry Tweed as well, but the boy had begged to ride on Dancer with him and Hueron had obliged.

They rode straight to Meachum. Sliding off Dancer's back, Hueron actually smiled at his overseer. "Two healthy bucks," he announced, waving a hand. "Lester and Simon, both under thirty. Lester worked cotton in Alabama."

Meachum cast an eye over the pair as they clambered out of the wagon. "What'd you pay?"

Hueron just smiled.

With a nod, the overseer strode out to the first unharvested row of cotton. "You two over here. Buster, give these men your bag, then go get me two more."

Tweed's brother raced to hand his bag to Lester and then sprinted away. Hueron turned to see Tweed clinging to the saddle horn, gawking at the distant ground. Chuckling, he plucked him clear of Dancer and handed him to Richmond.

Richmond set him in the wagon. "Is next Sunday all right?"

Hueron nodded.

Richmond shook his hand. "It's a fair deal."

With a death grip on the buckboard, Tweed swung his legs over and dangled a foot off the ground.

Richmond strode back to catch him. "Hold on there, little fella. You're too valuable to hurt yourself." Plopping him back on the seat, Richmond climbed up to join him and waved to Hueron. "Till Sunday."

An earth-shattering wail erupted. Tweed dove out of the wagon, scrambling to his feet to run. Quick as he was, Meachum was quicker. The overseer snatched him up, cuffing him on the ear. His howling ceased, though the tears did not.

Hueron felt a flash of remorse. Tweed was so young, so innocent. His whole world existed within the plantation boundaries. Still, he'd gotten a full hundred for the boy. He'd also gotten the use of two good field hands, though only for twenty days. Should be enough. And in truth, Richmond's plantation was a better place, with better opportunities for the boy. Richmond treated his slaves more like gold than basic brick. The boy wouldn't suffer overmuch.

⁓≫≫ ≪≪⁓

Maggie was in the back of the field, working far from the master. It was the only thing that saved them.

She'd known Tweed had gone to town but hadn't worried. The master was a father and would take care. Any lingering doubts faded when her son rode back so happily perched on that horse.

She held a fist-full of cotton when his howl pierced the afternoon. Pierced her soul. Even as it ceased, she felt Buster beside her, stock still and staring. Then the boy leaped to help his brother as he'd done countless times before. As he always did. Maggie leaped to catch him.

Buster was so much bigger than the last time she'd stopped him. He fought fiercely, forcing her to lock her arms around him. They struck the dirt together, flailing as the dust burst up, choking them.

"Hush, baby, hush," she whispered over and over. And when his struggling threatened her grip, "They'll kill you both. Tweed and you. They'll kill you both."

Finally, Buster stilled.

Maggie squeezed him tight before pushing herself upright. By the time she was steady on her feet, he was standing tall. Not working, not picking. But not running.

Through her tears, she looked to the wagon, the men. If they'd noticed the struggle, they were ignoring it. Meachum wore an amused smirk, and the two masters busied themselves in calm conversation. Tweed must have been tucked into the wagon, out of sight.

Buster finally bent, snatching at the white buds while tears streamed down his cheeks, tears at odds with his angry glare and the determined jut of his chin.

It was the last time she'd ever see Buster cry.

Maggie had done nothing. They'd taken her little boy, physically carried off a screaming five-year-old begging for his mammy. She not only let them but she'd stopped Buster from helping him. Weren't no use saying there was no stopping it. It might not have helped Tweed to watch his mammy and brother whipped while he was carted off, but seeing her try to save him rather than just pick cotton...

Buster had been quiet, terribly quiet. She'd tried to speak with him over supper, but all he'd said was, "I know." Just those two words and nothing more. He'd lain down in the straw—the bed seemed so big now for just the two of them—and turned his back to her.

Maggie hadn't seen Honey yet, which maybe told a tale on its own. Buster might not blame her, though she wasn't sure of that, but his sister might think anything. Honey might even think the mistress had sent Tweed to a better plantation for his own good.

Drying her tears, which she had only vaguely felt flowing down her cheeks, Maggie threw her wrap about her shoulders and strode out the door. Without the moonlight, it was hard going, but she went. Even finding the path to Sampson's back door was accomplished with just a scratch on her ankle.

It took a while for the door to be opened. When it did, the same little man stood there, gazing at her.

"Old mule threw his shoe."

He shook his head. "Not now, woman."

Maggie grabbed the door, refusing to let it close. "Inky done threw his shoe."

The man was shoving hard, trying to shut it. "No! No!"

"They took my boy," she growled. "I got one left, and he ain't spending his life afeared of what they'll do next."

At least the man quit shoving.

"I knows you ain't got Murphy," Maggie pleaded. "I knows you ain't got Rufus...but you must *know* something. If we'se get to Quincy, somehow..."

The Black face gazed at her with pity in his eyes, but pity didn't buy freedom. "My master done left a week ago. Say he's going to Quincy hisself, but I dunno. Been whispers lately, suspicions. He might not ever come back."

Maggie closed her eyes.

"All I know is it's the brown house by the church. No...by the church graveyard. There ain't no more to tell."

Church graveyard?

"You cross the river and head north. Don't seem to matter how you cross. When your feet step on that shore, you head north. First church you'll see."

"Thank you," she whispered.

"It's a free state over there." The man sighed. "But that don't mean all the White folks *approve*. Just you be as careful on that side as this one."

⟫⟩⟩ ⟨⟨⟨

Honey didn't understand Biddy's words at first. "Sold" and "gone" didn't make sense in regard to her brother. Tweed was too young. Shoot, even that mean overseer had quit trying to make him work. It just couldn't be.

Bibby patted her shoulder and walked away. The words, however, gnawed at her brain like a caterpillar on a sycamore leaf. Nibbling in the background, cutting up her peace. When Preacher appeared to walk her home, she took one look in his eyes and knew. Her baby brother was really gone.

She didn't want to see Mammy—she actually said Mammy instead of Maggie—but perhaps she ought to.

Preacher didn't think so. "She's holding together for Buster. You go there, you'll tip her over."

So they went to their own tiny cabin and found honeysuckle flowers filling the bowl again. Tweed must have picked them before...

Preacher wound up leaving them there as he cooked the corn-meal and bacon fat.

Honey kept trying to find the thing she wanted to say, but nothing was there. She really didn't want to say anything. "Maybe if I ask Miss Marianne..." was the closest she got. But exactly what could she ask that the mistress could actually do? What could anyone do? Besides, the mistress might not be so happy after not doing something about it. Honey'd learned enough about the woman to realize blame would fall on those around her.

She didn't eat that night, though Preacher did. And when he was done, he turned down the lantern and held her in the dark.

"Do you want to stay or go?" he asked the hair atop her head.

"Go." The word was out of her mouth before her mind knew it was there at all.

His chin moved in acknowledgment, and she knew—*she knew*—he'd find a way.

>>> <<<

Maisey had been hit this morning, much to her indignation. She was a good girl. Booker had never seen fit to so much as yell at her, although he never really did much yelling anyway. He did get angry, but his anger was short and funny to see. Meachum's anger was scary to behold.

She had long since learned to defuse men, knowing they liked her, admired her body, wanted to touch it. It was a way to control them, really. Stand with a hip thrust out, allow a blouse to gape a little in front, or pose, giving them an under-eyelash look. Never blatant...always accidental. Her mammy used to say it was survival.

Meachum had moved into Booker's cabin. She only knew 'cause she'd gone a week ago to find out all she could and get a little coddling. Fortunately, she'd seen the whip on the peg by the door—the peg she used to hang her wrap on when she went inside.

Now she knew nothing—same as all the other slaves. It made her feel vulnerable, without a weapon.

But when Meachum had hit her in the field, he'd noticed her body. His eyes had never looked at hers but downward, and they'd stayed there a while. She'd seen the same look from Booker. If she could get the overseer to lie with her, she could find things out again. Oh, not big things at first and probably not as good as the stuff Booker let drop. Booker liked to brag, and this new feller didn't, at least not to slaves. Still, just being in proximity would be useful sooner or later.

Maisey waited till supper was done and the others had bedded down, then rolled out of bed and made her way up the familiar path to the overseer's cabin. Booker had kept a pot of salve for injuries. She'd ask if Meachum had that, tell him it was for one of the others but rub her arm as if she was the one needed it. The bit right next to her breast. The path was familiar enough that even with the sliver of moon hidden by cloud cover, she found her way. A sycamore marked the last turn before she saw the light from the cabin. That light—full lantern not afraid to shine bright—was the mark of the overseer's place.

Stepping up to the door was scary. It must have been the whip hanging there threateningly that made it so, for once her ear was pressed to the door and she couldn't see its rawhide handle, Maisey relaxed.

She wrapped twice just like old times. Then the door swung open, and it wasn't like old times at all. Meachum was buttoning his shirt. Maisey smiled.

"What you doing here?"

"I came for the salve," Maisey offered, and set her hand on his bare chest.

The man stilled for a moment. "I see." His hand reached around her, not to pull her against him but to take the whip from the peg.

>>>> <<<<

With keeping an eye on Buster and trying not to think about Tweed, Maggie didn't notice other things going on in the field. There was a feeling of unease from Squint, but then unease was the general mood under Meachum. She did notice Oliver looking around, but then he did that now that he was picking cotton with the rest of them. He'd be better off minding his work.

The day was done and they were dragging their baskets to the barn when Squint asked her, "You seen Maisey?"

Maggie shook her head as Oliver helped her drag her basket onto the scale.

Meachum stood in his usual place, writing down where the needle pointed for each slave's cotton but saying nothing. Even when Oliver's was lighter than ever, he just scratched a number and stared off. Didn't even threaten a beating.

As Maggie walked away, she began to wonder. During Booker's time, Maisey was often late, so they'd grown used to not seeing her with the others. Perhaps she'd managed to worm her way in with Meachum. Still, the girl always worked the field. She never got a morning off, let alone a whole day, and Meachum didn't seem the type to indulge her more than Booker. Sneaking a look at the man's face as he weighed bags, Maggie got a nasty thought.

They found Maisey near the clearing on the path to the overseer's cabin. For an instant, Maggie thought the girl had gotten a new, darker dress to replace her faded rag, but she soon saw that the deep hue came from dried blood.

The girl had been whipped so many times you couldn't count the lashes. All the lines merged into a cross-hatched mess, half-hid beneath dirt and leaves and even insects. Maggie had seen only one other slave beat this bad, and Hank had died days later.

Truth was, she'd never liked Maisey. She resented her, the way she used her body to ease her workload. Maggie had often thought a beating would do her good. Now she felt guilty for ever thinking such a thing.

Squint fetched Bibby, who risked sneaking the mistress's best salve to Maisey's cabin. Maggie and Bibby cleaned up the blood, pulled leaves and horsehair from the wounds, and finally left the girl lying on her stomach with the salve thick on her back.

She didn't wake up that night and certainly couldn't work the next day, or the next few after that. Meachum never so much as asked about her.

⤜⤚

Lucy played with Ellen for hours. The puppy fell asleep in her arms and wouldn't chase the stick anymore. The sun had risen pretty high, and the air was warm and clear and blue.

She hadn't played with Tweed in a while. It wasn't the same without Buster, and Tweed tended to just run around and forget their objective. He wasn't old enough to work, he'd told her, so he was too young to play with her. But he might be less young now, and anyway, she was tired of her own company.

She ran to the Indian fort, then the riverbank, and even their slave cabin with the window. Wherever Tweed was, he was hiding pretty good. There wasn't even a trace of him.

Lucy's stomach rumbled, and she wound up running home. Cook fed her a plate of beef stew with a hunk of bread, and she forked out the beef and potatoes and carrots, leaving the peas behind. She didn't like peas.

When she was done, she shoved the bread into the gravy, scooping up a few of the peas as well, hoping that Maggie liked them. She folded the food carefully into her napkin to keep the gravy from staining her pocket.

She took her plate over to Cook, who stared down at her with that lopsided look she used when she suspected Lucy was up to something. One bushy eyebrow would shoot up while the other stayed in place, and her mouth thinned something fierce.

"Have you seen Tweed?" Lucy asked.

Cook, who never liked to move more than was needed to stir a batter or lift a roast, lowered herself to one knee. She hugged Lucy something fierce, something few had ever done.

The girl went still with the waiting.

"Tweed's gone, honey child."

"Gone where?"

The hug lasted a little longer. At last, Cook let go, using her hands to pull herself up off the floor. That was the signal for Lucy to skedaddle off to play, but this time she needed to know.

Cook's knee creaked upright, and she balanced herself before turning around, then noticed Lucy was still standing there. This time, both her eyebrows shot up her face.

"Cook, where did he go?"

Something changed in the woman's expression, maybe because something had changed in Lucy's expression first. "Tweed's been sold, honey. He's on another plantation now."

"But...his mammy's here..." A cold pit formed in Lucy's stomach, and she felt dizzy.

She tried to understand, to think about the words, but her brain felt numb. Was Buster gone too? Was *Maggie* gone? She whirled around and raced out the door, running past the puppy barn, into the trees. She sped down the Honey Trail, and for once, didn't sneak honeysuckle. Rounding the cotton barn, she saw the fields.

The slaves were there, picking cotton. Meachum sat on his horse, but he wasn't holding his whip. Preacher was closest to him, with Buster not far behind. It took only a heartbeat longer to spy the purple scarf, and when Lucy saw it, she gasped aloud.

Maggie was still there. She hadn't been sold with Tweed. But...that meant Tweed was all alone. No Buster, no Maggie. How could that be? He wasn't even old enough to work.

Lucy waited until Meachum walked away. He'd been doing that lately, moving off to eat his lunch. Not far, but far enough he couldn't rightly see everything in the field.

She crept through the last of the bushes to reach Maggie. The purple scarf was as cheery as ever, but the woman's face looked so sad. Lucy thought of the mama dog with her puppies. You couldn't take the puppies from their mama until they were old enough, Father had said. Surely Tweed wasn't old enough either.

When Lucy pulled the bread from her pocket, she felt a tiny drop of gravy on the material. She didn't care. Let them tell Mother.

"Maggie."

Maggie didn't hear her and kept working away.

"Maggie, here."

Lucy held out the bread in front of her, but the woman didn't take it. Lucy thought perhaps she was lost in thought, as her father sometimes was. Then Maggie looked at her, brown eyes blazing with anger.

"Go away!" she whisper-hissed. "You go away and don't never come back again!"

Lucy fell back, and the napkin dropped to the ground. It rolled through the leaves, stopping at Maggie's feet. That was the last thing she saw before she turned tail and ran.

≫≫⟩ ⟨≪≪

Maisey shared a cabin with Elvira, Hoby, and Oliver. There were empty cabins at Sweetgum, but Booker'd like to pack them in. Saved fuel for the stove, so he said. Bibby had cleaned Maisey's wounds again that afternoon, catching a few things in daylight that they'd missed by lantern. She couldn't stay with her the whole day, but then Maisey probably slept anyway.

Bibby was back after sunset, when Maggie came in from the field.

"How's she doing?" Maggie asked.

"She's alive," Bibby told her. "Ain't woke up that I've seen, but she's breathing."

Maggie sat on the straw, staring at the raw mess that was Maisey's back. "Ask Honey to feed the boys—boy."

Bibby nodded. "I almost told the mistress twice today. She'd not like this, not one bit."

"What would she do?"

The older woman shook her head. "She'd talk to the master, that's for sure. But what good would come from that, I don't know."

"Master would know what type of man Meachum is."

Bibby gave her a steady look. "You think he don't know now? You think he didn't know the day he sent Booker scurrying?" She wrapped her shawl around her. "There's chicken on that dish yonder. Honey can bring the plate back in the morning."

Maggie nodded. "Maisey always so proud of her looks," she murmured, smoothing her hair off her back. She'd always been a little jealous, she realized just then.

"At least two of those whip lashes caught her chin. She won't look quite so good anymore."

⤚⤜⤛ ⤙⤚⤙

Maggie expected Honey to pop by, maybe with a johnnycake. She needed to talk to her, ask about Lucy. Part of her worried about the child telling her father, but deep down, she didn't think that would happen. Still, it was one more reason to run.

As it turned out, it was Preacher who entered the cabin. "Oliver and the others sleeping elsewhere tonight," he told her. "Honey done fed Buster."

Maggie nodded. She felt the man standing at her back with one foot out the door. He was always like that with her, but maybe standing in view of Meachum's handywork, Preacher saw the need to run.

He did step closer. "Whew! That's bad."

"Only seen one worse."

He didn't ask, of course, but he didn't leave.

Maggie turned to look in his eye. "Hank. My man." With a sigh, she squeezed out the rag in the warm water and laid it across Maisey's back.

"Honey's father?"

She nodded. "Buster and Tweed's father was Skeeter. He's moved on. Alabama, I hear. He was nice enough, but Hank—he was special. Called me wife. Took good care of us and truly loved Honey. He named her Miranda. Prettiest name he ever heard, he used to say."

"How'd she get to be Honey?"

"Loved that honey tree. She'd climb it, sit under it, eat all the honeysuckle she could reach. Mistress—the old mistress—called her Honey, and it stuck. Only Hank, he wouldn't accept it. Never called her anything but Miranda. I used to dread the day when the mistress heard him. But she never did. Or never cared."

"Honey sure do love that tree." Preacher took a step away, hesitated. "That why he got beat?"

Maggie shook her head. "One day, she was near four, Honey wanted us to play with her. We were out in the field, working in the hot sun. It was so hot that summer. She came running up the row, begging me to play. I swatted her behind, told her to git. But she ran to Hank. She always ran to Hank.

"That man stared down at her for the longest time, even brushed the hair away from her face. My heart was pounding so hard. See, Meachum was near. He never saw it, but he might've." Maggie wiped her cheeks even though she wasn't crying. "Then Hank got back to work. That night he went to talk to Squint, and others the next night. Three days later, they strung him up on that honey tree. Hung there two days 'fore he was dead."

"Did Honey...did she see...?"

Maggie looked at Preacher but saw Hank's old grin. "Honey looked and looked for him. On the second day, she started running for her tree. I had to race to catch her, even though I'se supposed to be at the field. I was half afraid they'd string me up next to him, but I couldn't let her see that. I caught her up, cuddled her close and held her face against me as we hurried past. Pressed her nose to my shoulder so tight she nearly smothered. So she might not...smell it..." Maggie heard her voice quiver and caught her breath. Never in her whole life had she told anyone this. Some knew, of course, but she'd never spoken the words before.

"I sang, 'Swing Low, Sweet Chariot' to her. My baby giggled as we passed her dying father."

Preacher's face wasn't one to change much, but his body went rock hard like a chipped Mississippi boulder.

"The mistress saw, but there was no punishment." Maggie shrugged. "Hank used to say, when I told him it's too dangerous to run, that some things are worth it."

Surely Preacher could see they had to run. He loved Honey—anyone could tell that. If he loved her enough...

Maggie heard the door slam shut behind her. The big man was gone.

Honey came later with a whole chicken leg and word that Buster was asleep. She didn't say nothing about Preacher, and Maggie didn't ask. But even Honey must have seen it was time to run.

~~≫⫸ ⫷≪~~

Hueron dug his knees into Dancer's flanks, feeling the need to race. He used to do that for sheer enjoyment, as distant as that seemed now. All he wanted today was to inspect the cotton.

It had rained last night. Not a downpour but rain nonetheless. Cotton, he remembered the Alabama man telling his father, was a funny crop. It loved rain, needed rain as any crop needed it, but only while the buds were closed. Once they opened, once the white fiber burst free, rain became the enemy.

A little water in a warm setting would be okay. The cotton should dry, and you could still pick a valuable harvest. If it didn't dry, however, the fiber would discolor, which meant less money. More water made the cotton string out, or even fall away in a white string, or the seeds in the fiber might sprout. Any of those made it worthless.

Dancer thundered around the bend, and Hueron pulled back on the reins. The field was there, plenty of white still waiting to be plucked. He swung a leg over and slid off the horse, wrapping the reins round the same branch he'd been using all week. Sitting on his own horse, Meachum greeted him. Booker had always touched his hat respectfully, but this overseer eked out one solitary nod. Hueron really didn't like him.

The slaves worked away in the morning sun, backs bent, bags filling up. But were they really working any harder, any faster since the new overseer took control? Hueron walked a row, eyeing the cotton here and there. No sign of string-out. It all appeared pretty healthy.

He neared a woman—Maggie, he remembered. "Cotton still good, as far as you can tell?" he asked.

She looked up in surprise. "Yessir, cotton still good. Little bit of rain ain't hurt it none."

Her hands kept busy, and he paused to watch for a moment. She was quick, with a sure movement on the bud. "You do that well, Maggie."

She slowed an instant, then sped up again. He caught the startled look she cast him. "Thank you, Master."

He realized she was scared of him, and why wouldn't she be? Why wouldn't they all be nervous in his presence?

Spinning on his heel, he started back toward the overseer. He was relieved, seeing the crop was still good for the time being. And then he noted the rows, and the number of heads working them. Twenty-one. There ought to be twenty-one slaves working these fields, with the two new ones from Richmond. He counted nineteen.

By the time he reached the man, he was seething. "Where's the rest of the slaves?"

"Sir?"

"We're missing hands, Meachum. Where are all the slaves?"

Meachum just gave him that frown of his, as if Hueron was the one confused. Well, he'd have his answer one way or another. The older one—Squint—was working close by.

"Squint," Hueron called.

The slave straightened, staring at him as if he'd suddenly turned into a bear.

"Squint, what field hands are not here right now?"

The slave stared a moment longer, and he realized he was looking to Meachum for guidance.

"Never mind him. Answer me. Who is missing?"

"Oliver," Squint told him nervously. "And Maisey."

"Down two. Where are they?"

"In the cabins, Master. They's sick."

Hueron turned to catch the glare on Meachum's face. Being in ignorance, Uncle Jay used to say, was death to a businessman's business.

"Squint," Hueron said quietly. "Show me."

⇒⇒⇒ ⇐⇐⇐

The crippled lad, Oliver, had been beat.

"He needed it," Meachum said, standing beside Hueron without an ounce of remorse. "He'll be working tomorrow. Now may I get back to the field?"

"Where's Maisey?"

The overseer hesitated.

Hueron ignored him, prodding Squint instead. "Show me."

When he entered her cabin, his jaw dropped. He'd seen beaten slaves before, both in Baltimore and Missouri—that split in the skin from the lash of a whip, the cross-hatched look when the whipping had been severe. But this...

Dropping to his knee, Hueron checked the girl's pulse. She was alive, at least, but the rains would come and go before she'd be back in the field.

"What was her crime?"

Meachum finally blinked. "Sir?"

"What did this woman do that required such a horrible thrashing?" He turned to Squint.

"Don't rightly know," Squint told him in earnest. In fear. "We found her in the woods this way. She ain't said nothing yet."

Meachum shrugged.

"Squint, go to the house," Hueron said. "Tell Bibby to come take care of her, do everything she can. Fetch the doctor if she thinks that best."

The overseer protested, "That isn't necess—"

"If my wife asks, tell her I said to do it." When Squint hesitated, Hueron touched his shoulder very gently. "Go on now."

The old slave hurried away.

"Mister Hueron—"

"I can think of one place I can make up some of the money you cost me, Meachum." Hueron sighed. "You're fired. Clear your things out and leave."

❧ ❦

The stallion walked slow as Meachum's mind flew fast. He had actually tied his own whip to the saddle so he wouldn't strike his own horse on impulse. The overseer seethed. This was *his* job—it belonged to him. He'd created it, for Chrissake. Years of great tobacco yields, making a name for himself. Then that fool owner sold a thriving plantation to an idiot who wanted to pick cotton. Now the son was too timid to let him drive the field hands proper.

The horse stopped. Meachum had reached his cabin without even knowing. Packing was quick as he owned very little, really. He used to own more, living in this very cabin. He'd worked hard to get back here. Too damned hard. It was all that nasty woman's fault. She'd had no business coming to his cabin, even if he had gone a little overboard in letting her know.

Or maybe he hadn't gone far enough. His hands itched to finish the job, to rid the world of that thing that had cost him his carefully earned livelihood. For a moment he pictured it—his hands around her neck, throttling the life out of her—but he couldn't do that, at least not now. Hueron would know, even go after him. His slave-catching work would be impacted. There might even be men wanting to catch *him*.

Packing his things, he found the bottle he'd bought just last week—Old Bourbon Whiskey, according to the fancy label. Cost him a pretty penny, but he loved spending his money on such luxuries. That was the good thing about a job like this—room and board had been free. They weren't free anymore.

The whiskey tempted, but he stashed it in the saddle bag. Vaulting onto the stallion's back, Meachum wanted nothing so much as to ride Hell for leather out of there, work off his spleen while putting distance between himself and Sweetgum. Maybe get all the way to St. Louis. Maybe.

Then he remembered the shirt, the new linen one he'd just bought the same time he bought the whiskey. It was at the big house, being proper washed and pressed. His hand retrieved the liquor before his brain had time to think about it. Meachum drank a throat-full and pondered. And then drank more.

He'd lost everything else. Damned if he was gonna lose that.

⤜⤛

The master stayed in the field, overseeing after Meachum had gone. Maggie was real nervous, but he didn't yell or strut about and didn't slap a whip against the palm of his hand. He'd even praised her earlier. She couldn't remember ever being praised by a White man before.

When the master beckoned her over, his eyes never left the field. "Maggie, go ask Cook to send me something to eat. A piece of last night's fried chicken would be nice."

As she hurried through the trees, she realized she could slow down. Maggie always ran in case the master saw her, because deep down she doubted he knew Booker sent them for food. Between a master and an overseer was a terrible place for a slave to be. But the master himself done sent her now. Ain't nobody could get her in trouble if they saw her.

⤜⤛

"Bibby, please tell Honey I want scones for tea."

The "Yes, Miss Marianne" didn't come. Frowning over her sampler, Marianne realized she'd spoken too late. Bibby had already left.

Tossing her sampler aside, she pushed off the sofa and slipped past the drawing room doors, which needed polishing. Really, Mark had no business ordering the house slaves away from their work. She was relieved to hear the kitchen door open as she crossed the threshold.

"Bibby?"

As Marianne spoke, the door slammed against the wall. Mister Meachum stood on the threshold, his shoulders heaving with his breath, eyes glaring around the kitchen, landing on the table burdened with the start of dinner.

"Mister Meachum…" Her speech withered when that glare turned to her.

"Your husband fired me."

Mark had sent word for Bibby to help a sick slave. He hadn't mentioned anything beyond that. Her sympathy roused, Marianne stepped toward the overseer. "I'm so sorry."

He strode toward her, eyes bulging. His hands clamped down on her shoulders, holding her in place. She'd always been aware of that male strength, even found it attractive, but now she felt the threat behind it, a danger she'd never known, never truly understood.

She understood it now.

Marianne retreated a step, expecting him to let her go.

Meachum took an even bigger step to close the gap, his fingers biting into her flesh.

Fear flared in her throat, silencing her.

The back door opened, and that field hand with the purple headwrap stood there. Maggie, she remembered.

"Sorry, Miss Marianne," the slave murmured, lowering her head.

"Get out," Meachum barked, his clutch tightening in the cloth of Marianne's dress.

All she could manage was a gasping sob. She'd heard whispers of this man's violence and never believed them. She'd almost flirted with him by the store that day. Now he was going to hurt her bad.

"Mister Meachum," she heard a voice say. Unbelievably, that slave hadn't left.

⤜⟫⟫ ⟪⟪⤛

Maggie didn't dare step closer. Being within striking range of Meachum was never a good idea. But she didn't go neither, even though her feet wanted nothing else.

No good ever came from trying to stop a White man. No one knew that better than Maggie. Maybe it'd be good for the mistress to have just a taste of what slave women endured. A part of her—the part that mourned Tweed—relished that idea. But only a part.

"Get out of here, you Black bitch," Meachum growled. "This is White folks's business."

Maggie's mouth was so dry she had to work up spit to answer him. "Sir, the master will come looking for me if'n I don't get back soon with his chicken."

Stepping to the side, Maggie could see Miss Marianne's face. Pale and trembling, the woman knew she was in trouble, a trouble more primal than slaves and masters. Or maybe it was all the same. The Powerful and the Powerless.

There was a bond shared by women in being the powerless. Maggie hated to feel it with the mistress, but there it was. There'd be consequences in hurting a White woman where there were none for hurting a Black, but with no man here to stop him, Meachum could do anything he liked to the mistress.

With a primitive howl, he whirled.

Maggie froze, feeling like a hare facing a wolf.

The overseer rushed toward her—past her. Out the door.

When she heard the stallion's hooves pound away, Maggie sank to her knees. Miss Marianne was already on the floor, shivering amid her stiff skirts, which pooled across the pine. It was a full minute before either woman spoke.

"Thank you. Maggie...thank you."

"Yess'am."

The river. The way Maggie said it, the way Honey said it, they made "cross the river" sound as easy as "cross the field."

Preacher knew a little—only a little—about the Mississippi. He'd done asked before running away the first time. She was a wicked river, pretending to be so calm and pretty. "All you gotta do is toss a stick in it," Old Felix had told him. "That stick will be halfway to Vicksburg 'fore you can blink."

Getting in the water was easy. Getting out again was the tricky bit. Getting out where you wanted to get out, say in a free state like Illinois, could be damn near impossible. "Riverboat captains call it hard steering, boy. And they's got riverboats."

Maggie and Honey wanted him to build a raft. Just build one, as if roping a few logs together would answer all their prayers. Problem was the Drinking Gourd. Everything he knew, every piece of advice, said freedom was north. The Drinking Gourd pointed north. Canada was north. Chicago was north. The farther north you went, the better the chance of staying free. But that nasty Mississippi river ran south, and the farther south you went, the nastier it got.

That afternoon, while Hueron went to town and Squint was put in charge, Simon, one of the new hands, got to talk to Preacher. "This place sure is better with the overseer done gone."

Preacher kept picking.

Squint, anxious to please the master, wanted them all to work hard. Otherwise, so he'd said, the master might feel the need to get another overseer—the last thing they needed.

"This cotton stuff is a bit delicate for me," Simon kept jawing. "Don't rightly feel like men's work."

"What'd you do before?" Preacher spoke without thinking. Conversation wasn't something he craved.

"Worked on the river."

"You traveled the Mississippi? Steered a boat?"

Simon chuckled. "Ain't no Black men steering boats, son. I loaded crates. Onto boats, off boats. Worked the docks in New Orleans."

Across the field, Squint watched them nervously.

Preacher picked faster. "Do you know how to make a boat go upriver?"

"Power. Paddle, steam. Seen a big sailboat come in from the ocean and go up a ways." Simon gave him a level look. "No slave gonna make it up river without stealing himself a proper boat."

Preacher's impulse was to deny the implication, but he didn't bother. "Just thinking aloud. Case I ever wanted to get to a free state. Just...someday. Maybe."

Simon chuckled. "Illinois a free state."

"Yeah."

Simon's bag was three-quarters full before he spoke again. "You know Illinois is across the river."

"And north."

Simon straightened, stretching his back before grabbing another fist of cotton. "Yes, sir, it is north. And south...and due east."

"What you saying?"

"Illinois is directly across the river, all the way down to the Ohio. Ohio River, that is." Simon grinned. "You damn fool. If you went all the way down to St. Louis, the other side is still Illinois."

~~>>> <<<~

The raft Preacher had started constructing was coming along just fine. At first, it'd been so easy. Sneak a piece of rope out of the barn, use the old knife to cut it in two pieces, find two proper logs in the woods, and bind them together. He'd then carried his construction down to the river when the moon was near full to test it. The logs floated atop the water, barely sinking at all. The test also showed he needed to build the thing on the beach. Carting two heavy logs through the woods wasn't easy, and carting a whole raft would be impossible.

It didn't take long before other problems arose. One was building materials. Finding good wood got harder each time, and finding wood he could drag harder still. His visions of a big raft faded. He'd be hard pressed to construct something the four of them could fit on. They'd have to huddle close together to stay dry.

If good wood proved scarce, usable rope was rarer still. Preacher had found the first few pieces lying around the barn, unused and unnoticed, but they weren't enough to build the raft. The last thing they needed was anyone thinking stuff was going missing. A slave would get thrashed just as hard for stealing frayed rope as a gold coin.

The other problem was hiding the thing. Too big to bury in sand now, he found scattering debris atop it only covered so much. Every day the danger of being discovered grew, and if they'd thrash him for taking a bit of rope, they'd lynch him for sure if they saw what he was doing.

Preacher went out each night for a few hours, finding and dragging a tree. The third night, he also found a coil of rope, though he wasn't sure it was enough. Best wait till he had all the wood before trying to tie it together. He'd use less rope that way.

The work cut into his sleep, of course, but no one seemed to notice. When he did tumble into bed, another worry kept him awake. He couldn't swim. Preacher figured none of the others could either, or at least no one had volunteered when that White child floated down the river. But if something happened, he'd be the one they all turned to.

He had actually decided to learn the night Honey said she wished to leave, but there wasn't a daylight hour he weren't working in the field. Besides, the river wasn't exactly inviting on the cold waning nights of March. He'd even subtly probed, but Simon couldn't swim and Squint didn't know anyone who could. So, he reluctantly gave up on the idea.

They'd have to cling together, maybe tie themselves to the raft if they could find something to use. They had two blankets, after all—enough to tie them on. Course, if they didn't make it, the blankets would be gone. But then if they didn't make it, blankets would be the least of their troubles.

Lucy felt lonelier than ever. She took to carrying Ellen with her, showing her the Indian fort and the best beach for skipping rocks. She sat and played with her on the hill where you could see the whole river and went to the slave cabins to point out Maggie's window. And the cotton fields to point out Maggie.

The first time she took Ellen, the puppy cried and was happy to be reunited with its mother. After that, it seemed the puppy was happy to be with *her*.

Ellen wanted to meet Maggie. At least she whined when she saw the purple kerchief fluttering in the cotton field. But Lucy knew Maggie had been angry at her and might be angry still.

Waiting till Cook turned her back, with last night's chicken sliced up and the clean napkins all folded on the table, Lucy grabbed as much as she dared and raced outside. She'd gotten a good handful, enough for Ellen and her and more besides.

Today when Ellen saw her, she actually jumped and barked and wagged her tail. Lucy grinned and waved, feeling happiness leak through her bones. She had a friend again. She still had Buster too, of course, but Buster was a field hand now, with no time for nonsense. Least that's what he told her.

Lucy meant to go straight to the field, but her feet kept finding other places first. Ellen wanted to romp in the Indian fort for a while and then eat her chicken on the beach. They both got their feet wet there.

At last they found their way to the cotton fields. Maggie was in the far corner, far enough that Lucy doubted the man overseeing could see her. It was the perfect opportunity, as Miss Helen would say. Yet Lucy hesitated. What would she do if Maggie was still mad at her?

She and Ellen crept up on Maggie, keeping low behind the hawthorn. Lucy felt her heart beating in her throat. She really hoped the mammy wasn't angry now.

Maggie was working with her eyes on the cotton. She didn't look up, even when Lucy got real close. She didn't look up when Lucy held out the napkin, easing closer still. It wasn't till the purple cloth lifted that Maggie's dark eyes saw her.

Those eyes turned so sharp they pierced Lucy's heart. Tweed's mammy stared at her a full moment, without any smile. Without any lessening of that anger.

"I'm sorry," Lucy whispered, and set the napkin on the ground. "I miss Tweed too."

Clutching Ellen, she whirled around and ran away.

⋙ ⋘

Maggie watched the White child run off, feeling a surge of fury. Why did she get to run and play with a dog when Tweed was gone? Just 'cause she was born to a White mistress instead of a Black slave.

Squint hadn't seen nothing, and even if he had, he'd do nothing. Everyone kept picking. Everyone kept quiet. The world was quiet.

Maggie snatched the napkin from the dirt. Weren't no point in letting the ants get it.

⋙ ⋘

Preacher slid his arm out from under Honey, pushing himself up from the straw. Two nights ago, he'd gazed down on her sleeping form, silently swearing to take her to freedom. Tonight he couldn't see her at all. The clouds hadn't freed the sky.

He left her, hurrying through the woods, scanning as best he could. Only good thing about the storm last night—all wind and little water—was that it must have knocked a few trees down. Surely it had knocked trees down.

What he thought would be the easiest part hadn't been easy at all. Finding proper logs meant they had to be light enough to drag by himself, yet sturdy enough to construct a decent raft. Early on, Preacher had told himself the thing only had to float once, cross just one river, and after that, it could break apart and sink in the mud. But the Mississippi was a beast, and the far shore looked far indeed. Big paddle boats chugged by, fighting against her, and fighting hard at that. Anything carrying his Honey across that water had to be sturdy.

The raft trees weren't perfectly straight or the same length. Their shape varied, their weight varied, and laid side by side, they left holes an unwary foot could easily fall through. Preacher's vision of the final boat shrank over the weeks of assembling it, and still he had trouble finding trees. Two nights had passed when he hadn't found a single log at all, and two Sundays had passed as he built.

Now, slipping through the trees, he tripped and crashed into a bush. Biting back a curse, his hand explored the culprit—a long, sturdy tree, felled by the storm. It was long enough to use, though thinner than most. Its fresh roots made it awkward to drag.

Preacher wrestled the thing through the Hawthorne, tugging it over a rock and round a young pine. With the plantation in an uproar to clear the fields, he still worried someone might notice fresh drag tracks.

If we get caught...

A distant branch snapped, and Preacher froze. The back of his neck prickled, and despite the chill in the air, sweat broke out across his skin. Scanning the trees revealed nothing, neither body nor movement.

It took long minutes to convince his feet to get going. Good sense urged leaving the tree where it was, or at least stopping at the edge of the woods. He didn't, because deep in his gut he needed this over with. The sooner the raft was built, the sooner they dragged it into the water and floated to Illinois, the better.

He did have a wild idea about clinging to logs, never mind stringing them together. But they'd be borne downriver separately, with no control. Anything could happen. The raft might not work, but at least they'd be together.

Tugging his find over the embankment edge, Preacher eased it until the end plopped down into the sand of the beach three feet below the grass lip, which created a sheltered overhang that hid the logs he'd been gathering. Dead, leafy twigs were tossed on top of these to hide them. The first two or three had been near impossible to see from land or water, but as the pile now stood at seven, it spread out of the sheltering shadow, and Preacher had no idea what someone on the river might notice. Big river steamboats passed a fair distance out, but there were fishermen in rowboats, and others as well.

It would only take one...

In the stillness, another branch snapped.

Preacher dropped to a crouch, scanning the trees. A rustling caught his attention, and he saw what had dogged his steps. He waited till the boy reached the overhang before snatching him down to the sand.

"Buster, are you crazy?"

Buster gawked at the pile of logs. "You building something!"

"Hush!"

The boy stared at him, thoughts racing behind his eyes. He was just a kid but smarter than most, Preacher knew. Too smart for his own good.

"A raft! You're gonna raft away on the river."

Warnings rose up in Preacher's throat—admonishments, cautions. They'd be as useless as the wind, he realized.

"Will you take Honey with you?"

"And you," Preacher whispered. "Ain't leaving you behind. Even drag your mammy along."

"Tweed?"

The boy's plea pierced his heart. After a moment, Preacher shook his head. "Tweed's gone, Buster. We don't even know where he is."

"But...we gotta find him."

A hundred words rose in Preacher's throat, choking him. Unable to utter them, to even assemble them, he just shook his head.

Buster's lips trembled. He turned and ran off into the trees.

Later, dragging three more logs to his pile, Preacher counted again. He now had ten, though four were awfully skinny. Really only five proper ones, all told. The last was just too puny to use.

Each one he had to find meant another day or two, which meant more time for someone to discover his plan. But they'd only get one shot at this, so he decided to find two more stout ones.

As if that old luck had decided to favor him, he found one barely five minutes later. Dragging it back, Preacher laid it against the others, measuring the length. It was longer than most, but skinnier and a bit twisty in the middle. If he set it in the center, it would push the raft wider, although they'd need to be careful about setting a foot in the hole. Well, they wouldn't exactly be running around the thing.

A couple of branches snapped at the tree line. His heart stopped beating, but then Buster emerged, dragging a tree even better than the one he'd just found.

Preacher grinned.

Together they scoured the woods for one more but had no luck. Only when the moon sank in the sky did they stop the search. Just one or two more, that's all they needed, at least for the thing to be big enough to fit on. Tomorrow, they'd finish it.

As tired as he suddenly felt, Preacher bade Buster help him drag the wood into a tight pile and spread the dead leaf covering over it. No point getting caught now.

Here Comes the Rain

THE SECOND SUNDAY IN April started pleasant enough. Hueron felt hopeful. He'd spoken to Richmond yesterday, who'd pointed out that the rains could come late this year, as they sometimes did. Richmond thought Sweetgum might well get every bit of cotton from the field to the market.

The sun shone bright in a blue sky, and the buggy rolled past the fields on the way to church. Hueron looked out across his fields thriving with activity as Squint oversaw the slaves working away. Good signs, all this. Even the day's sermon supported hope. Reverend Jessop spoke of all things being possible, a strong departure from his usual promises of damnation. Marianne chatted to several townswomen before they left, and Lucy talked to a young girl. Maybe, *maybe*, everything was gonna be just fine.

Two hours later, Hueron knew otherwise. It wasn't so much the rain, which started mildly enough, a simple splatter on the dirt. It was the thickening clouds, seemingly piling atop each other. The blue sky evaporated into oily puffs that swelled and darkened as the afternoon droned on. If Meachum or Booker had been there, he'd have probed their brains for advice or wisdom or pure hope, but there was no overseer to ask.

Squint likely knew more than either one of them but answered only with platitudes—out of fear, Hueron suspected. Slaves probably knew more than any White man but feared the master's wrath and a good flogging.

And whose fault is that?

That afternoon they worked until the last possible moment of the day and were out again the next morning. The heavy stuff held off through the night and sunrise, waiting patiently until Monday afternoon. And then it came full on.

Marianne urged him to stay inside. "You'll catch your death!" she told him, exasperated or genuinely worried.

Some corner of his mind appreciated her concern. She'd been asking about a trip to New Orleans, and he'd decided to allow it. He'd send her and Lucy down to visit her aunt, then join her after the harvest.

The slaves worked, and he watched. They switched up the process, with Squint and Oliver and two of the women hauling baskets up and emptying them under a tarp in the wagon. Squint had them selecting the dryer cotton, ignoring the soaked buds. They kept picking till nightfall hid the white from the green.

That night it bucketed down, the winds jeering at Hueron through the mansion's rattling windows. The next morning, Squint showed him, though he already knew, of course. The cotton was wet, heavy, and stringing out. The fibers were falling from the buds to the ground, creating long strands where fluffy puffs should be. There was some good stuff still, but now the slaves would have to seek that and know what to pick and what to leave. That meant less than a normal day's pickings.

A lot less.

Worst of all, while the rain had tapered off, the clouds hadn't. They hung threateningly overhead, promising more damage at their whim. Nothing to do but pick.

Hueron and Squint walked the rows in the third field. There were a few unopened buds, and those might yield good fiber, but the vast, vast majority was ruined cotton. By Hueron's estimate, some twenty percent of the crop was gone. It could have been worse, much worse, but it was bad enough.

Ironically, the sun was shining the next morning, pink sky turning blue and bright. The damage had already been done, so the cheery warmth only taunted Hueron. By his careful figures, he would make a profit but not a big one. Not enough to take a year off to restructure Sweetgum to tobacco, at least not comfortably. They would have needed to plant tobacco two months ago to see any viable crop this year.

Turned out it was easier to switch to cotton than to tobacco. That was just like his father, taking an easy path to what he thought was riches, blithely leaving others to forge the difficult path out of trouble.

That night Hueron wrote a letter to a man in New Orleans, an old friend from his Baltimore days. He wasn't a plantation owner,

but he supplied equipment to them. Perhaps he'd know someone who could offer advice.

⟫⟫ ⟪⟪

In two more nights and with Buster's help, Preacher had
enough trees.

The boy had brought two half trees, not long enough for the
raft. When Preacher explained this, Buster said he thought the
two together would form one tree.

Perhaps they might, Preacher realized. The lashing together
would bear watching and might require an extra line or something. But the vines in the woods—vines he'd shied away from
using on the raft—might suffice to tie a few half-trees to a tree
beside them. Keep them in place. The raft didn't have to ferry
them around for years, after all. Just one night.

That was the challenge. He'd built other things, figured out
the how when others didn't have answers. But he'd built what
he was told to, and to the satisfaction of a White man. Success
was the master's approval. This time, success would be survival—a harsh measure if he failed.

When Buster found that last tree and they laid it by the others,
Preacher counted seven proper ones, all told. Three more that,
when laid with the others, were too puny. Spreading them out as
best he could, it looked like there'd be room for him and Maggie
to sit, but the raft wouldn't be long enough to fit both Honey and

Buster. Maybe if Honey sat on his lap, and Buster on Maggie's, it could work.

"Let's test it." Buster plucked up the smaller piece of rope. "Tie just a few together. See it float."

Preacher didn't like the idea because, he realized, he was afraid of the result. They could simply string them together and float away. If they tested it, if they discovered the actual risk...

Buster was already assembling four logs, logs barely thicker than the kid's arm. Preacher dragged a fifth over, just to be sure. They used the rope to secure them around the middle, wrapping it between and around. Knotting it was harder than it should have been because the old rope was stiff, but at last they had some semblance of a raft.

Towing it out waist-deep in the water, Preacher felt the cold river sap all his energy. When the thing actually floated, easily riding the surface, he felt elated.

"Works good!" Buster jumped up, half lying on it.

Preacher shook his head. "You're too light," he told him, and hopped up himself. Cold water struck his stomach, but the thing stayed afloat.

Surface ripples lapped the wood, and the platform teetered. Buster hopped off and skirted round the raft, leaping up from the other side. It wobbled. They balanced. For an instant, it righted itself. Buster climbed up to a sitting position, grinning ear to ear. Preacher swung a leg up, and the raft tipped over. Buster disappeared. The boy burst through the surface an instant later, spluttering.

Preacher stood up out of the freezing wet, wiping his eyes. The rope had failed, and half their precious logs were loosely floating down the Mississippi.

Buster coughed. Their eyes met, caught. They stared at each other. Preacher chuckled. Buster giggled. With the water trickling down the back of his neck, Preacher saw the boy's dripping face through the waterfall from his own head and burst out in a full belly laugh. When he yanked off his shirt and squeezed the water from it, Buster joined in.

They laughed liked fools. Too much noise, really. But laugh they did, and no one appeared to stop them.

Together they waded out of the water, walked up the sand, and headed home. There really wasn't much else to do.

"Preacher, what we gonna do?" Buster asked.

"We build it better tomorrow," he said.

Dragging logs again the next night was discouraging, but with Buster's renewed enthusiasm, the task seemed easier. They needed more, of course—surely twice as many to make it stable. But now they had a better idea of what logs worked, which somehow made finding them easier, perhaps because Preacher spent less time eyeing each one up and down to determine if it was suitable.

No, the problem wasn't the logs. It was the rope. The shorter bit was lost to the river, which hadn't worried him at the time. Thinking about it now, he decided to cut the coiled rope in two pieces, to tie the raft on each end rather than in the middle. It would take some sawing with a borrowed knife but would be well worth it.

Then they tried to uncoil it. It had seemed such a great find, but the heavy coil refused to straighten from its knot. Preacher tried soaking it in the river, warming it by the stove. At most, he got the end lifted, but it wouldn't bend. He couldn't wrap it properly around the logs, let alone tie it. Turned out there was a reason no one had touched it in years.

The only other piece he found was thin and tattered. Being more supple, it did wrap around the trees, but it wasn't long enough to bind even one end, let alone both. He needed more.

Sneaking rope from the puppy barn had scared him—still did. Preacher told himself no one had touched it in months, no one would notice the absence, but working the fields in daylight, he'd feel his shoulders hunch whenever the master approached. He dreaded hearing a shout of "Thief!" and feeling that bullwhip across his back.

Now he'd have to steal from the cotton barn. The barn the master went into every day.

Buster thought they should use vines from the woods and brought him long pieces for three nights. It wasn't until he asked the boy to try tying them that Buster finally gave up. The vines were nearly as stiff as the coil and lacked the strength to make up for that. Only one managed to secure one tree to another, and that only at one end. They'd need another like it just to secure the two.

Stealing rope was their only hope.

꘏꘏꘏ ꘏꘏꘏

Miss Marianne wanted to get more lace, and she wanted to take Lucy with her. Honey could guess where the child might be. She knew about the barn puppies, and knew Lucy had one in particular she played with. It'd be her own dog if her mother allowed that, but Miss Marianne wasn't fond of animals.

When Cook threw up her hands after calling and calling for the girl, Honey volunteered. "Bet she's in the barn. I'll go check."

"That child!"

Honey darted out the door, anxious to get back to the mistress. She'd want her hair done before they left.

Entering the barn was a gloomy process, especially when the sun was shining as it was today. Honey had to let her eyes adjust to the shadows to see proper.

"Lucy! You in here, child?"

Something fell in the far corner. Then silence.

"Lucy?"

Exasperated, Honey marched past the hay. "Your mother wants you. Now don't try to hide." She watched the rustling in the far corner, movement too small to be a horse and too large for a puppy. Darting the last ten feet, she grabbed hold of a slim shoulder.

But the shoulder belonged to Buster.

"What are you doing?" she demanded, more frightened than angry. He was supposed to be working the fields. His absence wouldn't sit well with the master.

"Leave be!" he told her, shaking free of her grasp.

That scared her all the more, for his words weren't those of a boy being caught out. They were a man's anger at being stopped.

"You can't be here! You have to—"

"I rightly know where I have to be." He glared at her, twisting something in his hand—a coil of rope, thick and new.

"Master sent you for that." Honey bit her lip. "I'm sorry, Buster. I forget you're a man now, a working field hand. He'll be wanting that rope Squint just bought. You seen Lucy?"

Buster looked away, toward the puppies.

"Is Lucy playing with the puppies?"

He finally shook his head. "Ain't seen her."

Nodding, Honey turned away to retrace her steps. She did glance back to see him carefully draping the rope on the stall peg, which, come to think of it, seemed odd.

⟫⟫ ⟪⟪

"Get me that white lace now. The pretty one...you know."

Honey did know. The delicate white, soft to the touch, with tiny rose petals woven between the vines. It'd look so elegant trimming Miss Marianne's new evening silk dress, the one in the dark blue.

She had to walk to town to buy it because Squint couldn't be spared to drive her. Truly a blessing, really, as the sun shone and warmed the day. Honey was a very lucky girl to be outside walking.

She heard a wagon approach, rolling wheels, horse hooves clopping in the dirt. Watching the way the sun sparkled on the dew drops, she was distracted and the man's voice that rang out startled her.

"You're one of Hueron's, aren't you? What are you doing out here?"

"Yessir," she said. "Mistress sent me to town to fetch her lace for her gown." She knew his face. Mr. Jevington.

"You got a pass?"

"Sir?"

"A pass. Slave ought to have a pass to be off plantation by themself. How do I know you ain't a runaway?"

Honey could only blink up at him a minute, then found her voice. "No, sir! Mistress sent me to fetch her lace."

Mr. Jevington frowned at her so hard her stomach went cold. Then, at last, he spoke. "You get in this wagon. I'll take you to town."

Honey didn't like the way he talked, nor the way he watched her climb up. She didn't like it at all, but there was no choice. So she sat in the back—as far from him as she could get—and the wagon rolled on to town.

>>>> <<<<

Bibby had carefully measured the dress sleeves and hem. It needed twelve full feet for lace, allowing for the seams. Miss Marianne wore wide, bell-like skirts. Honey had exclaimed over it, but the mistress told her the skirts in Baltimore had been even wider.

When Honey plucked the mistress's coins from her pocket to pay, it turned out she'd taken too much from the purse. Miss

Everette gave her a lot back. "Have a care for that money." The shopkeeper smiled. It made Honey feel very sophisticated.

Carrying the lace neatly wrapped in paper, she spied the wagon near the blacksmith. Mister Jevington wasn't in it.

Her feet moved before she even thought. Honey hurried in the opposite direction, down Main Street and to the tree line. It would take longer, but there was a path through the woods to the river. From there, she could follow the water to Sweetgum.

Preacher had told her that all men did what he liked to do with her. Some did it whether the woman was his wife or not, and some did it whether the woman wanted to or not. And a slave woman, she realized, had no right to refuse. She didn't know if Mister Jevington was such a man, but she'd rather not find out. Consequently, her mind was rattled when she returned.

Bibby took the lace, and Miss Marianne held it against the silk dress and laughed in delight. "Perfect! I still have the eye!"

"It'll be so beautiful in the candlelight." Bibby nodded, then set to work with her needle, and Honey was sent to fetch a pot of that new tea from China.

In all the excitement of tea and hem-measuring, she forgot about the money.

↬⟫⟫ ⟪⟪↫

That night as she made johnnycakes for supper, Honey found the coins in her pocket. Her first impulse was to run straight to the house and return them, but it was late and surely they'd keep till morning. Surely.

Sitting across the tiny round table from her, Preacher wolfed down his food. He'd been working hard, she knew, harder than all the other slaves put together. The cotton was done, so Weena said. She was back working in the house.

With a plantation full of eased work, of slaves slowing just a bit, smiling just a bit, Honey knew Preacher had more burdens, not less. He was up to something, and she could guess what. Whenever she tried to ask, he kissed her and winked and said not to worry.

Now, as she pondered that, Preacher rubbed his shoulder. There was a quick knock on the door, and Buster stuck his head in. "S'pose to be a rainy night," he told them.

"S'pose to be," Preacher said. "Ain't hardly so yet."

He and the boy locked eyes. Then Buster nodded and left. Honey's husband licked the last crumb from his fingers, stretched, and rose from their delicate little table.

"You awfully tired," Honey said.

He nodded, stretching. Moving toward the door, he cocked an eyebrow at her.

"Why don't you sleep tonight? Whatever you're doing, wait till tomorrow."

Preacher met her look without saying anything. One thing about her husband, he knew how to keep his face steady and calm no matter what he was thinking. Useful trick, that.

"Buster was playing with a rope today," she told him.

Preacher cast a side glance at the door, where the boy had disappeared.

One thing Honey had learned was when to keep quiet. If you waited long enough, heavy words were dragged out of people's mouths by their own weight.

"You said you wanted to go, sweetheart. I'm working on that."

She'd guessed, in some portion of her mind, but she'd wanted him to just whisk her off to safety one fine evening, not do crazy things, risky things. The sort of things that got a slave killed. Only a child would think there'd be no danger, and Honey was certainly no child these days.

She rose and moved to set a hand on his heart. "The rope?"

"Don't want you involved."

She didn't flinch, didn't move. Didn't withdraw her hand.

Preacher released a long sigh. "We need one."

"Preacher, they'll miss it! Squint bought it in town for something. You can't just take it."

"Be days before somebody misses it."

"Trouble when they do," Honey told him.

At that he came back to cup her face and kiss her long and thorough. "It's worth it. You're worth it. Anyway, the rope will only be missing a few days. Three at the most." With that, he left.

She stared after him, not daring to follow because she might make too much noise. He had tried to make it sound simple, but Honey was no fool. Some things could get a slave yelled at, some slapped, and some whipped hard enough to peel the skin from your back. Stealing new rope would get you killed. So Honey made a plan of her own.

The real challenge came the next morning. Honey slipped in through the kitchen at sunrise, beginning the day with cleaning the front parlor and dining room. Now that Weena was back, they were able to get the whole lower level polished proper. Next, she washed laundry and hung it out on the line. Normally she rushed through so she could help cook, but Weena was able to do that now. Problem was, Miss Marianne didn't wake up till the sun had half-climbed the sky.

Her nerves stretched, Honey finally took the mistress's tray up, ladened with toast and jam and hot chocolate. They didn't always have the chocolate, so Miss Marianne was quite pleased.

"My blue dress," she told Honey brightly. "With my new silk shawl. I've got tea this afternoon with Mrs. Jevington."

Chattering away, Miss Marianne was full of plans and gossip, which was a very good sign. Honey cooed at the right times, murmured soothingly upon occasion, and lastly, tried a new hair style that made the mistress gasp in delight.

Finally, Honey watched her climb into the buggy, Squint driving, as he was not so crucial to the field these days. It still wasn't truly safe, of course. It still was a fair-sized risk. But the decision had been made. Nothing occurred the rest of the day, up till Preacher walked her home, to change her mind.

Honey waited till Preacher blew out the light, till they lay in the dark, counting the minutes until he would slip out the door. She hadn't been sure even then that she would do it.

"There's coin," she whispered.

Preacher didn't react at all. She wasn't sure he'd heard her.

"Coin for rope," she prodded.

Again, there was silence, but this time she felt his surprise. "Where?" he asked.

She told him.

They lay still a little longer, Preacher holding her, her clutching him. They didn't talk none.

Honey wondered what it would be like to be free. Maybe have a cabin all their own and grow a fresh garden. She could almost feel the dirt beneath her hands as she tended potatoes and carrots and fetched eggs from their own chickens. Better to picture that than see them all running for their lives.

⟫⟫⟫ ⟪⟪⟪

Preacher was reluctant to approach her. In some ways he still blamed her for his being caught, he supposed. Though truth be told, he'd probably never have made it to Canada with that bum leg. Might not have made it anywhere alive. Still, he didn't want to tell her, but in the end, he did.

Maggie was in the good barn, checking the damp cotton spread out on the wood platforms. Seemed to Preacher if the cotton weren't dry and fit by now it never would be, but the master saw it different.

The woman was pulling up the planks off one of the platforms when he walked in. They all had work to do, but without a proper overseer, Master Hueron had a time keeping them all busy. He was worried about his cotton, not his slaves.

"Most of this done germinated," Maggie hailed him. "I don't think it's gonna be much use."

Preacher waited till he was standing next to her. The barn appeared empty, but he looked around a third time to be sure.

She was frowning when he turned back, fists upon her hips. "What you want?"

"Rope," said Preacher.

⋙ ⋘

That very night, despite the rain, Maggie walked to town. It was a long, cold trek, with the wind rising and blowing in her face. Tears sprang up in her eyes from it, and her fingers kept tightening the blanket wrapped round her. She'd given her coat to Buster, as he was out working on the raft.

The raft. Even thinking the word sent a thrill spike down her spine. Maggie knew a lot could happen, might happen to stop them. To get them caught, punished, maybe hung up like Hank on the Honey Trail.

But the Lord don't love no coward, she told herself.

The town seemed darker than usual. Naturally, she approached the store the back way, slipping carefully through the bushes, round the back of the buildings. At last she found the back door. She took a deep breath and knocked.

It seemed to take forever before it opened a crack. The Black man stood there, gazing out at her, frown growing. "Ain't helping with any mule tonight, woman."

Maggie's hand shot out all on its own, stopping the door from closing. "No mule. Rope."

At least her words stayed the door. "I got coin," she begged. "Need rope, a good strong length."

The man stared a moment more, then slipped away. She peered inside, seeing hay and supplies stacked everywhere. There were two lamps burning where there'd only been one before.

Could they be fixin' to get some slaves out to Quincy?

The White man appeared, striding toward her fast. Yanking the door wide, he glared down.

"I gots coin," she told him, her voice scratchy with nerves.

The Black man stood behind him. "What's you wan—"

The White man cut him off. "How much you got?"

Maggie held the money out. He took it, counted it, eyed her, and counted again. Shoving it all in his pocket, he turned and disappeared. A few minutes later—though it seemed forever—he came back with two thick, heavy coils of brand-new rope. Surely it was enough and more for Preacher.

"Anybody catches you with this, I'll say it's stolen. Don't care what they do to you."

Maggie was nodding before she understood his meaning. "Thank—"

The door clicked shut.

She tried carrying one coil on each shoulder, but the ropes were heavier than she'd imagined. She then dragged one coil a ways, stashing it under a shrub before fetching its twin. Twice more she'd drag one, hide it, drag the other. Finally, admitting she'd never be done before sunup, Maggie ran to fetch Preacher.

›››› ‹‹‹‹

With the field now clear, they prepped the soil for new seeds. In four months, a whole new crop would be ripe for the picking.

Preacher found himself plowing and, being alone, started thinking. He had always figured the rope would keep the logs together, and with them all riding on top, the raft would float gently across the water. But now, idly following the old horse, he remembered rescuing Lucy. That river hadn't been so gentle. Riding down the mighty Mississippi on a bunch of loose trees seemed nothing short of foolhardy.

Back on his previous plantation, he'd once watched a guy build a logged roof on a shed, weaving the rope carefully around each separate log. Surely that would make it more stable.

The sun had set and the moon risen before Preacher finished for the day. Picking cotton needed proper sun, so the master said, but they could plow well enough in the twilight. Squint sent him home late to finally eat his dinner.

The knock on the door—*since when did Buster learn to knock?*—roused him from falling asleep at the tiny table.

"He's tired," Honey whispered softly.

Preacher pushed upright, shaking it off. "Not so tired."

Honey touched his arm. "You should get some sleep."

"Won't be long," he told her, and meant it. He just wanted to try weaving the rope around the logs.

Honey shook her head, disbelieving he'd be back so soon.

Laying a couple of trees out by the water, they set to weaving. It was easier in the sand as the twine could be threaded below or above without much effort. And it seemed there'd be enough, using one coil for each end. Preacher's only concern was the stability.

Buster—that bright boy—had the answer. "We tie that long log across, corner to corner! See...it'll stiffen the raft right up."

Son of a bitch! It should work.

Even as they grinned at each other, Preacher heard the running. His heart dropped to his stomach, and he shoved Buster down below the sandy bank to keep him hidden. Too late to hide himself.

Squint burst through the trees. "Both you boys, run to the cotton barn. Hurry!"

Preacher didn't move. Truth was, he couldn't.

Squint had to catch his breath to talk. "Master done sent me to gather all the men. There's a fire in town, Sampson's Store! We're riding the wagon in to help put it out."

Both Preacher and Buster started running with Squint. Briefly, Preacher worried about the raft not being tucked away, but they'd already left it.

"Will we be in time to save the store?" he gasped out. That fire must have been burning awhile already for the word to get all the way to Sweetgum.

"They's worried about the whole town burning," Squint said.

⟫⟫⟩ ⟨⟨⟨⟵

Buster clung to the wagon as it flew down the road. He'd never ridden in the wagon, never been to town. Tweed had, and Honey had been in that fancy buggy more than once, but he'd never so much as set foot on a street.

Light blazed up ahead, flickering like a giant lamp. Except a lamp was all contained like, safe behind the glass. This was wild and raw. Outta control. Scarier than the brightness was the sound, a sort of low roar like an angry bear. It wasn't screaming exactly, but you knew you had to be wary. Rousing a bear was never good.

I wish Tweed was here to see it.

The wagon rolled right up the street, past buildings with lamps on, past people scurrying around like squirrels. The night had been chilly, but now the heat reached them, warming his face up past comfort level to hot. A sort of frightening hot, with your skin knowing the truth before your brain puzzled it out. This was danger, pure and evil, staring them down.

The master yelled at them to jump out of the wagon, to get a move on. Buster clamored down to the street, but Preacher seemed slow to move. Men raced past him into Sampson's, racing out with stuff in their arms. Bags of chicken feed, oats. Baskets for collecting eggs, piles of ropes. Buster couldn't help but stare at those. Fleeing the blaze, they dumped it all a ways up the street and spun back for more.

"Preacher!" shouted the master, striding up to the wagon.

Preacher roused, hopping down and heading for the store.

"Don't touch the hay, mind!"

Buster stepped to follow, but the master grabbed his shoulder. "This way."

They hurried around to the back, keeping a wide gap between them and the building. The front had shown signs of fire, but not too bad. The back was a blazing mass of flames.

Men stood in four separate lines. Buckets passed up two of the lines, where the final man tossed water at the store. Then the empty bucket slipped down another line and back to the well. The master inserted Buster into one of the lines and an empty bucket was shoved in his stomach. Quickly he passed it on. Didn't seem to him they'd stop a fire this way.

The odd thing was, the line was mixed. Men and women, Black and White. A White woman was behind him, working away just like the men. Except for Lucy, he'd never in his life been this close to a White woman.

When he stared too long, she smiled and tugged the bucket from his hands.

By the time the dawn trickled through the sky, Preacher was exhausted. He sat by the empty water trough, back against the sharp-edged wood. The wet chill was welcome. He was soaked from poorly aimed pails and his own sweat and barely moved when the White masters walked past.

Heaps of burned embers rose like tiny tombstones from the ground that had held Sampson's Store. Even the wooden sidewalk in front of it was a charred hole, looking like Hell itself had boiled up from the earth to smite the place. The Emporium and the cafe still stood flanking the gap, singed but whole. Word was Sampson himself was at the doctor's in none-too-good of shape.

They'd been fortunate, very fortunate, to save the rest of the town, let alone the very buildings beside it. Some were calling that a miracle.

Another shadow approached. Preacher barely had the energy to turn his head.

It was Squint. "Got some water here."

Oliver had already passed, dragging the empty bucket to the well. Squint offered a drinking cup on a long handle, brim-full of liquid.

Preacher's hands snatched it greedily, pouring it down his throat before his mind stepped in. He managed a grateful nod.

"Fortunate none of the other buildings burned," Squint told the air. "Seems word got out fast, real fast. Our old overseer Meachum gave the warning...saw the blaze early-like."

"Meachum?"

"'Parently he was just passing through. Lucky timing." Squint gazed down, his face disappearing with the sun-glint behind him.

"'Bout me at the river..." Preacher began.

Squint stopped him. "I don't need to know, boy." In the distance, Oliver hauled the bucket back up from the well. "I don't need to know nothing. *You* need to know 'bout Meachum."

"Meachum set the fire?"

Squint took the cup. "It's what you call one of them coincidences. Time was that store helped slaves, so they said. Now it can't help 'em no more."

⤙⤚

Maggie awoke with fear burning her belly. The sun had already breached the horizon. It weren't bright yet, but she could see the blanket lying over her. Squint should have long since strolled past with the summons.

Then she saw Buster's side of the bed—empty. She was sprinting for Honey's cabin 'fore another thought entered her head.

When she got there, her daughter's cabin was deserted.

"They's gone to town," a voice said. Maisey's voice, coming from the slave clearing. The girl stood there, shoulders bowed beneath a blanket wrapped about them. Her face would never be as pretty as it once had been, but she had a certain dignity now. A maturity.

"Town?"

"There was a fire last night. Squint fetched all the men to fight it. Left the women 'cause we wouldn't all fit in the wagon."

Maggie closed her eyes. They hadn't been caught, hadn't been hauled off to be whipped or hung. "Fire."

Maisey nodded.

"They say those forge things get way hot," Maggie said. "Black-smith," she added when the other woman looked confused.

"Weren't no blacksmith fire," Maisey told her. "'Twas Sampson's Store that was burning."

Maggie's belly went cold.

Without the master or Squint, there were no orders for the field hands. Maggie hurried to the house only to be told by Cook that Honey was way too busy to talk. Miss Marianne had done thrown a fit when the master was gone and wouldn't let Honey out of her sight.

Maggie next went to the river. She didn't know exactly where they worked, but she knew it was somewhere near there. Walking the shore, eyes peeled, she finally came upon the three logs with ropes twined about them, just lying out in the sun for anyone to see.

Struggling, she managed to slide them under the overhang with the rest of the logs. Then she noticed the tree branches and scattered them atop the pile.

Better, she decided. If you walked along the top part near the trees, on the actual dirt path, you couldn't see the logs. But if you dropped down to stick your toes in the Mississippi, the raft components stood out like a purpling bruise on pale skin. In the end, Maggie realized there was nothing more to be done but cross her fingers and pray.

The wagon rolled in a little before noon. To Maggie it seemed forever. It was bad enough she'd had to hide the raft, which was just barely hidden at that, but Sampson's Store...that was a worrying bit of knowledge.

The men were stuffed in the wagon the way a fat White woman stuffed herself in an old dress. Buster was wedged in between Squint and Oliver somehow, while Preacher sat in a corner, waiting till the way was clear before climbing down. Maggie felt a wave of relief at seeing them all whole and safe.

Even Miss Marianne welcomed them home. She kissed the master, who slid off his horse and held her for a long time. He was soul-weary, Maggie realized.

"You men go rest," he said. "We'll get back to work tomorrow." Arm around the mistress, he started walking toward the house, then paused. "You all did real good. You saved the town, maybe saved lives. Thank you."

Maggie stared after them, hardly believing it. Standing there, praising the slaves, the master seemed almost decent. Hard to think these were the same folk that had sold Tweed.

The others slowly walked away, even the prospect of the day off failing to lend them energy. Preacher was the last to move, and when he did, he headed in the opposite direction from the cabins, straight for the beach.

Maggie hurried to catch him, matching his slow step. "I covered it as best I could. You don't need to go there."

He kept walking.

"You don't need to go to the beach. I took care of it."

Buster appeared out of nowhere, striding with them. The boy had more energy than the rest of them put together. "Preacher..."

"'Twas Sampson's that done burnt, and Meachum set the torch to it," Preacher told her in a soft and pleasant voice.

Chilled by his words, Maggie stopped in her tracks.

"One way or another," he said, "we go tonight."

Somehow the strength flowed back into his body, in his arms when he needed to lift logs and his legs when he needed to drag the raft closer to the water. Preacher started out cautious-like, worried over noise, over someone out for a walk, but as the afternoon chugged on, he gave up all that worrying to just work.

He never spoke a word to Buster, but the boy knew when to lift, when to wrap rope, and how to keep his mouth shut. Maggie appeared early on with two water gourds and four johnnycakes. She, too, stayed silent.

It wasn't till Honey appeared in the late afternoon that Preacher opened his mouth. "Go back to the house," he told her. "Go to the cabin when day is done. I'll come git you when it's time."

Her sweet lips twitching in a fleeting grin, she held out two chicken wings. "Yes, sir," she told him softly, cupping his face with her hands despite his grime and sweat.

The sun had disappeared and the moon climbed high when Preacher straightened, rubbing his back, to watched Buster tie the last knot. They'd intended to flip the raft over so the cross-supporting log was on the bottom, but honest to God, Preacher didn't know if he had the strength.

"Come on," Buster urged, dragging at a corner.

Preacher grabbed the opposite side and pulled. It slid, reluctantly, toward the ripples lapping at the shore. Spots of light shimmered on the surface as if eerie ghost candles flickered beneath the water.

"Not too close." He stopped the boy. "Don't want the Mississippi to take her till we'se ready."

Preacher didn't know what to expect at the cabin, but there was Honey and Maggie all set with water gourds filled to the brim and a passel of johnnycakes they'd baked. They'd even put the bacon fat all in them.

"You've used up all the food." He frowned at Honey.

"We'll need it," his wife told him, and he felt a fool suddenly, realizing how little point there was in leaving any behind...no matter how the journey ended.

Slipping silently through the woods, Preacher stared up between the trees. For the first time since he'd left Mississippi, the Drinking Gourd hung in the sky, bright and pretty and pointing the way. They could follow it easy once they crossed the river.

Determination rose in his chest like a grizzly, strong and angry. He would get them through. He would get them safe.

God damn it, I'll get them free. Every last one of them.

⇢⇉⟫ ⟪⇇⇠

The raft lay at a slant on the bright sand, just a few feet away from the river. Maggie thought it the most beautiful thing she'd ever seen.

"Why's that tree set wrong?" Honey whispered.

"Meant to be on the bottom," Buster whispered back. "We need it."

"For what?"

Maggie stepped up to the far corner, trying to lift it up. Preacher took the other corner. The thing was heavy, heavier than she'd have thought, but with Buster and Honey's help, they flipped it over. Her end got too hard to hold and dropped, slapping the water. They all fell quiet.

Certain they'd been heard. Maggie strained her ears for the sound of men running. She caught the rustle of leaves, seemingly stirred by the breeze as it danced around them in circles. The air filled with the song of the whippoorwill. But no human, White or otherwise, appeared.

Preacher latched hold of the raft and started dragging it into the river. Buster and Honey hurried to help. Snatching the johnnycakes folded up in Honey's spare skirt, Maggie waded into the Mississippi.

The other side of the river, the land of Illinois, seemed a lot farther in the moonlight. She'd heard the river was narrower here than in Hannibal, but exactly how narrow? It would have been smarter to remove her shoes, she realized as the cold seeped up her legs. Quickly she hitched up her skirt, but it got wet as well.

One second the raft was level with her knees, easy to sit on and ride. The next it floated waist-level and kept rising.

"Hold still," she whispered to Preacher. With the moon behind him, he seemed in control, but she realized he wasn't.

"Damn river's got it," he told them in a hushed voice. "Get on."

Honey levered herself out of the water, swinging her leg up, kneeling. She reached a hand out to help as the water rose up above Maggie's waist.

Maggie clambered on, lying on her stomach on the hard logs. Buster and Preacher struggled up as well, Preacher rolling himself to lie on his back. With him sprawled like that, there was hardly room for the rest to sit. Buster rose to one knee, looking out across the rippling water.

The raft picked up speed, aiming not for the far shore but down river. Past the big house, heading straight for Hannibal itself. There was nothing to do but hang on.

~>>>> <<<<~

It was late when Hueron guided his wife and child onto the wharf. The steamboat was supposed to have left Quincy at nine o'clock, then ten. Now nearly eleven at night, it at least appeared the *Annabel Lee* was preparing to depart. Her gangplank was finally in place. Marianne was smiling at the lights and music of the big boat, and Lucy hopped up enthusiastically on the wood dock. Odd to see his family so lively so late in the evening when Hueron's own bone weary body wanted nothing more than his bed. *"Soul-weary,"* he recalled grandmother saying.

His grandmother—Elise. She'd been the smartest businessperson he ever knew. His grandfather had a reputation in Baltimore, having built a store near the harbor that became *the* place to go. He had everything there from clothes to food items to household goods, and Grandmother Elise had a way of displaying them. People—groups of women, young men looking to sharpen their image—would come to walk through, to see what was there. It was Elise who tired herself diligently working. Once she passed, the store was never quite the same again.

Music was coming from the steamship. A calliope, the purser told them, ushering them up the gangplank and pointing the way to their cabin. Lucy smiled and held her father's hand, and Marianne echoed the same excitement as she clung to his arm.

Hueron wished he was going with them, but there was work to do. He needed to push Sweetgum into the category of thriving plantations before visiting relatives in St. Louis.

⤐ ⤎

Preacher swung his legs over the side as they lurched yet again. Not satisfied with controlling the raft, the river was bent on shaking them off. He grabbed hold of the binding ropes and prayed they wouldn't shake loose. Kicking with all his might, he tried to push the thing across the water.

They'd passed the big house and then some, going so fast it made him dizzy to see the shore racing by. Buster splashed in next to him, legs churning in the foam. Thing was, the Mississippi appeared smooth—rippling but not frighteningly so—until she sped you along.

Slowly they were edging closer to that shore. Honest to God, he didn't know if their kicking was helping that or just wasting breath. For every yard the river yielded toward Illinois, she bore you twenty toward Hannibal.

·»»⟫ ⟪««·

The steam whistle blasted twice. It was time. Hueron kissed his wife and daughter. Wistful, regretful. *When I've got the cotton sold, I'll join them for a few days. See St. Louis with my family.*

Men in uniform stood at the gangplank and the ship's mooring lines. Everyone was all smiles to the passengers and guests alike as the business moved on beneath the trappings.

Standing on the wharf, Hueron watched the boat slip away. The big wheels started churning, the stern moving backward, pulling her out deeper, allowing the bow to follow, to swing into position. Then the paddle wheels reversed direction. She headed off.

The engine wasn't a quiet thing, and with the spectators at the rails of the ship and standing beside him, it took a minute before Hueron picked up on the odd cries. People were pointing, murmuring. The voices grew loud, peppered with cries of, "Oh my God," and, "Sweet Jesus," and, "It's runners. Runaway slaves."

Up river of the docks, pretty much in the center of the mighty Mississippi, was a flat thing racing through the waters. A thing with shadows on it—people, Hueron realized. Slaves fleeing their masters.

Except they didn't seem to be riding the thing so much as clinging onto it for their lives. The raft was aiming to crash against the paddle boat. He could only hope Marianne and Lucy wouldn't witness the carnage.

⤞⤝

Maggie was holding onto Preacher with all her might. Honey lay next to her, holding Buster. She wasn't sure they needed to hold the two in place, but it was better than just watching.

They'd made it farther out, but getting past the middle of the river seemed to be impossible. The raft raced down river, bumping and wiggling as if determined to knock them off.

"Jesus," Preacher gasped, his gaze was locked on something behind Maggie.

She didn't even want to turn to look. But she did.

When they'd rounded the last bend, there'd been light in the distance. Town light, lots of it. Now she spied the buildings, the people. Talking, pointing. Completing the turn, she saw the big thing in the water, giant wheels churning. Giant wheels that the raft was aimed toward.

The big boat shrilled a warning. As if they could do anything.

People lined the rails on the ship, White faces gawking, hands pointing. The raft was close enough that Maggie could see their open mouths, hear cries above the tumbling waters. One scream louder than the rest.

"Maggie!"

She knew that voice. Standing at the rail, blonde hair glinting in the oil lamps and her eyes just skimming the top, was Lucy.

The raft zipped toward the churning paddle wheel looming up out of the raging river, making the bundled logs look like twigs beside it. Maggie saw the spray, felt the throbbing. Foam flecked her face as if to soften the approaching death.

Beyond the deluge of water, she watched Lucy press her head through the railing, one arm reaching out. Reaching out to *her*.

"Maggie!"

Miss Marianne stood beside the child, never touching her. Not pulling her head back, not minding her safety. Preacher scrambled up on his knees beside Maggie, and Buster gasped. If the menfolk saw the danger, why didn't the girl's own mother?

Somehow, the raft slid by the huge wheel, jerking wildly, but they passed. The river bore them down the side so close they could almost touch the painted planks of the boat. Every master and mistress was staring, their fancy clothes splattered with Mississippi.

Then the big ship gathered speed, now staying with the raft, then pulling ahead. They hovered almost even with Lucy.

"Maggie!" The child's high-pitched scream pierced the night, the noise—the heart.

Too late the mistress looked down at the girl, too late her hand reached out, more likely to slap than to steady her daughter. The child's face was so exactly like Tweed's had been when they snatched him from Maggie, from all he knew and loved.

Lucy popped through the railing to jump, or fall. The tiny splash was lost in the ship's churn. Not one of those smart White folks so much as moved.

Heart in her throat, Maggie watched anxiously as the little head flew past the great spinning wheel. For an instant, she went under—if indeed Maggie had seen her at all.

Then something did surface. Hands beating the water, a choking cry carrying in the air. "Mammy!"

Maggie's own sob was a faint echo of the child's as the boat steamed away. The raft would pass Lucy next, too far away to help.

Rising up on her knee, Maggie rolled into the water. She heard another cry of "Mammy!" before the waves swallowed her up—this one in Honey's voice.

Maggie broke through the surface, gasping and thrashing. Lucy was actually moving toward her, hands and legs working to keep her afloat. It was so much farther than Maggie had thought. So very far.

She kicked against her skirts and the water, fighting old man river himself. *"Lay on the water,"* she remembered Hank teaching her. *"Kick your feet like a pair of scissors. Cup your hands so they can push against the waves."* Not too different from that paddle wheel, Maggie realized, and that sure seemed to work.

A trailing wave from the boat tossed Lucy closer. More waves, fainter than the first, helped. They lifted the girl and shoved her nearer. Maggie was less affected as she swam through the swells. They collided. Little arms flung about Maggie's neck as Lucy stilled. Her own arm hugged the child close, even as the other worked with her legs to keep their heads above the river.

When she looked up, the raft was so far away she couldn't even see the faces on it, and it was drifting farther. At least its course now aimed for the Illinois side.

~>≫⟫ ⟪≪≪~

"Preacher," Honey gasped. She'd meant to shout, but somehow hadn't because there was nothing he could do.

He touched her arm and pointed. A rowboat had left the docks, two men inside. It was minutes away from Maggie. A second boat launched even as they watched. She saw Maggie—Mammy, her mammy who had always loved her—bobbing in the water. So very far away.

"They won't hurt her," Preacher said. "She saved a White child."

The raft angled closer to the shore, though not near enough yet to hop off. At least those rowboats wouldn't get anywhere near Preacher and Buster and her.

The first boat reached Mammy, and Honey started breathing again. She saw Lucy's little body being lifted up over the side and waited. And waited.

The man bore down on the oars. The boat pulled away, leaving Mammy alone in the middle of the Mississippi as the raft sped on.

Honey sat, watching the spot where Mammy had been. Where she wasn't any more.

"She's gone," she whispered to Preacher, who seemed busy with other things.

"We don't know that," he gasped, and the raft beneath their feet trembled.

Honey's body wobbled above the shifting logs.

Preacher strained with a rope, pulling up as hard as he could. She realized the water on his brow wasn't from the Mississippi. The logs quivered again, threatening to come apart. Buster leaped up to help Preacher.

After the bright light of Hannibal, they now glided through the dark. Closer to Illinois, much closer, but not there yet.

Honey's fingers latched on as best they could. "How do we get there?"

Preacher just shook his head. The river curved, the raft skimming over a darker patch, close enough to shore she could see an owl in a tree.

"We're gonna jump."

Honey shook her head, but Preacher kept talking.

"At that point up ahead, where that willow dangles. Shoot, might even be able to grab it."

Honey didn't think so. "Can't we just wait till—"

"No." It was Buster who told her that. "This raft goes where she wants. She's close to Illinois at the moment, but she might just change her mind again."

The willow was coming up fast. A black willow, she recalled. The same as her honey tree back home.

There is no back home now.

Buster leaped, water splashing all about, even hitting Honey's cheek. Preacher put his arm around her.

"I don't—"

He slid her to the edge, and a splinter dug into her thigh. Then the river engulfed them.

Honey fought the water, trying to find the surface in the second before Preacher lifted her out. The Mississippi rushed on, bearing the raft away, but Preacher held fast. His feet reached the bottom, she realized.

They walked to shore where Buster waited. Honey fell to the ground, landing in a rush of dead leaves. *The water gourds are gone,* she thought. *The johnnycakes, gone. Mammy, gone.*

"Sweetheart, we gotta go."

When she looked up in confusion, Preacher stroked her cheek. "Whole town of masters saw us. Somebody gonna come looking."

Hunted

ONCE THEY WERE OUT from beneath the willow, the sky sparkled in glee and the Drinking Gourd shone proudly, as it hadn't done for the last week of Preacher's other escape.

This one will end better, he promised himself. *Just follow the river to Quincy.*

"There's a trail," Buster called from above them, having started exploring as soon as his feet hit the shore.

Preacher guided Honey up the bank. Midway, she started to slip, and before he could react, she caught herself, reset her foot, and scrambled up. Maggie had told him Honey would be a help. If only she could see how right she was.

With much less grace, he followed.

The trail proved no more than a horse path, in some places not even good enough for that. A tree here, a vine there overgrew it, proving it wasn't well traveled. Worse, they couldn't always see the river. The Gourd itself, bright in the sky, was harder still to navigate

by with the overhead branches obscuring it. Preacher had waited for a full moon so they could follow it.

"Can't see the Mississippi," Honey spoke softly, yet her voice
carried clearly on the night air.

"I can hear it," Buster answered, his hand pointing. "Keep
going."

Keep going. It became their prayer.

>>>>> <<<<<

Meachum hung back, watching. He'd followed Hueron to
Hannibal with vague notions. Maybe he'd discover his profits,
if indeed there'd been any, find out just how desperate he was.
See why the man needed a hotel room away from his wife.

Nothing turned out quite as juicy as Meachum had hoped.
Oh, Sweetgum hadn't made a fortune, but the money was better than it should have been. Apparently, the Southern plantations hadn't brought their cotton to market yet, which put
a premium on Hueron's crop. Sweetgum's master had left the
office with a smile on his face.

As for the hotel room, Marianne herself had emerged later.
Both mother and daughter had walked through Hannibal on
Hueron's arm, laughing and shopping.

Meachum had wound up in a saloon, drinking early. He'd
had several but pulled himself back from the brink of being a
true boozer. Instead, he'd acted on that enticing aroma from the

kitchen, ordering a bowl of rabbit stew and taking his time over it. Thinking.

Truth was, the plantation seemed to be doing okay without him. It would be better with him, of course, but the master was the stubborn type. Truly, he wasn't the type of man Meachum wanted to work for. He lacked the stomach to do what was needed.

It was a short jump from this thought to deciding to find a new job. Hannibal was a thriving place, more so than he'd realized. Might be a good place to look.

Thus, Meachum had been walking by the river, heading back to his horse and gear, when all the commotion started. He saw the big riverboat heading out, heard the cries, saw the pointing. He watched the raft sailing right for the paddle wheel, the child leap into the water, the boat heading to pick her up. He saw the raft survive the encounter, disappearing into the night, bearing at least three.

Runaway slaves. Now *there* was his calling. His feet raced off before his mind had even reached its conclusion.

Though past its zenith, the moon was still visible in the sky. The Mississippi had gotten a little too far from view, so Preacher herded them down to the muddy bank. Their feet slipped along slowly, but at least they knew where the water was. A small island popped up, reducing the river to a narrow channel, and he feared losing sight of it altogether.

Besides, the path itself had joined a larger road. Any pursuer would use that way, and no matter how he pondered it, Preacher knew they'd be pursued all the way to Quincy.

Buster took the lead now, and keeping up with the boy was a challenge. Honey was keeping up, though the bottom of her skirt was in tatters. She'd *tsk* and yank her hem free of the briars each time one would snag it. Preacher had counted four angry *tsks*.

Unlike Hannibal, no lights or town noise emanated from Quincy. Buster halted, turning his back to the river, then began walking away from it. Honey followed.

When they climbed the bank, Preacher could see a pasture beyond the trees. A farmhouse perched near it, or maybe a barn. Even in the moonlight, it was hard to tell.

A house by a graveyard, was what Maggie'd said. It was close to the river but on a street, he was sure. Not some farmhouse by a pasture.

"Buster," he whispered, and winced at the noise. "I don't think this is the right place."

The boy turned, retracing his steps. Honey followed, revealing her tense, tired face. Preacher would have liked to reassure her, promise they were safe, that it'd all be over soon. But he knew it had only begun.

⤜⤜⤜   ⤛⤛⤛

They hadn't walked very far when Buster spied the graveyard. He saw the house first, a modest sort of place, tucked away safely from the town. It was near the river, and when he stole up the hill, one large tombstone gleamed beneath the moon. A town could only have one graveyard, right?

"Preacher, that's the one?"

Preacher stared at it so long Buster worried he'd fallen asleep where he stood. "Go find out," the man finally said.

Buster stole quietly to the door, looking everywhere as he approached. The moon was getting low now, and he knew some folks started early. Slaves started early. But there weren't no slaves this side of the river.

His ears strained to catch any noise. After a long moment, he knocked. Immediately a dog started growling within. Not a loud bark, thank the Lord, but a noise all the same. A long moment later, the dog stopped. Buster was two steps away when the latch clicked.

The door swung open, and a White man stood there, candle in hand. "I wasn't expecting anyone," he said softly.

Buster could only stare. The man had a white collar like the Reverend Jessop, and he dreaded the man's reaction.

The door swung open wide. "Come in, my son."

⤜⤜⤜   ⤛⤛⤛

Crossing the river would be the trickiest bit. Meachum considered the ferry, of course, one of Hannibal's pride and joys. But it wouldn't be crossing till tomorrow morning, and that might just be too long.

Peter could be persuaded to take him in that old rowboat of his, but then Meachum would be on the other side without a horse. Although he could pick up one in Quincy, that was a good two-hour walk.

Truth was, he hated being without a horse. Walking put him on the same level as the slaves, and it was important to establish his superiority so they knew right away, feared right away.

He'd known a guy, Jaigger, who taught him a lot about being a slave catcher. The man helped Meachum see how the money flowed and swelled, how masters got so angry they'd agree to fees and conditions smart businessmen would normally refuse. And the slaves—well, they never complained about treatment. There was no point.

Jaigger and Meachum had gone on many a hunt together, making a lot of cash. Been good days, those. Just what he needed after being let go by that idiot who purchased Sweetgum.

They'd been on separate bounties one summer, for whatever reason. Meachum had a fat commission job that was as soft as butter. Caught an old slave whose value laid not in his strength but in his skill. He was a genuine blacksmith, earning a ton of money for his master. The master hired him out to all the surrounding neighbors.

Only thing the master told Meachum was to make sure the old guy could work afterward. He figured injuring his legs would be just fine.

When Meachum returned, grinning from all the cash in his pocket, he got word Jaigger'd been injured. He'd been chasing two young ones, so young their heads didn't rise above a man's chest. One of them was a scrawny girl. Jaigger'd gotten off his horse to chase them through a swamp. He'd loved that horse and didn't want no accidents as sometimes happened in unknown swamps, with the soft mud and the gators. But being low to the ground made him vulnerable. That scrawny girl had cracked his skull with a tree limb. Jaigger'd lived to tell the tale, just.

Meachum himself had hunted down the pair. The boy was returned to his master with a broken arm and a few cracked ribs. The girl died in transit.

In the end, he went searching for Peter, finding him in a whorehouse near the quay. The man didn't even need persuading, as his pockets were empty. Meachum figured the slaves were heading to Quincy and should be there by the time he'd covered the distance. He'd tame them proper before heading back.

⟫⟫⟩ ⟨⟨⟨⟩

Once inside the reverend's house, Preacher sat on the rug. Reverend Murphy had offered his chairs—big, soft chairs in his pristine parlor—but Preacher felt too scruffy to sit in them. Instead, they all sat on the floor.

There was a proper fire burning in a proper fireplace, and while the night wasn't exactly freezing, it was amazing how warm and comforting the flames could be. Even Honey held her hands out, as if warming her palms would warm everything. And funny enough, it did.

"You...didn't come with Rufus?" the reverend asked.

Preacher shook his head.

A Black woman hurried into the room, solemnly gazing at them. She shook herself, wiping her hands on her apron and clucking like a hen at feeding time. "I'll fix 'em some vittles," she announced. "Hot and fresh. That's what I'll do."

"Thank you, Belle."

Preacher frowned. He didn't think there were no slaves here, but this Belle was doing work for the reverend. But, she seemed to lack the fear most slaves had.

Even as he pondered, the reverend smiled at him. "Belle is a free woman. She keeps house for me." Belle nodded and left, and the reverend waited to continue till she was out of earshot. "Rufus was Belle's husband. He was a good man."

Reverend Murphy stepped next to Preacher, making his way down to the floor. He sat beside them, like an equal. "Robert, my son, will take you to Beardstown. He's not here at the moment but should be back sometime tonight."

"Take us?" Buster burst out, then looked immediately embarrassed. He still had that boy spirit, not having learned to keep his head down and mouth shut.

The reverend only smiled at him. "That's the next stop, Beardstown. From there, you can choose to go on to Chicago, or Canada."

"Choose? We can choose?" Buster asked.

Preacher roused himself, thinking it a bad thing to let the boy do all the talking. "Canada," he murmured, then cleared his throat. "I want out of this country."

Reverend Murphy turned his head. He might have been a White man, but he had soulful eyes. They were an odd blue, startling really, but they shone nothing but kindness out into the world.

"Then you shall get out of this country," he said.

***

Meachum had energy to spare when he leaped from Peter's rowboat. The hunt did that to him, spurred him on when the lack of food and sleep should have slowed him down. He'd feel it later.

Quincy was the destination. It had to be. There was someone there helping them—a White man, unbelievably—but Meachum didn't know his name. Even after sticking Rufus's feet in the fire, he'd never gotten it.

But where they'd go after Quincy, he didn't know. That thought alone made him run.

***

An hour later, a door opened. Not the one they'd come in, which Preacher'd had his eyes glued to. A metallic latch clicked in another room, and cool air tickled his face.

A White man appeared, skinny as Buster and not much taller. He had a crooked nose, unlike the reverend, but his eyes were the same odd blue and his hair the same yellow-tinged red. He smiled, striding forward with a master's stride, hand out for a shake as if Preacher were White himself. "Bob Murphy," he said warmly. "The reverend there is my father."

Preacher clasped his hand, marveling at the gesture. Turned out when someone opened his hand like that to you, your own hand moved before you could think proper.

"Preacher," he said, his voice sounding scratchy. "They call me Preacher."

"Sounds like you came to the right place."

Preacher trusted these men.

Bob—he insisted on them calling him Bob just as if he hadn't been White—had them in the wagon quick. Belle made him pancakes, not with cornmeal but flour and milk and butter. He rolled them up and ate them on his way out the door, inviting Preacher, Honey, and Buster to do the same. Belle had made a whole passel of them, and what they didn't eat she stuffed into a wicker hamper.

The wagon was loaded with hay, both loose and in bales. Bob vaulted into the driver's seat and bade them climb in, warning them to keep low. "Doubtful anyone's about," he said, "but no point in giving them a chance to see. We'll be clear of Quincy in fifteen minutes."

They thanked Reverend Murphy. Clasping Preacher on the shoulder, the reverend wished him a safe journey and happy life. Preacher was almost to the point of believing that could be.

They rolled through the town slow. Lying in the hay, straw atop him, Preacher watched the lightening sky above. The stars faded, and the soft gray wisps of cloud were just showing themselves. He wanted to ask Bob to spring 'em, but of course he didn't say a word.

The path led through the last of the trees, and Meachum found himself on a slight hill, peering down at Quincy. The night was seeping away, and he could make out the different buildings, the town center with the warehouse, and the church. It seemed quiet as a tomb.

He couldn't see the whole thing, of course. More houses lay beyond the center, and some of those weren't visible. A whole train of men could leave from there and he'd never spot it. There were homesteads beyond that, separated enough that their own neighbors wouldn't know what they were about.

Illinois folk weren't supposed to help runaways, but he knew some did. Others just didn't like being woken up to see if they had missing slaves in their cellars. And while the constable there would hand over any runaways, he wouldn't arrest citizens for holding them and certainly wouldn't pound on someone's door in the early morning without a good reason.

As Meachum pondered this, he spied movement down below. A wagon slowly rolled through the town, already at the last buildings. As soon as it was clear, it picked up speed.

Meachum sprinted, then fell. The other reason he'd wanted to quit slave chasing, the one he'd forgotten, was that he was getting older.

He got up quick and went to Reeves Stable. He'd take a horse and leave a dollar.

⋙ ⋘

As the wagon lurched forward, Preacher's head lurched as well, bumping into Honey's. They lay side by side, not touching exactly, but close enough he could feel her warmth—and she his, he promised himself. To draw whatever comfort she could. She hadn't spoken much since Maggie went into the Mississippi, and he couldn't be sure she knew what was happening.

The air was cold, and fear was cold. Together, they froze Preacher's soul. Even as the wagon left town rolling toward the dawn, he couldn't relax. A whole city had watched them run, fleeing down river. Damn, the *master* himself had seen. Someone would be chasing them.

And all he could do was lie there by his wife and strain his ears, listening.

⋙ ⋘

Meachum found the stable gate locked but vaulted the fence easily enough. Reeves had three horses in the barn, one of which was his own. The white mare was long in the tooth but would serve his needs. Only problem was, he doubted she could jump the fence.

Fortunately, the side door in the barn wasn't locked. He pulled the horse through, even took the time to saddle her, and was leaving the town behind in just a quarter of an hour.

Ten minutes after that he reached a fork in the road. The sky was lightening, so he climbed down to check. The east route had two fresh tracks in it, while the north route appeared unused.

A farmhouse stood off to the right, a cornfield to the left. It was a big one, as the Illinois farmers loved corn. They didn't like cotton, but then cotton didn't like Illinois.

The sun snuck a peek over the hill, revealing a rambling shadow a ways up ahead. Meachum dug his heels in. Reluctantly, the mare snorted.

⋙ ⋘

Preacher heard the echo first, then odd clips that weren't a part of the wagon noises. It was a horse coming up the road behind them. For an instant he thought it was moving too slow to be chasing them—probably just a farmer off to do farmer things. After all, he wouldn't have slaves to do it for him.

"Mind if I check your hay," a familiar voice said. It weren't no question.

Preacher's stomach clenched so tight he couldn't have moved if a copperhead reared up. He felt Honey tense beside him, heard Buster's hiss. No one who'd ever worked under Meachum could forget that voice.

The wagon kept rolling. "You can buy hay in Quincy," Bob Murphy said, real friendly-like.

The metallic click that answered him didn't sound like no horse. "Stop."

The wagon ceased rolling, though no brake had been applied.

"You planning to shoot a peaceful man?" Preacher marveled at how calm Bob sounded.

"I'd be shooting a thief."

"That what you did to Rufus?"

Bang. The wagon lurched, the horse cried out, and a body thumped against the wood up front. Preacher shot up out of the hay to see Meachum wrestling to control his own mount. Bob Murphy lay slumped across the bench seat.

Meachum stared. "You," he said, a slow grin spreading across his face. "So glad it's you."

The man raised his pistol. Preacher'd seen only one of those before—but one was enough. Meachum fired—

—and the gun exploded. The barrel split as smoke billowed all around.

Preacher was unhurt, but Meachum shouted, dropping the weapon and fighting to hold his horse in check. Vaulting the wagon side, Preacher grabbed the man's arm, yanking him off his mount. Meachum fell heavy, and the white horse took off. Dodging the mare, Preacher turned back, and a powerful fist felled him.

Meachum had sprung up pretty quick. His boot kicked Preacher hard as he sprawled in the dirt, aiming for his head but striking his shoulder. Good thing really, as it would have dented his skull.

The second kick sent the toe deep into Preacher's ribcage. Meachum leaned down to survey the damage, grinning. "Always knew it would come to this," he snickered. An unholy light burned in his eyes.

Suddenly, with a loud crack, the man dropped atop Preacher and lay still. Honey, standing behind him, tossed her big stick aside.

"Preacher?" She leaned down, fingers roaming his face. When he grasped them, she smiled.

Getting up wasn't easy. Meachum was a dead weight over him, and that chest kick burned when he tried to breathe. He struggled to his feet and had to cling to the wagon to make his way round the front, where Bob Murphy lay unmoving.

The man had blood on his jacket but was still breathing. Preacher pulled back the cloth to find more blood on his chest, near the top of the shoulder. Far away from the heart, at least.

"What do we do?" Honey asked.

There was only one thing, really. Preacher lay Murphy gently in the straw and turned the wagon round. Seeing Meachum lying there, alive but unconscious and very much in the way, he wound up pulling him off the road, into the grass. He drove slowly back to town.

A White man came out of the cornfield, studying him and the wagon. "Hey, that's Bob Murphy," he said.

Preacher nodded. "I gotta get him to his pa."

The man moved to Bob, checking his wound. "I'll get him there."

Preacher sat still, pondering. He honestly didn't know what to do. The farmer yanked his own jacket off, using it to stanch the wound. "He's not that bad, truly," he said. "I'll take care of him."

"Sir..."

"You need to get your family on now. Take your wife and your kid outta here." The man picked up Bob and gently laid him in the grass.

Honey touched Preacher's arm.

"Beardstown," a voice cracked. Bob's voice. "Blacksmith...Henderson. Tell him Bob Murphy recommended you."

A dozen thoughts ran through Preacher's mind—a dozen things to say, a dozen things to do. Instead, he yielded to Honey's tug. *There's a time to run, son.*

"Yes, sir." Preacher nodded, then told the farmer, "There's another one a little farther up."

"That one can wait." The man eased Bob gently back to the grass. "East. You head straight where that sun's rising now. Take you till the sun sets to get there, I reckon."

Preacher turned the wagon round again, careful to stay far from the two White men. It was easier the second time. Within a minute, the mule was back on the road, pointing toward the dawn.

"Here." Bob was holding something in his hand, something small. Before Preacher could tell the boy, Buster leaped down to get it.

"Preacher." Bob was already sounding stronger. "You're a family, mind. Anyone asks, you tell them that."

Buster clamored up beside him, and Preacher clapped his shoulder. "Yes, sir. We're a family now."

For the most part, the road was empty of other travelers. More importantly, it was empty of choices. Occasionally paths would break off, but they were sufficiently smaller and less traveled that Preacher was never tempted to follow them.

Buster sat beside him, staring ahead without saying a word. Honey lay in the wagon, not wanting to be seen even if they were in Illinois. He let her lie and was rewarded when she seemingly fell asleep.

Early on they'd all kept quiet, fearful of disturbing the world and thus getting noticed. As the sun climbed higher and the road stretched unending, Preacher found his tongue. "You all right there, Buster?"

"Yes, sir."

Silence fell again, lasting as long as it took the wagon to reach the end of the woods and roll out to a flat bit of open land. On one side crops grew, though Preacher didn't recognize the plant. It was young, whatever it was. On the other side stood a house a fair distance off the road and a few fruit trees.

"Your mammy wanted you free, you know," he told Buster. "She started pushing me before she'd fixed my leg that day and never stopped till the raft was ready."

The boy didn't so much as turn his head. He'd lost his world, Preacher reminded himself. Despite his tall, little body, despite his smart thinking and somber way, he was just a child. He'd only seemed older because of Tweed. No kid brother to shore him up now.

"Honey and me, we'll take care of you now. Buster, I promise we'll take care of you."

The little head turned. His hair was getting longer than usual, probably 'cause he'd been busy helping with the raft. It aged him, somehow. Booker'd put him to work for sure, if he saw him now.

"I can take care of myself," the boy said, no defiance or anger in his tone, no mulish look to his chin. Just a sincere, honest belief.

And looking at what the kid had just survived, Preacher realized he might be right at that.

⇥⇤

They passed their first wagon when the sun had reached its zenith. Honey lay somewhere between asleep and awake when the clip-clops approached. She curbed the impulse to sit up. Coming from ahead, it wouldn't be someone chasing them. It couldn't be. Illinois was a free state.

But her throat went dry as the sounds grew louder, and her stomach dropped completely when they stopped altogether.

"Where you headed?" a deep man's voice asked. It sounded unfriendly, although she realized that might just be because it sounded White.

White men here are different, she reminded herself.

"Beardstown." That was Preacher, sounding so polite.

"What for?"

To Honey, the silence that followed seemed far too long.

"Looking for work," Preacher said, and she could hear the grin in his voice.

"What kind of work?" The questioning was too long, surely too long.

"He's a blacksmith." Buster spoke up, sounding enthusiastic somehow. "A good one!"

Honey heard cloth moving and wondered if Preacher was hugging the boy. She would have if she could.

"Well now, if your pa's a good one, he should talk to John Henderson on State Street. He's the blacksmith. He might can use you."

"Thank you, sir," Preacher said.

The clip-clop sounded again.

"Watch that Tom at the ferry, mind," the man called after them. "He'll try to charge you two quarters for your wagon. You tell him it's half that, you only got one horse."

"Yes, sir," Preacher answered.

Honey lay there, waiting till the wagons were surely out of sight. She didn't know what a ferry was, but then they didn't have no money.

"I sure is hungry," Preacher announced to the world.

Honey pushed herself up, reaching for the hamper Belle had given them, looking for those pancakes. She found them in a red checkered napkin, atop another napkin stuffed full.

"Fried chicken! Preacher...there's fried chicken! Lots of it!" Suddenly Honey's stomach gnawed at her ribs, demanding she devour that food. All her caution about who else might be traveling that road evaporated like the morning dew in the bright sun.

"Well, stop that jawing and hand it out." Preacher grinned. "First piece to Buster, for being such a smart lad."

Honey wasn't so sure. "What if that man comes asking at the blacksmith's? Why aren't you working there?"

"Blacksmith's where we're going, Honey. Anyway, that man's heading to Quincy. We'll be long gone before he gets back."

Honey shook her head. Too many possibilities, too many assumptions. What if that man wasn't going that far? Handing out drumsticks, she asked instead, "What's a ferry?"

"Man gets himself a flat boat, takes people across the river on it. It's good money."

"We ain't got money," Honey told him as she bit into her piece. The meat was so juicy, the fried crust so crunchy. She'd never had anything like it in her life.

Buster dug into his pocket, fishing, then pulled out a handful of shiny metal. "Silver dollars," he told them. "Mister Murphy gave them to me."

Honey leaned in, staring at the handful of shiny coin. "How many?" she breathed.

"Seven," Buster told her.

"You can count that high, Buster?" Preacher grinned.

"Buster can do anything," Honey said.

⇢⇢⇢ ⇠⇠⇠

The day the wagon rolled into Chicago was one Preacher had dreaded for thirty-two years. Mister Henderson, the gentle blacksmith who'd looked too puny to wield a blacksmith's hammer, had said the road to the city was three days long. It had taken them five, partly because Preacher decided they needed a proper night's sleep and partly because the blacksmith had warned he should drive through the city itself before dawn. "Best go when they's all still abed."

Thing was, his daddy—Big Anthony—had lived in Chicago. Worked in the stockyards, a proud freeman. Then some White fellow with a scraggly beard offered him a better job and took him to a bar and bought him a drink. Big Anthony had woken up in a slave pen in Missouri.

When he told them he was a free man, they beat him senseless. On the auction block—some place called the Forks in the Road—Preacher's daddy was sold for seven hundred dollars, an amount that made the White man who'd kidnapped him slap his knee in glee. Big Anthony had been as big as Preacher, with powerful muscles and a dumb brain. That last—the dumb brain—was what he'd always told Preacher, because only a dumb brain would think itself free in Chicago. That was why Preacher wanted to go to Canada. Slavery was illegal all over Canada, not just bits and pieces. Big Anthony had said that up there, they didn't like slavery and didn't like Americans trying to reclaim them.

But, the road to freedom went through Chicago. All he could do was not drink with White men. Which, Honey insisted, was not that hard to avoid.

The road changed rapidly, from dusty and empty to muddy and bustling with people, even in the dark before dawn. Chicago had pretty near thirty thousand folk living there, so Preacher had been told. As the sun sneaked a peek, people walked the sidewalks and a few wagons rolled in different directions, the roads becoming a maze of crisscross paths.

"There's a Black man riding that horse," Buster whispered excitedly, pointing at a tall man dressed in decent clothes. He looked like a master, right up to the hat on his head—a hat he tipped to Honey, grinning as he rode away.

"That a free man?" Buster watched him trot down the street. Preacher nodded. "That's a free man." *At least for now.*

He steered the wagon through the busy streets, catching occasional glimpses of the water on his right. Lake Michigan—his daddy had said it was big. When he saw the tall ships, he headed toward them.

Preacher rolled right up in front of the Sauganash Hotel and pulled on the rein. There was no one about, which was worrying. He handed the reins to Buster and climbed down.

"Where you going?" Honey seemed nervous, and he realized she had reason.

He didn't like the idea of leaving her alone in this city any more than she did. So he opened the door of the hotel, keeping one foot outside.

The interior had a few oil lamps burning, highlighting a sort of counter with a man behind it. A skinny man with bushy eyebrows, he looked up and studied Preacher before making his way around and striding up to him.

"Good morning," the man said, soft and friendly-like.

Preacher lifted his chin. "I'm looking for work. Was told Mister Claridge was the man to see."

The man nodded and disappeared through a door, soon returning with a large woman in her fifties. Wiping her floured hands on her apron, she approached Preacher.

"You looking for work?" She smiled. "How many of you?"

She weren't as tall as him, but she came closer than any woman Preacher'd ever met before. He ducked his head instinctively. "Pardon, ma'am. I was told to speak to Mister Claridge."

The woman grinned, and he saw there was also a spot of flour on her cheek. "Ain't no Mister Claridge." She chuckled. "But if'n you was a White man looking all mean and determined, I'd a told you he was out hunting bear."

The man behind the desk cracked a smile.

"Now, I got a room in the back you can have for a few days till we get you set up proper-like."

"I want to go to Canada." Preacher hated to say it and waited for her to ring a peal over his head.

She frowned a moment but didn't yell. "Shame, that. Could have used your muscles there. But you ain't the first to ask, and I can understand." Turning, she called to the desk guy. "Send a note to Captain Berl on the *Arbor*." Then, with a wave of the hand, she offered him a seat at a table.

"I gots my family outside," he told her.

"Well, go get them."

⟫⟫ ⟪⟪

Sitting around a table just as nice as Miss Marianne's, Honey felt warm and safe. Miss Claridge being kind and a good cook made Honey want to stay.

"I want to go to Canada," Preacher said, neither demanding nor insistent.

"Then let's go to Canada." She smiled. Truth was, she shared his need to get far away, to be as safe as could be from Meachum and his like. She suppressed a pang for Tweed. There were other things to think about now.

Captain Berl turned out to be a close friend of Miss Claridge's. "Sure, I can take them with me. We leave in two days for St. Joe."

"That's in Canada?" Preacher asked.

"Lord bless you, no. Michigan. Start of the St. Joseph Trail."

"I thought we could sail to Canada."

Honey worried that the captain might get annoyed, but he just chuckled. "No, sir. Canada is a long way from Chicago, too far for the *Arbor*. The entire state of Michigan lies between. But it's a shorter journey overland. Go to Detroit and look for the ship *Home*. Captain Nugent's boat. He'll take you to Canada real quick from there."

⟫⟫ ⟪⟪

Buster, having never so much as set foot in Blanten, couldn't quit staring at all the Chicago bits. Wooden platforms built just so you could walk above the ground. Roads meant for carts and horses crisscrossing between buildings that weren't houses nor barns. Stores selling stuff he'd never heard tell of. And people moving—even in the dark—to do things he couldn't even guess at. They was free, every one of them.

What do they do all day?

Beside him strode Miss Claridge, walking purposefully through the city. She was a determined sort, reminding him just a little of Mammy. Just a little. They marched past all the citizens of the city and into a store filled with food.

Filled with food. Buster couldn't tear his eyes away. "What is this place?"

"Green Grocer's," Miss Claridge said. "The Lake House on Kinzie has a good dining room, but I'm a better cook."

Buster just nodded. Mammy had wanted to grow food by the cabin, but there never seemed to be the time. He and Tweed had started to plant stuff twice, but they'd had no idea what they were doing and none of the adults had the time to tell them.

Crates of green spread out before him, lettuce and onions and potatoes. People were weighing the vegetables like Mister Meachum had weighed cotton. There was an excited hum in the air at all this food. When Buster saw a Black man buying carrots, he gasped aloud. A Black man putting carrots in his basket, actually waving at the White man who gave them to him.

Tweed would have loved this, he thought before suppressing the image. No point in thinking about that. It was gone, just like Sweetgum and Lucy and the puppies. *Like Mammy.* But it was time to stop thinking about her as well.

"You all right there, boy?" Miss Claridge nudged him.

"Yes, ma'am," he said, taking the basket she held out to him. They strode off to get carrots themselves.

〜≫⟫ ⟪≪〜

Ten days later, Preacher stepped on the land he'd dreamed about since he was Buster's size. Sailing on Lake Michigan had been a scary thing, with the wind a whipping something fierce. But a day later, Captain Berle had set them down on land again—Michigan land. He introduced a friend taking the captain's cargo of grain to Detroit, and Preacher, Honey, and Buster had hitched a ride. Three days after that, they stood on another wharf.

This time it was the sailing vessel *Home* they boarded, under the watchful eye of Captain Nugent. He was a gruff soul who made Honey nervous, but in mere hours he set them down in a town called Amherstburg.

"Where do we go from here?" Preacher asked the captain.

"This here's Canada," Nugent told him. "This is as good a place as any."

Buster, who was already speaking up more than ever before, frowned at the settlement before them. "I always thought Canada was bigger."

At first look, Amherstburg didn't appear any different from parts of Missouri. Down the gangplank to the wooden wharf, which was smaller than the city's, the dirt road was just a step farther on. Honey clasped Preacher's arm, and he noticed how Buster flanked her protectively.

"We'se safe here," Preacher murmured, reminding himself as much as them.

Across the road was grass, another road, and the buildings of a town. People strolled on wooden sidewalks, horses clopped along, and a buggy rolled past. There was more grass here, marking the dirt roads clearly, and the land was flat as far as he could see. It looked bigger than Blanten, but not as big as Hannibal.

Preacher almost felt like they'd run all this way to still be in Missouri, but then two Black men walked by, dressed just like the Whites, talking about the weather. Black men conversing on the street—he'd never seen that in the South. Slaves didn't talk where White men might see them in case it annoyed them, or they thought of some work for the slave to do. Slaves didn't draw attention to themselves.

The two men stopped conversing and smiled at the three travelers. "Well now, you just arrived on the *Home*?"

"We did," Preacher said.

"You're welcome here. Go see George Bullock at the Boarding House. He's got some rooms, and he knows where the work is."

"I'm Oscar." The second man smiled, stepping close and offering his hand just like a White man.

Preacher shook it. "I'm Preacher."

⇢⇢⇉⇉ ⇇⇇⇇⇇

Amherstburg was a magical place. Buster found he could walk freely, anywhere. He could run errands for Miss Bullock without worrying about where he went or who saw him. He could work for Oscar at the stables, grooming those horses and earning coin for doing so. Even dangling his feet in the water off the pier was fine. The men who saw him just smiled and waved.

Best was the food. Miss Bullock was a fine cook, so Preacher said, and they ate regular hot meals of chicken and pork and bread and apple pie. It took a bit to get used to a White woman serving them food at a proper table, but after the apple pie, Buster thought more about the smells that made his stomach growl than skin color. Not once did they eat johnnycakes.

To pay for their room and board, Preacher worked round the docks and Honey helped round the boarding house. Two days later, Buster found a job at the stable. Imagine, getting paid to tend to horses. He'd been shooed from the barn often at Sweetgum.

It was a fine afternoon when he was currying Onion, an old horse "that could make you cry," so Oscar said. Buster wanted to try fishing off the pier, but he didn't want to shortchange the horse's currying time. If'n he was getting paid, it was important to give them their money's worth.

Voices were carrying on the breeze, rising in volume and number. He didn't think much of it till one man's shout cut through the others.

"Oscar is going back with us. He belongs to Emmit—he's a fugitive."

Buster's instinct was to hide, and he almost tossed the curry brush to run. But Canada was free, he'd been told and told, and he didn't have to hide there. Besides, Oscar was his friend, and a man helped his friends.

The men faced off near the lawn overlooking the water. Two big White men with clenched fists were glaring at Oscar and Mister Bullock. The bigger man leapt forward, grabbing Oscar's arm. "He belongs to Emmit."

Mister Bullock, also White, stepped between the man and Oscar. "Oscar don't belong to no man but himself."

Two more men, both Black, came sprinting from the docks. They added to the flesh-wall protecting Oscar. "Ain't no slavery here," one of them said, gentle-like.

Stiffening his spine, Buster hurried on to join the wall, although he wasn't as tall as the others. One of the intruders glared down at him, dug in his back belt, and produced something Buster had seen before—a gun. This one looked like Booker's old weapon, rusted and falling apart.

"You know what this is, boy?" the man demanded.

The others stayed quiet, so Buster answered him. "Yes, sir. It's a gun."

The man laughed, angry-like.

"I seen one like that blow up in the hand that shot it," Buster added. "Burnt him good."

The other man clenched his big hand into a fist, and suddenly Preacher was there, standing beside Buster.

"There's a lawman coming," Preacher told them. "He says Oscar is free, but kidnapping is against the law."

The man with the gun clutched it, weighing its use, as two more Amherstburg men and a woman joined the wall. "Oscar is free," Mister Bullock said.

The two men finally stepped back, still angry but seemingly defeated. A man with a gun fastened to his belt came striding up, and Buster guessed he was the lawman. He *seemed* like a proper lawman.

The two intruders turned away, walking back to the docks. Buster watched until they climbed a gangplank and disappeared.

Preacher clasped his shoulder. "Buster, what you doing? You coulda got—"

"He was being a man," Oscar told him.

Buster nodded.

FREE

HAVING NEVER CONSIDERED LIFE after he was free and never able to take this freedom for granted, Preacher found himself enjoying each new day.

Oscar's brother was a farrier, which meant he shoed horses and mules. As he said he needed help since business was good, Preacher gladly learned the art. The man owned a barn with a forge and never bothered with any other blacksmithing work even though he was often approached. He had no interest in it.

Preacher did. Thus, he turned a fair job into a very good one, and in time bought himself and Honey a little house all their own. Honey was heavy with their first boy by then and just as proud as she could stare.

Buster helped at the forge, running errands and currying horses. Preacher tried to teach him blacksmithing, but he loved the animals more. In his teens, he bought his first one and sold it to a farmer in need of just such an animal. By the age of twenty, he was buying and selling proper quality-bred equines. A real horse trader.

Mister Lincoln of Illinois became President Lincoln, and the United States went to war with itself. In 1863, the Emancipation Proclamation said that every slave was now free even as the civil war raged on. Missouri, so they heard, stayed out of the thick of it.

Preacher's firstborn was fourteen when news broke that the war was over. The Confederate States of America lost, and slavery was indeed abolished. The South was beaten, the former slaves all told each other in the Canadian streets.

As their children—five big ones, all smart and proud and free—grew to adults, Honey asked about traveling to Missouri. Their home was and would always be Amherstburg, where their kids now had kids of their own, but she wanted to find Tweed.

"We ain't gonna find him," Preacher told her.

"But we can ask. He went to that plantation of Master Hueron's friend."

Honey wanted to go back, he knew, just to see. To see where Maggie had once raised her, to see where Buster and Tweed had played by the river. He wasn't so keen, knowing those old masters the way he did. They might not be allowed to have slaves these days, but that didn't mean they were sitting at tables drinking tea with their old servants. They'd hold grudges, blame their former slaves for causing all their grief. Losing a war wouldn't turn them up sweet.

When Preacher and Honey's youngest, Maggie, got married, he finally agreed. Honey hoped Buster would want to go, but he was busy with his own family. Honey thought he was too sensitive to look for his brother. Preacher thought he was too smart to look.

The trip back to Sweetgum was very different. They had good money, for one thing, and could afford accommodation. Keeping a firm grip on their purses, Honey and Preacher booked passage on a schooner to Detroit.

In Detroit, they took the St. Joseph train, which followed nearly the same route they'd taken when running from Chicago. This train had existed back then, but they hadn't dared ride it. Now they sat calmly in upholstered seats, watching the landscape pass by.

There were rumors that a new railroad could take them all the way from Chicago to New Orleans, which proved true. Preacher booked them two seats to Hannibal, marveling that this large iron monster could carry them that far. "In the lick of a cat's ear," he was told when he asked how long it would take.

It took two weeks.

The closer they got to Hannibal, the more nervous Preacher got about going there. They were still in Illinois and wouldn't cross the Mississippi until Hannibal itself, but gazing out the window, things didn't seem all that different. The land appeared the same as it had when they left, as did the roads, the wagons and farms, and particularly the people. How different could Missouri actually be?

Eventually they crossed the river that had claimed Maggie's life. Soon after, they stepped onto the platform in the city Preacher still had nightmares about escaping. He looked around, saw the old saloon on that same street corner and would happily have taken the next train back to Chicago.

Honey didn't share that urge, so he rented a buckboard and, tired as they were, took the familiar road north to Blanten.

Unlike Hannibal, Blanten had grown some. Everett's Emporium was still there but in a different spot. The corner where it had stood near Sampson's Store now held three large buildings, including a town hall. They were brick construction, every one of them, including the new Everett's across the street. There was no sign of Sampson's.

The blacksmith was still there. In truth, it was the only place that remained where it had been in the old days. They stopped because Honey needed a stop and Preacher felt more comfortable in a blacksmith's.

Inside, an older woman sat on a stool, wiping her brow. It was early May, but the day was warm and a blacksmith's was rarely comfortable.

"My man's out at the Leonards' place. Won't be back for a while."

Preacher pulled his hat off his head. "Yes, ma'am. Sorry to trouble you." He turned to leave.

"Say...don't I know you? Preacher, right?"

For an instant, he felt that rope looping over his neck, but when he turned back, the woman was smiling, not racing for help or nothing. He bobbed his head.

"Caused quite a commotion when you ran off down the river. Folks could talk of nothing else for weeks."

She thought it funny, he could tell. A night of absolute terror, a night when Maggie had drowned in the Mississippi. But events had a way of becoming tales, and he supposed this one had been quite a story.

"I always thought old Meachum'd bring you back," the lady continued with a hint of a smirk. "I'm glad he didn't."

Preacher studied her face as the questions surged. What exactly had happened? Had Meachum returned, told them a tale of his own? Had they never seen him again? Had Honey killed him with that blow? He daren't ask.

"Preacher?" Honey entered. "Knew I'd find you..."

"Honey," said the woman. "Still together, I see." She smiled. "I'm Linda Adams, by the way. The blacksmith's my man."

Honey smiled back, seemingly without feeling any ropes at her throat.

Though Preacher judged it time to go, he did ask one question before leaving. "Mister Meachum around?"

The look the woman gave him was penetrating. Very penetrating. "Ain't seen him since the war. There was a rumor of him getting killed in Vicksburg, but I think it was just a rumor."

When the buckboard drew close to Sweetgum, the familiar hills rose up. Then the cotton fields appeared, though now covered in tobacco. Preacher had to suppress the urge to turn around.

There were still Black men in the fields, working away. It made his skin crawl to see it. Then the skinny man standing where the overseer should be turned around. He, too, was Black and familiar—older, but very familiar. He burst into the big grin Preacher remembered.

"Oliver!" Honey cried.

They actually hugged, those two, and while Preacher didn't join in, he found himself smiling. Talking to Oliver would be easy.

"Miss Marianne's at the house. Young Master Richmond—he came along a year after you left—is down in New Orleans looking at horses. He's a fine man...wants a proper bred 'un."

"He should talk to my boy," Preacher said, looking over the field. He recognized a few faces out there, working away just as if nothing had ever changed. "You all know about the Emancipation Proclamation?"

Oliver chuckled. "Yes, sir. But a man's still gotta work, freed or not. And this work's good as any."

Honey frowned. "Is it?"

"We gets room and board, Miss Honey. Every Sunday we gets a silver dollar and the day off!"

"Did...did you ever hear tell about Tweed?"

Oliver blinked. "Why...why yes. Of course. We'se so proud of him."

"Proud?" Honey asked.

"Master Hueron and Master Richmond sided with the Unionists. Master Hueron got bushwacked for it. Some folks here thought they should have seceded and fought with the South. The war outside Missouri weren't nothing compared to the war inside the state.

"That was supposed to shut the other Unionists up. Instead, Master Richmond went off to fight, and Mister Tweed went with him. Mister Tweed fought in the 62nd! The First Regiment of Missouri Colored Infantry! He was at Forks of the Road for a bit."

Preacher frowned. "Forks of the Road was a slave market."

"Yes, sir. It got sort of freed-like, and the 62nd was stationed there."

Honey was stock still at Preacher's side, so he asked the question he knew she had to know. "Did Tweed survive?"

Oliver's grin faded. "Battle of Vicksburg. Master Richmond died there, and they pretty sure Tweed did as well."

"Pretty sure?" Preacher prodded.

"They didn't keep as good of records of the colored infantry."

⟫⟫ ⟪⟪

With Tweed truly gone, there was no point in staying. Honey wanted to go home. But even as her hand clasped her husband's arm, she realized she'd have to wait. Oliver was calling an early lunch—*imagine, an early lunch for the field hands!*—and Preacher was fixing to sit and jaw. He had come a long way, after all. He deserved a little jawing with old friends.

So, after careful thought, Honey walked the Honey Trail. The old dogwood tree was there and blooming something fierce, welcoming her as nothing else could. She lingered to pick honeysuckle and savor the honey out of each blossom.

No conscious decision was made, but somehow she strolled on, finding herself at the kitchen door. She knocked. It was yanked open by a huge White woman, her mouth sneering something fierce. "We ain't got no work, and we ain't giving handouts.

"Miss Tully, who's that at the door?" It was Weena's voice, and Honey's smile overcame her startled reaction.

"Just some Black trash—"

"Weena!" Honey called.

Miss Tully was shoved aside, and Weena filled the threshold, beaming from ear to ear. They hugged like long-lost sisters. "We always wondered," Weena murmured over and over. "So you did make it clear to Illinois."

"Made it clear to Canada," Honey told her.

Despite Miss Tully's disapproval, Weena dragged her inside.

"Will she want to see me?" Honey asked, suddenly worried. Everyone was being all friendly-like, but truth was, she'd run away from Miss Marianne. Slavery being over didn't change that.

Weena nodded. "She's asked about you often. Did I think you made it over that river? Had anyone ever heard from you? She missed you."

Walking through the familiar halls, Honey's doubt grew. Then they entered the foyer by the front parlor. Miss Marianne sat there knitting in a rocking chair Honey didn't remember.

"She took up knitting when the master died," Weena whispered. "Miss Marianne, look who's here to see you."

The mistress looked up and smiled. "Honey! I always knew you'd come back." She rose gracefully, setting aside wool and needles. The sun through the window revealed a few lines on her face, a bit of gray in her hair. "I don't really have room for you in the house," she told Honey seriously. "Weena's been taking care of me for a while now."

"She knows that, Miss Marianne."

"She'll have to work in the field."

The tales on Honey's tongue—about the Mississippi escape, her life in Amherstburg, Buster, her children—all died stillborn. "Yes, ma'am." She smiled gently. "You don't need the likes of me anymore."

⟫⟫⟫ ⟪⟪⟪

Preacher could have talked to Oliver all afternoon, but the man needed to do the work he was now getting paid to do, and anyway, he'd learned all he truly needed to know. Squint and Bibby had passed peaceful-like. Simon had also died, but not so peaceful. He'd run off to fight in the war.

Honey had come back as they were standing up, and she heaved a deep sigh. "Let's go home," she told Preacher. He decided to ask about Miss Marianne later.

Oliver peered at them for a long moment, and then thought for a long moment more. "You seen Miss Lucy, down near the docks?"

"I don't want nothing to do with that girl," Honey said, real anger rising. "She killed my mammy."

Preacher knew she'd never forgive that child.

"She did not kill your mammy," Oliver said in a tone Preacher'd never heard him use before. "Miss Lucy's a teacher now. You go see her." It was a real command, from a real overseer.

Honey scoffed, but it was Preacher he was ordering.

"You do it," Oliver insisted. "Won't take long."

Well, the way home was through Hannibal, and Oliver seemed to think it important.

⟫⟫ ⟪⟪

Their steamboat didn't leave for two more days, and Hannibal being, well, Hannibal, it didn't feel like a place they should happily wander around. Honey preferred to sit in their room.

Preacher wound up near the docks, near the place Oliver had told him to go. It was a small office next to a shipper's office, with a blue door and a hand-painted sign: Freedman's Bureau. There were two Black women inside, and two White men. They were all working away with papers and drawings.

One of the men looked up. "Can I help you?"

Preacher, looking around, nodded. "I'm looking for Miss Lucy. Lucy Hueron."

The man walked closer, looking him over. "She's Mrs. Styles now. My wife."

For an instant, Preacher worried, but only an instant. Mister Styles was tall and strong, but he was smiling and actually holding his hand out. A firm handshake was offered, which Preacher accepted.

"Did you know her from Sweetgum?"

Preacher nodded.

"She'll be back in an hour. We're building a school a little ways out of town, and she likes to check on the progress."

So they returned an hour later. Honey didn't see the need, but they'd never be here again and Preacher couldn't help but feel they ought to talk to Lucy. She'd always been a good child, after all. It weren't her fault what happened to Maggie.

In the end, he simply said he was going and if she didn't want to come, he'd see her later. Honey wrapped herself in her cloak, muttering under her breath. He heard the word foolish three times and wasn't sure if she was referring to Lucy or him.

More people bustled about the area, both outside and in, but it was a mixed-race group and somehow not so scary. When they entered the Freedman's Bureau, Preacher felt Honey's surprise. The little room had a sort of warm energy, and he couldn't help but think that, if it were up in Amherstburg, Honey would be working there. But maybe not.

There were several White women there, but only one had blonde hair. She was facing away, struggling out of her hat. Another woman touched her arm, nodding at him. The blonde turned around.

She had some of Miss Marianne's beauty, though not all of it. Miss Marianne had always been delicate, seemingly unable to do more than glide across wood floors or arrange roses in a vase. Miss Lucy emanated capability. She was a grown woman with a real purpose. An important purpose.

Now she beamed at them. "Preacher! Miss Honey!"

She strode forward, hand out, just like her husband had done earlier. When Honey didn't move, Preacher took a step and clasped it.

"I'm so sorry," Lucy continued. "Mister Preacher sounds completely wrong."

"Miss Lucy." It was fortunate he was smiling, because he couldn't think of a single thing to say, but luckily she did most of the talking.

"I'm so glad to see you! We never knew what happened, if you made it to freedom. How nice to see you did."

Honey reacted then, and Preacher had to keep himself from clamping a hand over her mouth. "Unlike my mammy!" Her voice rang out in the room, stilling all other sounds as people paused to look before resuming their tasks.

A Black woman hurried over protectively. "Don't you dare talk like that to Miss Lucy. Shame on you, Honey!"

It was Maisey, her hair turned white and her hands shaking. "This woman has been working every day helping us, all us freed slaves. She's building a school for us right this minute." With that, she whirled around and marched off.

Lucy smiled, seemingly not offended in the least. "Oh, Honey, I'm so sorry. You've lived with that your whole life, haven't you?"

Confronted, Honey wrapped her arms about herself, and Preacher wrapped his around her shoulders. "We're glad to know you were unharmed, Miss Lucy," Preacher said.

At the back of the room, a door opened, and a moment later, Maisey returned with another woman on her arm.

Honey went still beside Preacher.

The woman was Maggie.

Ten minutes later, they were in a back room, the door shut and steaming cups of tea before them.

"Why didn't you..." Honey started.

She wanted to blame someone, Preacher knew, but she couldn't figure a way to do that.

"Now I raised you sensible like," Maggie told her, a wide grin on her face. "Get word to you, indeed! Why didn't you get word to me you was up in Canada?"

Honey sat next to Maggie, touching her every chance she got. Truth was, Preacher couldn't believe she was there himself.

"Mister Styles," Maggie said. "They'd pulled Lucy out of the water and rowed off. Later they said there weren't no room in the rowboat, but no one ever believed that. So there I was, making my peace with God. And out of nowhere, another oar flips by my head and there's this new boat—tiny one, with just one boy. Mister Styles."

"It was a canoe." Lucy smiled. "He had himself his own canoe and went to rescue her."

"He went to rescue you, child." Maggie gave her a devilish smile.

Preacher thought he'd never seen Maggie smile so much in all the time they were back on Sweetgum as she did now.

"He couldn't rightly get me in that boat. It wiggled like a slippery fish. But he told me to hang on, and I did, and he rowed me back to town."

"They must have beat you something fierce," Honey said.

"No, ma'am. Master Hueron was there, on shore, and came for me. He asked where you was heading, and I told him wherever the Mississippi took you. Maybe I coughed more than I needed. I worried for days about punishment. Would they beat me as bad as Hank? Would they string me up? When we got back to Sweetgum, Squint asked him what to do with me. All the master said was, 'She jumped in to save my daughter.' And that was that."

"Hank...?" Honey barely mouthed the word, but Preacher heard. His arm clasped her shoulders, and she gave him a soft look. She'd known, he realized. In some dim recess of her brain.

"Sweetgum raised cotton one more year before we switched to tobacco." Lucy was talking now. "When we made the switch, Father moved Maggie to the house. He started going to meetings, and they elected him as the delegate to go to the state convention. He voted against succession."

"So Missouri stayed out of the war?" Preacher asked.

"Tried to." Lucy's smile faded. "Didn't truly succeed."

Their train left the following afternoon. Honey stayed with Maggie every waking minute until then. She told her all about Buster and his family and his horse trading. Maggie said she'd seen Tweed once more, just before he marched off to fight.

"He was so proud. I told him he didn't need to fight in no war. And he told me a man has to stand up for what's right." Maggie shook her head, then smiled at Honey. "He did well at Master Richmond's place. Grew up real good."

Honey invited her to come live with them, to walk the streets of Amherstburg.

"I got things to do here," Maggie told her. "Important things, Honey child. We're building a school."

So they left Maggie and Lucy standing arm in arm, waving, on the docks. Honey cried, but they were the good kind of tears.

To Preacher, the two women seemed right together. Lucy had been attached to Maggie as long as he could remember, and despite all her denial, Maggie turned out to be a bit attached herself. Now they were doing good work and pretty pleased about it.

Seemed like a good thing to him.

The End

Gratitude

So many people – so many friends – helped bring this dream to reality.

Ann Albers, who coached, coaxed, and created a marvelous image.

Debra Hartmann, of theprobookeditor.com, a talented editor who truly makes the story better.

Hannah Gomez of KAA, who gave me the confidence to publish. And Jessica Pryde, who helped find the words.

The Plymouth Writers Group in Devon County, UK, who kindly critiqued and improved the initial manuscript.

And to Maggie, whose generous spirit enriched me in ways beyond measure.

Thank you, too, for reading this book. It is for you we all strive to tell a worthy tale.

Also By Jo Sparkes

Wake of the Sadico

On a Caribbean dive vacation, five friends discover a centuries old shipwreck – and a karmic debt past due.

The Legend of the Gamesmen Fantasy Series

The Birr Elixir – She's a talisman for a daring Gamesman -- and a weapon against a prince.

The Agben School – Hiding from an evil that stripped away friends and support, Marra must risk all to save her world.

The Dim Continent – Marra travels to the heart of a fabled Continent - and the center of a fight she doesn't know exists, among men she thinks an ocean away.

ABOUT THE AUTHOR

As a contributing writer for the Arizona Sports Fans Network, where she was called their most popular writer, she garnered popularity with her humorous articles, player interviews and game coverage. Jo was unofficially the first to interview Emmitt Smith when he arrived in Arizona to play for the Cardinals. While feature writing on ReZoom.com, one of her subjects received the website's 'Man of the Year' award. Her body of work includes scripts for Children's live-action and animated television programs, a direct to video Children's DVD, commercial work for corporate clients.

Jo served as an adjunct teacher at the Film School at Scottsdale Community College, and made a video of her most beloved lecture. Her book for writers and artists, "Feedback How to Give It How to Get It" was born to help her students — and indeed, all artists.

Her original script, Frank Retrieval, won the 2012 Kay Snow award for best screenplay. Her fantasy series, The Legend of the

Gamesmen, has garnered two B.R.A.G. Medallions and a 2015 silver IPPY award for Ebook Juvenile/YA Fiction.

When not diligently perfecting her craft, Jo can be found exploring her new home of Plymouth, England, where she and her spouse have embarked on a new adventure.